DOG WITH A BONE

Rocky McAfee

This is a work of fiction. Names, characters, businesses, places, events and incidents are either the products of the author's imagination or used in a fictitious manner. Any resemblance to actual persons, living or dead, or actual events is purely coincidental.

Copyright © 2013 by Rocky McAfee
Cover by Author
All rights reserved

No part of this book may be used or reproduced in any manner whatsoever without written permission of the author, except in the case of brief quotations embodied in critical articles and reviews.

www.rockymcafee.com

Copies of this book may be purchased at
www.amazon.com

This story is dedicated to all the victims of crime and their families, who were failed by the justice system.

Acknowledgements

It gives me great pleasure to say thanks to my family, Adina Markin, Anne, Ron, Shannon and Emma McAfee for believing in my ability to write this novel, for your reading pleasure.

Many hours were spent hidden away from my loved one's flesh and blood just so I could make it happen.

I also want to thank Virginia "Dolly" Rogers, Monika and Karlisle Gobeil for their expertise in computer knowledge whenever I needed some technical advice.

Many thanks to the great folks at Createspace, for all the guidance they gave me.

And last, but not least, thank-*you* for purchasing this book and I do hope you enjoy it!

ONE

"What's down this road?" Sunny asked the stranger sitting in the blue Pontiac Tempest.

No answer. Just a domineering, sinister glare!

Sunny shouted out loud, as if to try and silence the hysterical, sonorous barking from his yellow lab in the back of the truck. The angry dog was frothing at her jowls, from forcing the unnatural, resonating screams from her belly. Hanging her front legs over the edge of the black Chevy S10 pickup, Babe's dark chocolate brown eyes were fixated on the icy-blue eyes of the man in the Tempest.

Sunny had never in his life, ever witnessed the crazy behavior of his female dog, as he had at this moment. A twinge of uneasiness set into his body. The quirky guy in the car kept looking at Babe as she bared her teeth and howled, him looking at the dog and then shifting his eyes back to Sunny. Back and forth, back and forth!

Again, Sunny shouted, "HEY, what's down the road?" At that moment, Sunny Kruzik realized, that the man sitting in the blue car, only two feet away, was perspiring excessively on his weather beaten forehead.

Sure it was August, and the burning hot sun was beaming down, but something didn't fit. This guy wasn't sweating from the scorching heat! Sunny and his friend

Ellen, were definitely hot, sitting in the truck, but it wasn't that bloody hot, to be sweating like a damn pig! The dude was nervous, not hot! But why? Babe was in the back of the truck, he was safe in his car. She couldn't reach to bite him.

"The guy's a frickin' weirdo, let's get out out of here!" Ellen charged.

"You're right Elly, let's book it!" Sunny agreed.

The dirt road was really only wide enough for one vehicle and Sunny already had the Chevy up on the edge of the chiseled-out embankment. The truck was over as far as he could edge it, without scraping the side on the dirt bank. The Pontiac was also over as far as it could fit. Both vehicles had managed to move over with just enough space, between them, so that they could pass each other.

All Sunny had planned to do when they had come upon this stranger, was to ask him what lay ahead, since this was a newly bulldozed road, through the woods, he and Babe hadn't explored yet.

Sunny shifted the stick into first gear and then eased the truck slowly around the car, with only a couple of feet between them. Slowly, the Chevy crept past the Tempest and gradually eased back onto the rough, uneven dirt road. Looking ahead, it seemed as though the road abruptly ended, forest all around, and only a small clearing ahead. No exit?

"He's gotta GUN! Ooohhhh my God!" Ellen screamed.

"Are you kidding me?" Sunny quipped.

"Noooo! ... LOOK!" Ellen cried.

"Damn it! He's aiming it right at us!" Sunny Kruzik checked out his rear-view mirror and to his horror, saw the reflection of the psycho, pointing a big handgun right at the back of the truck rear window. The madman had both hands on what seemed to be a large caliber revolver. A .357 or maybe a .44 magnum, the kind Clint Eastwood used in the Dirty Harry movies. Only fifty feet from the back of the truck!

"Shit Sunny! He's fucking crazy! What are we going to do?" Ellen asked hysterically.

The road ahead, seemed to go nowhere, it looked like a dead end! No wonder this creep jumped out of his car and pulled a gun on the unsuspecting couple.

He has us trapped! Sunny thought to himself.

"Ellen! The road ends ... we have to make a run for it through the bush, right now, just run, we'll separate, he can't get us both!" Sunny instructed.

"I can't, my legs are numb, I can't even move them!" she cried. "I can't move, I can't!"

Babe was wailing, sounds that would make even the devil himself run. She wanted that son-of-a-bitch in the worst way! Babe was trained not to jump out of the pickup, unless Sunny gave the word. Her fore-legs were hanging over the edge of the tailgate as she barked and frothed from her jowls.

Sunny could feel the fine hairs, on the back of his neck rise, as he scanned the surrounding bush line, about seventy yards away from the truck. He didn't have a gun in the truck, and the knife he had under the seat, was no match against bullets anyway.

But Sunny did know, that a handgun was only accurate within fifty feet of the intended target, and that, in order to hit a target, the shooter would have to be very experienced with the "piece".

It was a gamble, but there was no other choice! As if instinct had taken over, Sunny jumped out of the Chevy and grabbed Babe by her pink, nylon collar with his left hand. He never once took his eyes off the crazed dude with the long barreled revolver, not even for a second! He had a firm grip on Babe's collar, and was ready to pull her over the edge of the truck. She wanted a piece of that guy, and Sunny was ready to let her go get him!

At that instant, the madman dropped his aim, held the gun by his right side and then side-stepped over to the edge of the dirt road. He crouched down, never losing eye contact with Sunny. He then began picking up some small loose branches that had been cut by the road crew, who had obviously left them there after the road had been pushed through previously, some weeks before. The wacko, then moved over to his car and without breaking his stare at Sunny, set the branches on the top of the car's roof.

It's now or never! Sunny let go of Babe's collar and then jumped back into the cab of the truck. The motor was still running, so Sunny threw the shifter into first gear and gunned it! He spun the tires so hard that the dry dirt and gravel spewed into a nasty cloud of opaque grayness!

"I can't move my legs Sunny!" Ellen was hysterical, she was paralyzed with fear and was sobbing uncontrollably.

Sunny was shifting into second gear and kept the revs up high, still causing a major dust storm. Driving erratically, Sunny was planning on propelling the Chevy into the bush ahead, and then Ellen and him could jump out of the truck and run through the woods for safety.

"Pass me another Timbit, Gordo!" said Constable Larry Roberts.

Roberts was reaching across the gray table top for the box of donuts as Officer Gordon Smith was fixing up his coffee with some more sugar, as the drink wasn't sweet enough.

Officer Smith pushed the box of Timbits towards the cop, across the table as he stirred his drink and checked out the busty blond at the table next to him. She paid no attention to the overweight policeman, although she could feel his horny eyes burning right through her clothes.

The donut shop was buzzing with the regular crowd that craves their sugar and caffeine fix. Not an empty seat in the place. *Doesn't anyone work anymore?* Smith thought to himself. *Should have invested in Tim Hortons stocks!*

Just then, a dirty looking fellow, unshaven, matted hair and ragged clothes, started hassling the Asian counter clerk. He was telling her to go back to wherever she came from. But she stood her ground and told the bum to leave the store immediately. He looked her up and down, mumbled a few choice words and then turned around and headed for the door.

He hadn't noticed the policemen sitting at the table, over by the window. They noticed him and watched him go through the exit.

Officer Smith got up and followed the miscreant out the door and then asked the guy what the problem was. He almost jumped out of his weathered up skin, when he realized a cop was right behind him.

"Holy shit! How did you get here so fast?" the bum croaked in his raspy, cigarette voice.

"I've been following you and if you don't smarten up, your going to jail! Do you understand !?" Smith barked at the unkempt man.

"Yes ... sirrr ... I didn't mean what I said to her, honestly, I didn't," answered the bum.

"What's your name?" Smith asked the vagrant.

"Bob Singer, sir."

"Well, Bob Singer, I want you to go back in there and apologize to the nice lady, okay?" Smith directed, "and don't forget ... I'm watching you!"

"Okay, I don't want no trouble sir!" Bob Singer stumbled back into the donut shop and went right up to the counter and told the clerk how sorry he was for bothering her. She nodded, but proceeded with her job and then ignored the man.

Officer Smith sat back down at the table with Roberts, and shook his head from side to side slowly in disgust and said, "sometimes, I feel like a goddamn baby sitter! And the poor bastard shit himself, to boot! What a stink!"

Constable Larry Roberts just laughed, "donuts and bums ... is that what we signed on for Gordo?"

Roberts was a fifteen year veteran, with the Vancouver City Police. After he graduated from John Oliver Secondary School, he decided to enlist in the Police Academy, just like his father had done. It was steady work with good pay and full benefits. Larry was in great shape, always working out and running, unlike his partner, Gordon Smith.

Smith was a little overweight and didn't work out much at all. But they seemed to be a fine match for police work.

Roberts' cellphone went off. "Yeah, we're in the vicinity ... we're on our way! Another body, over on Broadway! Finish your donut, Gordo and let's get a move on."

Smith grabbed a couple more Timbits and crammed them in his mouth, he got up from the table, scanned the donut shop like a hawk seeking its prey and then headed for the door. Roberts was already in the cruiser.

The cop cruiser sped out of the parking lot, headed for Broadway.

A small crowd had started to gather behind the vacant lot on Broadway and Knight Street. The sky was clear with only a few clouds, birds in a nearby mountain ash tree were chattering excessively!

Gasps and shocked looks came from some of the curious onlookers, others were snapping photos from their cellphones.

The lot was overgrown with weeds and somewhat a garbage dump, bottles, cans, old paper, a real mess, but the most obvious thing in the lot, that stood out, was a body! A lifeless body, not a drunk or a homeless person, but a dead one.

Every now and then, one of Vancouver's two thousand transients or homeless, would occasionally take up residence in this vacant, dirty lot. But not this time, this was a real dead person!

With the siren and strobe lights flashing, the cruiser pulled up to the gathering crowd, with a screeching sudden stop. Sirens could be heard about a block away ... from the bright red fire engine, that was also on route.

Constable Roberts jumped out of his "ride" and headed towards the crowd. He asked the people to move aside as he gestured with his hands, in a swimming motion. The gathering responded, by opening up and letting the officer get through. Officer Gordon Smith was grabbing some yellow "Crime Scene" ribbon from the trunk of the cruiser.

DOG WITH A BONE

The ear piercing siren, coming from the approaching fire engine was now deafening, as the mammoth machine had come from the opposite way, as the cops cruiser had, and arrived with full staff in tow. All the firemen were jumping off, as if they were rushing to a massive fire!

This was just standard procedure, in the big metropolis of Vancouver. Anytime a phone call to the 911 emergency personnel was made, the dispatcher would send out all available units, usually more than needed, at the expense of "Joe taxpayer".

Another car pulled up to the commotion, with a man and a woman inside. Both casually, but smartly dressed. They pulled up behind the cop car and both got out.

He was wearing designer jeans, (probably from Bootlegger) and a collared shirt with embroidery on the chest area. His shoes were of the Doc Martin style. She also had jeans on, kinda tight, with white Sketcher sneakers and a short sleeved pink sweater, hiding a pair of 38's.

As they walked up to Officers Smith and Roberts, the sun was shining brightly. The female adjusted her designer sunglasses, to keep the heavenly rays off her orbs.

"Who do we have this time?" the guy asked Roberts.

"Looks like another young boy, Mike," Larry responded to the couple.

"Shit! Not again!" the man replied.

A few of the firemen were helping to push the crowd back to the sidewalk. Smith handed the Fire Chief, the roll of yellow tape and told him to cordon off the area to keep the people away.

The couple that got out of the car were homicide Detectives, specially assigned to the Fraser case. Detectives, Mike Kuban and Jane Rhodes have been on the Fraser case since day one. They were both assigned to the case, because of their experience with murder investigations.

The case was named the Fraser case, because fourteen months ago, the first young boy was found dead on Fraser Street and 41st Avenue at the corner of the cemetery. The boy found today makes the count eight. Not all were boys, four boys and three girls, all under the age of twenty-one years, now another one.

The lifeless body lay face down, in some long weeds, with what looked, like some more weeds strewn over top of the back of the young boy, as if to cover him up. One sneaker was missing and he had no shirt, only blue jeans, one sock and one runner. Dried blood was evident on the left side of the boys face and neck. It was a gruesome discovery for the lady that had been walking her dog by the empty lot!

Mike Kuban started with the Vancouver Police back in 1999, he enlisted after he resigned from the Canadian Armed Forces. He felt that he could go farther with the police, than he could with the army. After working five years as a Patrol Constable, he posted for Corporal, got that job, did that for two years and then applied for the posting in OIS, (Operations Investigative Section) which deals with all the murder and homicide crime scenes. It was right up his alley!

Jane Rhodes became a member of the Vancouver Police, because she felt she could do a service for her country! Always active in high school, involved with the Student Council and one of the best on the track and field team, she was a prime candidate to join the Police Academy. Jane was very proud to be part of the Vancouver Police Department, since it was the first Canadian police force to hire a female officer and first to start a Marine squad. She had heard that the VPD had a great track record for treating women as equals. Rhodes got into the homicide department after a good friend of hers was raped and killed by a psychopath. She was "hell bent" on bringing these kinds of scum to justice!

Kuban radioed for Forensics to arrive on the scene, only after making the confirmation, that in fact it was a dead body and not some drunk passed out. All too often, reports about dead people are phoned in to the police; only to discover someone sleeping off a good night of drugs or alcohol.

TWO

Business was brisk at Black's Lock Shop, keys being cut, locks being sold, customers inquiring about the new digital safes, all the usual stuff that makes up a day.

The owner, Merick Black, was on holidays, but he had the best employees, money could buy. Merick was on vacation in Hawaii, a long needed break.

Being self employed has its advantages and disadvantages. The advantage of course, is being able to take your holidays when you want and for as long as you want, providing you have great staff, to run your enterprise! The major disadvantage being, if you have unscrupulous employees, well then you're just a glorified babysitter.

One of the newer employees working at the lock shop is a guy by the name of Ike. A tall, fit younger dude about twenty-eight years old. Ike is very energetic and is on his way to becoming a certified Locksmith. He needs a minimum of two years apprenticeship under the professional training of Merick, in order to get his Canadian Journeyman Locksmith license. Ike's a guy that can do lock jobs with ease. He has a natural ability to fix all things in the lock business, and an uncanny reputation for picking locks!

If someone loses a key, or has trouble opening a lock, well they just call Ike; he is the shop's "pick pro" as they call him. Of course, you have to be "bonded" in order to legally pick locks out in the real world, otherwise you could end up in jail. Picking someone's lock is a federal offense, unless you have their direct permission.

Ike always had an interest in locks, ever since he was a small boy. His father lost the key to the garden shed one day, when Ike was about eight years old and his dad couldn't get in to the shed, to get the lawn mower out. So Ike asked his mother for a bobby pin. He took the bobby pin and bent it a certain way, (something he saw in a comic book) then he manipulated the pin inside the key-way and *bounced* the tumblers of the lock and within minutes, he had the lock open. His dad was so proud of him, he bought him an ice-cream cone. Ike was hooked! He practiced on just about every lock he could get his hands on.

As he got to be a teenager, Ike would by-pass any damn door lock he wanted to open. There were no boundaries, when it came to picking locks. As a matter of fact, his buddies gave him the nickname "Pic". Ike Cross knew his calling was to be a Locksmith. Born to pick!

Besides working in the shop, Ike is also busy "on the road" doing service calls for clients. The busiest time seems to be at the end of the month, when people are moving in or out of their houses and wanting their locks changed.

"Black's Lock Shop! Jim speaking, how can I help you? Mmmhmm ... just a sec please ... hey Ike, a guy wants to drop a safe off today ... says the combination is screwy?"

"Is it a floor model or a wall type?" Ike asked.

"Is it a floor model or a wall model, sir? He says it's a floor model, about two cubic feet," Jim replied.

"Tell him ... that he can open the door, wide open and then lift the door straight up and off the safe and then he just has to bring the door in, not the whole safe," Ike explained from the back of the store.

"That's the problem Ike, he can't even open the door, cause he said the combo is screwed ... so he should bring in the complete safe, right?"

"Righto Jim, and tell him, we get to keep the contents of the safe, for cracking it for him ... just kidding man, don't tell him that!" Ike burst out laughing! He was a bit of a joker, always in a good mood.

Jim got off the phone with the customer, looked at Ike and said, "you're fuckin' crazy, you know that?"

"Of course I know that, I'm not stupid, I'm just crazy!"

Ike said, as he slapped his thigh with an open hand and laughed out loud hysterically!

Jim starts to laugh too, but rolls his eyes and walks away into the back of the shop and mutters to himself, "what a nut-job!"

The shop door opened, and in came a Purolator delivery person, with a package.

"Hi Ike, I have a package here for Sunny Kruzik, c/o Black's Lock Shop?" queried the driver.

"I can take it Keith," Ike said, setting a wrench on the counter.

"Yeah, but I'll need a signature, must be important stuff," Keith said.

"Okee-dokee Keith, you're the man!" chirped Ike.

Forensics had finally arrived at the crime scene. The four persons sent, from Investigative Services were part of a larger group that formed the "Forensic Identification Unit" otherwise known as FIU.

All of the long term serving members, got right to work. One shorter term member was taking pictures, while the other three were checking around the body and the area close to the body.

Homicides are always troubling, especially when it's a very young person. A death is called a "homicide" until it's been proven that the death was met with foul play, then it's classed as a murder.

The cops and detectives among the scene were fairly certain, that this was in fact a murder, just by the characteristics of the way the body was laying. Both hands of the young boy had been placed underneath his body, like he was cupping his hands together and then laying on them. This was the exact same way, all the other victims had been found.

It was evident that the police had a serial killer at large! Some sick bastard was preying on these poor young people. Most of the victims had been sexually molested in one way or another. The boys orally and the girls both ways. Raping them was the most horrific crime these kids could endure, and then kill them, why? Their young lives snuffed out for the sexual gratification of some demented serial killer. Detectives Kuban and Rhodes, were sickened to the bottom of their stomachs. They were determined on catching this sick bastard! Kuban lay awake at night, wondering what he might do, when he caught up to this monster. Rhodes lay awake at night, knowing exactly what she would do and it sure wasn't a pleasant thought!

The police didn't have very many clues to go on, but they did have three. One clue was the DNA of the killer. The killer was obviously a male, because a female doesn't leave sperm samples. Some of the victims had dried semen on their bodies. The DNA samples were run through the DNA database, but no matches were found. The police figured that the murderer left traces behind on purpose, because he possibly hadn't been charged with any offenses in the past, and therefore never had to submit DNA samples to the courts.

The second clue was the tire tracks left in the dirt near the body. The tracks were very faint, but in three of the murders the tread prints matched up to be from the same tire. The only trouble was, that there are thousands of different tire treads out there. Some companies change their patterns every year, sometimes, twice a year. And tires can last for years before they are discarded. The forensics department, had submitted digitally enhanced image copies of the tire tread to all tire companies in Canada and the U.S.

After two weeks of waiting, one major tire company sent the information to the police, the tire that they felt was a perfect match. The tire was a Hankook 639, 15 inch summer car tire, produced about two years ago. The company had sold thousands of those tires over the last year and a half, but they stopped making that particular tread style about six months ago.

Because the tracks were very faint, it was an indication that the tires were well worn. This led the investigators to believe that either the tires were purchased when they were first available to the buyers or that the owner of the tires did a ton of driving, putting lots of wear on those rubber skins.

With this information, the police did an online search with the tire shops in B.C. And Alberta. First they pinpointed all the stores that sold Hankook, and then they requested a list of all the names of the clients who had purchased the Hankook 639, 15 inch model. What they came up with, was a huge list of customers, totaling two thousand, seven hundred and eighty-nine. It wasn't the best clue, but at least they had that.

The third clue was a chopstick that the killer had left imbedded in the heads of four of the victims.

"Hey Mike, what do you make of this?" asked one of the forensic investigators, named Louie.

"Not too sure Louie ... grass, to cover up the body maybe?" Kuban answered.

"Nothing, nothing at all, not much to go on, same as the others. This guy is a cocky son-of-a-bitch! Leave's a friggin' sperm sample that we can't even match up," Louie fumed.

Detective Rhodes walked over to Kuban and Louie and in an angry, upset tone said, "looks like the same MO as all the others."

"Seems to be, Jane," Kuban answered. "Bruising on the neck ... hands folded underneath the body; strangulation no doubt was cause of death."

"Look at this Mike!" Louie groaned, as he turned the boys head, ever so slightly with his gloved hands. "Another damn chopstick!"

"Shit! Louie, it is ... just like the little girl that was found down on Marine Drive about four months ago. Maybe death wasn't caused by strangulation after all, maybe it was brain trauma from the chopstick!"

"That sick bastard! I want him dead!" Rhodes cried.

As the forensic team and the detectives looked on, they could see, what looked like a round piece of bloody wood, protruding a few inches from the boys ear. It was evident, that the murderer had hammered this object into the side of the kids head.

"Are you guys done here Louie?" Kuban asked.

"Yes, we are," Louie replied.

"Okay, then lets get this poor boy down to the pathologist, so we can find out the cause of death and try to identify him, so that we can notify next of kin," Kuban ordered.

The Province and Vancouver Sun newspaper reporters were milling about taking pictures and jotting down notes. Sometimes the media was an advantage and sometimes it was a big thorn in the side of the investigation of the crime.

The advantage being, to inform the public about a serial killer on the streets and to be aware. The big thorn being, too much information given back to the murderer, so that he may be able to keep one step ahead of the cops. Some of these sick bastards get a real hard-on reading about them- selves in the newspapers.

News travels very fast today with online social media. As fast as the reporters can type the information into their net-books, it is already being downloaded into the online news reports. With the "click" of a button, the tragic event would be on Global TV, for the six o'clock news.

THREE

27 YEARS EARLIER

"You stupid sissy ... you little wimp, I'll teach you who the king is, on this block!" screamed Denny Barker, as he sat on the back of little Sunny and kept slapping him on the back of the head. "What kind of a stupid name is Sunny?"

The side of Sunny's head was bright red and he had some scratches on his cheek, from being pushed to the ground, by the big, mean bully! Moments before, Denny had grabbed the smaller boy, by the shirt collar and then asked him, "do you want it in the face or the gut, shit-head?"

Before Sunny could answer, Denny slugged him in the stomach and knocked the wind right out of poor Sunny! As he was gasping for air, the bully tripped Sunny and then knocked him to the ground. He then jumped on Sunny's back and sat on him like a cowboy on a buckin' bronco! Denny then proceeded to slap Sunny on the side and back of the head. Tears were welling up in Sunny's eyes and he still had trouble breathing from the punch in the gut.

A few of the East Vancouver neighborhood kids gathered around the unfair fight, but nobody said a word. They just watched as the small kid took a beating from the bigger kid. After a few minutes of head slapping,

Denny spit on the back of Sunny's head, then he got up and gave him a kick in the side of the ribs. Denny looked at the other youngsters and asked them if they wanted some too. The bully then turned and walked back down the alley to where he had come from.

Sunny, slowly turned over and then sat up holding his side, where he had been kicked, crying but not too much, as he was trying to hold back the tears in front of the other kids; especially since one was a girl. A girl that Sunny had a crush on. Her name was Valerie. She and two other boys helped Sunny to his feet. They asked him if he was okay.

"I'm okay, I just want to go home," Sunny told them.

East Side, as it was called by the people that lived there, was home to average wage earners and mostly blue collar workers. The houses on the east side were about half the market values as the Vancouver west side.

Sunny and his family, which included his mom, dad, older sister Angel, and the family dog, named Lady lived in an eight hundred and fifty square foot bungalow, just down half a block from the "Projects" as they were referred to. The projects were cheaply built, low-rental units for low income families. Built in the early sixties, the rundown apartments housed single parents on welfare, alcoholics and people with disabilities who couldn't afford anything more. It was a real tough neighborhood! Robberies, suicides, rapes, break-ins, beatings, car thefts and the occasional murder happened weekly in the 'hood.

The Kruziks home was very secure. Sunny's father, Wade had everything locked down, double good. And then there was Lady, the cocker-spaniel, mixed with daschund, her bark was worse than her bite! The slightest noise and she would let everyone know she was there.

Sunny walked down the lane towards his home, crying softly and kicking the rocks that lay scattered in the alley. One big rock, he wound up to kick hard, but when his foot connected, he let out a yelp! Now he had something else to cry about. The pain in his big toe made him forget about the ass kicking he just received from the neighborhood bully, Denny Barker.

I hate that bastard! Sunny thought to himself. *He's going to get his, one day.*

Sunny entered through the basement door and went upstairs into the kitchen. His mom was sitting at the kitchen table, reading The Province newspaper. She looked up at Sunny and her smile turned to an instant frown.

"Not again, honey!?" she asked.

"I'm okay, mom."

"You're not OKAY, who did it this time, Sunny?"

"Denny Barker."

"That little armhole! That's it! I'm going to talk to his parents. He can't keep beating you up and getting away with it. How many times has it been this year, six, seven?"

"I don't know mom, maybe that, maybe more that you didn't know about. He's a bully, he doesn't just pick on me, he picks on other kids too ... like Stevie, his brother and even Andy Jones. He's a creep. He always makes fun of my name, he says it's a girls name! It's not a girls name, is it mom?" little Sunny wondered.

"Of course not, honey ... it's English for "son of mine" and because you're so "bright" as well!" reasoned Annie.

"And he bullies kids for no reason, just because he can! Please don't tell his parents, cause that will make him madder. His dad's a drunk and his mom is in the hospital most of the time," Sunny pleaded to his mom.

"Sunny, if you don't want me to tell his parents, that he's picking on the smaller kids around the block, then you are going to have to do something about it yourself. Can you not get all the other boys that he bullies, to help you stand up to him?" Annie asked.

"It's not that easy mom, most of the other boys are my size or smaller, and then Denny would just get them, one by one, when they are by themselves."

Sunny was a small kid for his eleven years. Smaller than the average size. The kind of small kid that bullies love to pick on.

Denny, on the other hand was a larger than average boy for his age and somewhat bigger boned.

Bullies aren't tough. They are generally cowards to stand up to someone their own size. The only way they actually feel tough is to push around, someone smaller and weaker than themselves. They get a sense of satisfaction from being mean to others that they can control. Sometimes bullies are bullied at home by their own family member. So then they take it out on others, to make themselves feel better.

Denny's dad wasn't a big guy, but he was an alcoholic. He always went to the bar after work and Denny's mom was sickly all the time, so she was either in bed or at the hospital getting treatment. They were never around for him growing up.

Whether or not, this had something to do with his mean, nasty ways towards the other kids, it was no excuse to bloody Sunny's nose twice a month!

Denny had one sister, but she was older than him and he wasn't mean to her, in fact they were very close. This may be due to the fact that both of them were adopted.

DOG WITH A BONE

But she wasn't around much either; she was usually out with one of her boyfriends. Being alone, made him reach out to the other kids, but in a hostile way, not in a friendly manner!

Nobody on the block liked Denny Barker, most of all Sunny Kruzik.

When Sunny's dad got home from work, Annie told her husband Wade about the horrible incident with Sunny and Denny. Wade was furious! He was all set to go pay Mr. Barker a visit, and tell him to discipline his goddam son. But Annie calmed him down and explained, how it may make matters worse.

Wade was a truck-builder Supervisor at a plant in Burnaby. On the job he got things done right and put up with no crap from anyone! If you slacked off, got caught stealing company property or were late too often, you were toast! Quite often the Union would get the employee back on the job, even if they were a huge liability for the company.

Time after time, Wade would fire someone and they would be back on the job within weeks. This would infuriate him and when he got home, you would know that some jackass was back to work that day.

This day was one of those jackass days and Sunny's dad was really pissed! So, had he went down to see Mr. Barker, there surely would have been trouble in East Side.

Sunny went to bed that night, but couldn't fall asleep. He tossed and turned and kept thinking about how that big creep, made him eat dirt in front of Valerie. He shuddered. Sunny was embarrassed and humiliated by that asshole! How could he go to school and face Valerie, knowing that she watched him get pummeled by "big nose" Denny. Maybe that was what made him mean. He had a big honkin' shnoz! Kinda like a hook, like an eagle's beak. *If only I could break his big honkin' eagle shnoz! That would be awesome. Teach him a lesson.*

Then it clicked! Sunny had a plan, a really great plan. In fact why didn't he think of it before. Well because, it didn't occur to him before; except that something that happened today gave him a brilliant idea!

Now he could sleep, and sleep he did. Sunny pulled the covers up over his chest and laid on his back. He fell into a deep sleep with a smile from ear to ear on his scratched up face. Tomorrow was a new day!

The kids at Tecumseh Elementary School playground were involved in various activities, the usual stuff; jumping rope, running around chasing each other, playing tag and of course some were playing hopscotch. But not Sunny. He was keeping his distance from the other kids.

One reason was that he had scratches on his face and was a wee bit embarrassed about it; especially if Valerie was around, even though, she was there when it happened and already saw the scrapes. Well it just wasn't that cool for her to see them again.

The other reason was that he was doing a little surveillance. He was scanning the playground for the "big nose" bully. Sunny didn't want to run into Denny just yet. Not at school, it wasn't the place and time!

After dinner, Sunny went outside to play. There was usually some kids around outside to hang out with. He really wasn't too interested in hanging with anyone in particular on this warm, but overcast evening. It was still quite light out, as it was May and the days were starting to get longer.

Sunny didn't wander too far from home, just down the back alley a ways. He picked up a few stones and started to peg them at the back fence of a neighbor, about three doors down from his house. Sunny was a real good shot, when it came to rock throwing. He had lots of practice, since the back alleys in East Side were gravel, not paved. Most kids in the area, at one time or another were involved in some kind of rock fight. Getting hit in the head with a stone now and then was a part of growing up in the 'hood! A good many windows had been broken too.

One day Sunny broke the church window that was on the corner of 45th and Gladstone Street, by accident of course. He got caught, cause a neighbor saw him break the window. He told his dad that he was chucking a rock at Dougie and he missed and it hit the window! Well his dad had to repair the window, but the cost of the glass came out of Sunny's allowance. He was careful from that day on.

Out of the corner of Sunny's eye, he saw a figure moving towards him, from down the alley way. Sunny turned just a little bit, to get a better look. Denny Barker! It was the bully making his way towards Sunny.

Sunny could feel his heart racing! Any other time, he would have started running for home. He could outrun Denny by a long shot. Sunny was the second fastest kid at Tecumseh School. Barry Sinky was the fastest. On Sports-day, Barry would get all the blue ribbons for first and Sunny would get all the red ones for coming in second.

His heart was pounding so hard, he could feel it in his little ears! Denny was getting closer! Sunny crouched down for a moment and then stood back up and turned towards Mr. Big Nose. *Man, that shnoz is big!* Sunny thought to himself. Sunny just stood there with his hands behind his back, as if he was some kind of human sacrifice for the bully. A lamb for the wolf! Denny was getting closer, with a big shit eatin' grin on his ugly mug.

"Hey, you little puke, aren't you goin' to run home to your momma?" Denny taunted.

Sunny never said a word; fear had taken his words away.

"You're dead meat, you little goof shit!" screamed the "big shnoz." Denny took a few more steps towards little Sunny and then grabbed him, with both hands, by the collar and pulled the collar up tight, ready to shake him.

With lightning speed, Sunny's right hand came from behind his back and he propelled it right into the bully's face. Sunny had an oblong boulder, just big enough to fit the whole inside of his hand with fingers extended, but curled enough, so he wouldn't drop it. It was a perfect fit! It was just like that rock was made for his grasp. Sunny smashed that big rock as hard as he could, straight into Denny's big beak.

Denny let out a blood curdling scream and released his grip on little Sunny's collar. The big bully slumped to the ground, still screaming! Blood spurted every which way from Denny's face. Holding his hands over his damaged big nose, the "not-so-tough-now" bully was crying and making some guttural noises. He was thrashing around on the dirty ground.

Sunny tossed the boulder into some grass over to the edge of the alley. He couldn't believe what he had just done. His heart was still pounding, but at the same time he felt an overwhelming feeling of relief. *Take that you big lump of shit!*

"What's going on here boys?" old man Johnson the neighbor asked, pointing with his crooked finger towards Denny laying on the ground.

"Denny tried to beat me up again, so I "rocked" him a good one, Mr. Johnson," Sunny answered smiling.

"Yes, Sunny you sure did, boy, you sure did." Mr. Johnson bends over, with a smile on his face and whispers into Sunny's ear with a cupped hand, "that boy finally got what he deserved, no doubt, yessir, David and Goliath!" cracked old man Johnson.

By now, a few kids from the neighborhood had started to gather around, watching Denny on the ground still crying hysterically. Valerie was there too. She looked at Sunny and smiled. Sunny felt like a hero!

Annie Kruzik could hear the commotion from her back yard. She was hanging out the wet laundry to dry on the clothesline. She wandered over and when she saw Denny bleeding on the ground and Sunny beaming, she knew something must have happened between them. She asked Sunny what was going on, so he told her what he did to Denny. Mr. Johnson told Annie that maybe someone should call an ambulance for Denny. Sunny's mom agreed, so she went into the house and made the call.

Ten minutes later, the ambulance showed up. They took Denny away to the hospital. It turned out that the impact of the rock, broke Denny's big nose and split his forehead wide open. His nose had to be set and twenty-two stitches were required to close up his forehead wound.

Denny's dad, Mr. Barker came down to see Annie Kruzik and started yelling at her. She told him, that his son was a bully and got exactly what he deserved and to get off the property. She also said if he was man enough to come back when Wade was home, he was more than welcome. Mr. Barker never came back.

Society itself, has indirectly created the "bully system". It seems that gradually over time, as each generation comes of age, parents do not want their children disciplined by school teachers. From the parent to the teacher, it's the old adage, *you can't touch my kid!*

So in essence, the parents took away the right, for the teachers to administer discipline to badly behaved children and teenagers. Sure, the argument goes like this ... too many students were being abused by certain teachers and principals of the school system, so the government stepped in, and implemented laws to protect students from being disciplined.

The dreaded "strap" was outlawed, as well as the yardstick, chalk-brush, pointer and any other implement or tool that could be used as a form of punishment.

Detentions aren't even handed out anymore. There is basically no type of punishment or discipline for any wrong doings by the students, in the school systems in Canada. All punishment in Canadian schools has been abolished by the government.

In other words, the students have no fear, whatsoever of the teachers, principals, their own parents or even the police! Nothing can happen to them, by Canadian law, and they know it.

So, nowadays, lots of the kids going to school, show very little or no respect at all, to their teachers. They know, that they can say or do just about anything and get away without any consequences! They have "No Fear".

With the majority of students that want to learn their studies, *respect* can be built through the "teacher/student" learning process. Some students who want to achieve a high degree of knowledge, will no doubt, have the highest respect for their mentors. These students are the future building blocks of human existence. Without these productive members of society, the human race as we know it, would self-destruct.

However, the other element of kids and teenagers that give the school system a hard time and always cause trouble are a drain on the system. These rowdies are usually the ones that start to bully the other kids, or turn to a life of crime and drugs. And they can usually get away with it, because there is no form of discipline or any consequences to keep them "on track" with society's rules.

Now if the strap was readily available punishment for the bullies, you can bet your last nickel, that there would be a lot less bullying going on in schools. Some respect can ONLY be built through "fear" for certain types of individuals. There are just some congenital, bad personalities out there, whether we want to believe it or not, and there is nothing that can be done about it. Or is there?

FOUR

After Denny got out of the hospital and healed up, he was a humbled kid. He never ventured down the alley towards Sunny's house and if he did have to go that way, he would go around the block. Denny never bullied any of the kids in the neighborhood ever again! He stayed away from Sunny at school as well. Even when Denny and Sunny entered David Thompson Secondary School, Denny stayed away from Sunny. By this time Sunny had grown in size and although he was still shorter than Denny, he had learned to fight.

Since the day that Sunny rocked Denny in the face, Sunny had gained an immense amount of confidence, to handle himself. Even though, he had a rock in his hand, he didn't feel it was cheating, anymore than a big guy outweighing a little guy.

After gaining the confidence, Sunny enrolled in Judo, then Karate and boxing too. He felt that expanding his fighting skills would only improve his ability to kick any bully's ass! Sunny started pumping iron at seventeen. He made his own bench press out of wood, and bought some weights. His dad brought home some weights that the welders had burned from one inch thick, heavy steel plates. He had built a mini home gym, in the basement of his parent's house for working-out.

DOG WITH A BONE

Sunny loathed bullies! He would never again be pushed around by anyone, no matter how big they were. If they crossed his path with any intimidation towards him or his friends, they were going down, one way or another!

When Sunny was nineteen, he and his sister Angel, and a few other friends went to a house party on the west side of town, on Dunbar Street. The party was rockin' and the booze was flying! Some hippies were there too, smoking that shit they call dope. There was a covered back porch that had a big comfy sofa. Sunny and two buddies were sitting on the couch drinking beer and Angel and her boyfriend were standing near the couch drinking and having a good time!

Sunny got up off the couch and went inside to go get a beer. He mingled with some of the wild party pigs that were crowded around in the kitchen. It seems that no matter how big a house is, the party always has the largest gathering in the kitchen. Maybe it's because the beer fridge is located there.

Just as Sunny stepped through the the back door, leading to the porch, he saw a blonde haired dude about six foot two, and about two hundred pounds, bitching to one of Sunny's buds seated on the couch. It was skinny little Ben, that the big guy was belittling.

"You're sitting in my seat!" big Blondie shouted at Ben. Then he proceeded to slowly pour his beer into Ben's lap. Ben just sat there as the creep laughed at him and slowly emptied the cold suds. Ben was no scrapper, he only weighed about one hundred and forty pounds soaking wet! Sunny was outraged! "Actually, that's my seat," Sunny taunted, as cool as a cucumber on a cold November day.

The big fellow snapped his head around to see who said that. "Who the fuck are you!" Blondie yelled through his walrus mustache.

No more words came out of Sunny's mouth, as he took four steps towards the "bar-star". Then with the speed of a rattlesnake, Sunny drove his right fist, up and into the bottom of the guy's nose. Three times, his fist jackhammered the pudgy face of the over-confident bully! The blonde man let out a groan and fell backwards into the wall and then slumped to the floor. He was out cold! Blood was starting to ooze from his battered face. Sunny brushed off his hands and asked Ben if he was okay.

"Yeah, I'm fine, just soaking wet in the crotch from his beer, that's all. Thanks a bunch Speed!" Ben gratefully said.

Sunny received the nickname "Speed" from his good buddies, cause he was lightning fast, when it came to disabling an assailant. Besides, Speed has a swell "ring" to it. So the name just stuck, and Sunny kind of liked it anyway.

Sunny was only 5' 7" and 178 lbs., but that didn't seem to matter, as many bigger guys found out. What he lacked in height, he made up for in swiftness!

Back when Sunny was taking Karate, his instructor told the class, that size doesn't matter, when it comes to a life or death situation. It's not the size of the dog in the fight, it's the size of the fight in the dog.

The Master explained that quickness will overrule size, every time, as long as the strikes are executed to the detrimental points on the body. He also told the group that when you size up your opponent, you look at them eye to eye, and then you imagine, instead of looking upwards, you are actually on an incline, with the opponent being on the upper end of the incline. With this mental image in your mind, no one is taller or larger than yourself. Now the odds are in your favor.

The Master also taught Sunny, that there is absolutely no reason to expend energy by talking or yelling at your opponent, before taking them down. You need to focus all your energy, like a "dog with a bone", on striking and winning. This, Sunny Kruzik has never forgotten.

The owner of the house came out onto the porch and asked what happened. He was informed, by the party goers that were standing around. The owner then told Sunny and his friends that they should leave the party. Apparently, the guy that Sunny knocked down was the house owner's cousin.

"No problemo, we'll be glad to leave, I have zero tolerance for bullies!" Sunny quipped. "He got exactly what he deserved!"

By the time Sunny Kruzik was twenty one, he was bench-pressing three hundred and twenty pounds of steel weight! He was able to do, three sets of twenty repetitions (or reps as it was known in the gym industry) and was curling one hundred and eighty-five pounds. That amount was more than his own weight! He became obsessed with working out. Six days a week. Sunny became very strong for his size. He was kind of a health nut, he drank carrot and apple juice daily.

As time progressed and Sunny went through his twenties, he got into all kinds of fights and scrapes. Some were in the bars or nightclubs and some were just on the street. He never started the fights. Sunny was taught by his Master, to never instigate a fight, but if someone was acting in a threatening manner, then by all means he would protect himself and put the attacker down, anyway he could. This code of ethics was taught to him by his Karate Master.

Sunny Kruzik would not tolerate the strong, picking on the weak! Whenever Sunny came across someone, (man, woman, child or teenager) getting harassed by someone else that was bigger or stronger, he would make it his business to intervene.

First, by talking to the bully, and if that didn't work, then he would "bash" the bully. Yep, Sunny the "Bully Basher". That's who he became, because he had zero tolerance for bullies. They needed to be destroyed, taught some lessons, so to speak.

This belief of Sunny's, was extended to animals as well. Sunny loved all animals, especially dogs. To him they were definitely "man's best friend". Never, ever, mess with man's best friend!

One day Sunny was driving down the street and saw a man kicking his dog. He quickly pulled his car over to the curb, got out of his car and approached the bully.

Sunny asked the man to stop booting the dog, and the guy told Sunny to "fuck right off" and mind his own business. Sunny dropped the guy right on the spot and started kicking the dude right in the ribs. Then he asked the guy if he liked how it felt.

The guy pleaded for Sunny to stop. The man apologized, said he wouldn't mistreat the dog anymore. Sunny warned the man, if he ever saw him do that again, he would send him to the hospital and take the dog away from him!

FIVE

The compact Chevy sped towards the overgrown bush. As the truck neared the thickness of the forest, a black area caught Sunny's sight from the corner of his eye. He turned to the left to see. It was an overgrown path, or maybe even an old road; there was a rusty chain secured completely across the opening, from tree to tree, about four feet high from the ground.

He didn't give it a second thought! Sunny gunned the accelerator and swerved over towards the overgrown path. Dust and rocks flying everywhere! He headed straight for the chain and kept the "pedal to the metal"!

"Twaaaang"! The chain snapped as the raging truck crashed through. Sunny never bothered to look in his rear-view mirror as he gained momentum going through the rusty old chain.

Branches from the old growth trees were scratching both sides of the truck. It was at this moment, Sunny realized how glad he was, to be driving a small truck and not one of those "big ass" trucks that were a menace on the roads and highways. He hated those big gas guzzlers. Most guys that drove those trucks were bullies anyway, always tailgating people and thinking they own the road!

"It looks like this old road keeps going, Sunny!" Ellen cried nervously, with relief in her voice.

"You betcha, what luck!" he agreed.

The road was rough, covered with moss, leaves, old dried branches and lots of rocks and potholes. It was about a ten degree slope heading downwards. The bush was so dense, that hardly any sunlight at all crept through the trees.

Babe was bouncing around in the back of the truck, but she curled her paws, hanging on with her nails dug into the plywood that covered the truck box. She was in the low crouch stance on all fours. Sunny loved his dog. He told Ellen to keep looking back to she if she was okay.

Ellen was bouncing around too, she banged her head a few times on the ceiling of the Chevy. She felt like puking! It was like an emotional merry-go-round for Ellen. First the freak-show with the gun and then the bumpy, torturous, hill ride, down the heavily forested road!

It seemed like hours, but it was only about ten minutes of "rough and tumble" off-road driving. As they were coming to the end of the path, they could see the sunlight breaking through the forest.

"Oh my God ... Sunny! We're almost out ... safe!" Ellen was crying uncontrollably and could barely get the words out. It was as if, her mouth was full of peanut butter. "I thought ... he was going to kill us ... I did ... I really did!"

"Elly, it's okay now, we're safe ... he's not going to hurt us, it's okay. How's Babe doin' back there?"

"She's holding on, but looks scared, Sunny."

They finally came to the end of the old road. It emptied out onto Marine Drive, with an endless line of cars zooming past them. Sunny eased the truck out of the dark forest and waited at the edge of the street for all the traffic to go by. He then turned right and floored it! The three of them were cruising along Marine Drive, all in shock! Neither one could believe what had just happened about fifteen minutes ago.

"We have to phone the police, Sunny!" Ellen shouted, as she was calming down slightly.

"No Elly, not right now ... I have to clear my mind ... I need some time to think about what just happened back there!" Sunny insisted.

"Listen Sunny, that psychopath is going to get away if we don't call the cops right now! He's probably gone from that area already," Ellen surmised.

"Elly ... take it easy, okay, I know your upset, but I really need to think this over, okay ... just please trust me."

Ellen had known Sunny Kruzik since grade five. When Sunny said "trust me", she knew full well, he meant it. He was the kind of person, a good friend could trust with their life!

Sunny and Ellen were best friends, they weren't lovers, although they had made out a couple of times over the years, when they were teenagers. But the two of them realized, that they were better friends than boyfriend and girlfriend. Besides, Sunny had a girl he was seeing on a regular basis and Ellen was happy being single.

Every now and then, Ellen and Sunny would hook-up and hang-out, just for fun and to catch up on life; like being chased by some weirdo in the bush with a gun!

Neither one of them were on Facebook, it was better seeing each other in person than going online. They both thought it to be too impersonal, to sit in front of a computer and talk back and forth when they could enjoy each others "real" company.

"Let's head back to my place and 'take five', I just have to think this thing over, Elly," Sunny said.

"Okay Sunny, I think I need a smoke or a drink or something to settle my nerves," Ellen said.

"Ha, you don't even smoke girl!" Sunny laughed.

"I know, but maybe it's a good time to start."

After a tense, twenty minute drive, Sunny pulled into the back alley, off of Victoria Drive and 44th Avenue, behind Black's Lock Shop. He pressed the transmitter "remote" button and the automatic garage door opened. Sunny pulled the Chevy S10 into the garage, up beside his other ride, a shiny new, pearl black Honda Accord. Sunny loved black vehicles. They showed the dirt more, but there was a car wash just down the block, which he frequented weekly.

Sunny and Ellen got out of the truck. Sunny let the tailgate down and Babe jumped out. He gave her a good head rub. "Good girl Babe ... good girl! You did real good hanging on for dear life, come on, let's head up to the loft, you two."

Ellen just laughed and shook her head at Sunny. He talked to Babe as though she was a person. To Sunny, Babe was smarter than most people, that's for sure. Truth be told, it's a scientific fact, that ninety percent of human's brains do not develop mentally, past the age of a fifteen year-old. Lot's of people are running around with no common sense. Maybe that's *why* all the prisons are overcrowded.

The three of them headed up the spiral staircase, from the garage to the loft. Sunny unlocked the inside door that led to the apartment.

Once inside, Sunny went into the kitchen area and grabbed a bottle of Sailor Jerry's Rum and poured both Ellen and himself a two finger shot of the smooth spirits.

He then poured some cold milk into Babe's bowl. She lapped it up right away and then went and laid down on her round, fluffy bed. She obviously had a hard day, bouncing around in the back of that bloody truck!

The loft was the epitome of "cool". It was a spacious open floor design. There were three good sized windows with a street view of the bowling alley across the way. It's bright red, neon flashing sign, radiated into Sunny's place at night.

The kitchenette was small, but had lots of counters and a sit-up bar. All of the appliances were stainless steel. The Italian leather couch and chairs separated the eating area from the TV room. A fifty inch flat-screen TV was mounted on the wall, but Sunny didn't watch much of that "reality TV" crap, his main purpose for the flat-screen was keeping up on the news and to watch rented movies now and then. Over in the far corner, hanging from the ceiling, was a speed bag and a heavy kick bag. The bedroom had three bamboo dividers, surrounding it for privacy.

Babe's round, fluffy bed was on the floor about six feet from her master's bed.

On one wall, hung Sunny's collection of swords. When he was studying Karate, he got interested in katanas and other samurai swords. He also had some very cool machetes and hatchets. The flashy collection of "cutlery" were mounted on the wall between two Van Gogh reprints.

Ellen and Sunny dropped onto the couch. Sunny slung his feet onto the glass and black wrought iron coffee table.

"I still can't believe what happened … can you?" asked Ellen, taking a sip of her rum and screwing up her face from the bite. "That's strong stuff … yewwww!"

"No Elly, I can't ... but it's a damn crazy world out there, and the creeps are endless!" Sunny said.

"I'm still shaking Sunny ... look at my hands," Ellen said, as she held her arms up and stretched her fingers out straight. The tremors in her hands were obvious. "What are we going to do Sunny? Shouldn't we phone the cops? That guy is going to get away!"

"Look, that guy is long gone, like a turkey through the corn. We need to close our eyes and reflect on what just happened and what we can remember about the complete incident. What the dude looked like, his car, the gun he was pointing at us, anything at all ... we need to remember! Close your eyes Elly and try and relax and think about what you saw," Sunny said, as he threw his head back and downed the rum, then wiped his mouth with the back of his wrist.

Ellen laid back on the couch and put her feet up and closed her eyes. She tried to relax and think about what she had seen earlier today. Sunny walked over to the bar and poured another rum, but this time added some diet-Pepsi. He wasn't much of a drinker these days. He liked having a clear mind, but sometimes a guy just needed a shot or two of good rum! "Yes ... yes Sunny. I did see something, now I remember, I think I was in shock at the time ... but I do remember now," Ellen exclaimed.

"What Elly, what did you see? Tell me what you remember seeing there!" Sunny asked excitedly.

" I saw ... "

The Vancouver City morgue was generally always full of bodies. Some from accidents, some from overdoses, suicides, gang warfare and the occasional domestic dispute. It seemed as though people were "just dying to get in there". They should almost have a sign up that reads "You stab 'em, we slab 'em"!

It was late afternoon, by the time the coroner brought the little boys body into the morgue.

The pathologist was a short chubby, bald man with thick glasses. His name was Larry Sweet and his twenty-five years in the field, made him one of the finest, in the City of Vancouver, employed at the morgue.

Larry summoned the coroner and his assistant to lay the body on the stainless steel examining table. The experienced pathologist had a frown on his weathered face. He could already tell, by the protruding wood shard stuck in the side of the boy's head, that it was another Fraser case statistic.

" What a waste!" Larry mumbled. "God damn it ... haven't those boys in blue, caught that asshole yet?"

"Not yet Larry," said the coroner's assistant. "Sounds like they may have a couple of leads though."

"I've been in this business a long time son, and after a while, every dead body that comes through those doors, is just like another ... well, I think you know what I'm going to say ... another number. And, I don't mean to sound harsh but, a person gets hardened over time. But, when they bring me a young child ... that's entirely different! It breaks my heart, to know that this kid or any other dead child, never even got a chance to grow up to live life! It's not right. And those asshole judges, they let the killers back out on the street, so that they can hurt someone else again. We need some of those judges bumped off! Maybe then, they would get tougher with the criminals," Larry ranted.

Larry Sweet was all business and no nonsense, when it came to his job. Larry put on his mask and gloved up before he attended to the young boy, who was by now, identified as Randy Dickinson and was only nine years old.

Larry had his assistant, Granger, remove the clothing from the body and took pictures from all angles. Granger snapped several photos around the head injury, from where the wooden spike protruded.

It takes a certain kind of individual to work in a morgue. There are all kinds of gruesome sights and nauseating smells. Some of the deceased are in advanced stages of decomposition. Others have limbs or other body parts missing. The occupation is not for the faint of heart!

Larry examined the boy visually first and had Granger take notes. After a thorough check from the outside, Larry picked up a scalpel and started to make an incision from the neck down to the navel. He then proceeded to open the boy up and remove the innards. One by one, he handed the soft, bloody organs to Granger, who then weighed each one on the shop digital scale and recorded the weight. Each organ was also digitally photographed for record purposes.

The pathologist then slowly removed the long, thick sliver that was lodged in the little boy's ear canal. It had been driven in so hard that Larry had to use locking pliers to pull it out, twisting and turning as he pulled. It had been driven into the ear canal about four inches. The end of the doweling was mushroomed over, indicating use of a hammer or something hard. Dark red blood oozed out of the ear. It was a horrible sight. Granger shed a tear!

Larry walked away for a moment, to gain his composure and then asked Granger if he was okay.

"Yes sir ... I'm okay, although it's very tragic and upsetting," Granger answered. "When I signed on for this profession, I didn't realize we would see these kinds of tragedies. The world, really is messed up sir."

"No doubt about it son. Now measure it out for me Granger, and see if it's the same as the others, cause it sure looks the same to me," Larry instructed.

"Eight inches, sir! And also, taking into account the flattened end ... I would estimate total length at about eight and a quarter inches, to be precise. One quarter of an inch, in diameter."

"I knew it ... it's another fucking chopstick Granger! The same kind as the other four ... identical to the others! The guy is either Asian or has a liking for Chinese food!" remarked the pathologist, angrily.

Larry checked the boys neck and had Granger make some more notes. There were bruises around the thin neck of the dead youngster. The bruises were long and several, almost like finger marks. On primary assumption, pathologist, Larry Sweet made a recommendation that little Randy Dickinson had been strangled by the killer and after death, had the chopstick hammered into his ear canal. But why? Was this some perverse, sexual satisfaction the murderer got off on? *Sick bastard! A fucking paraphiliac,* Larry thought to himself.

There was a knock on the back balcony door. Sunny jumped up and went to the door and looked through the little spy hole in the steel door. Babe gave a long, low, quiet growl.

"Don't answer it Sunny!" Ellen whispered. "It might be that crazy guy, maybe he followed us here!"

"It's okay, it's just Ike, from downstairs," Sunny opened the door slowly, and said, "hey Pic, how the hell are you? What's up, man?"

Babe started thumping her tail, and then got up from her comfy, fluffy bed and started to wag her tail back and forth, as she waddled over to Ike.

Ike bent over and started rubbing Babe's head, like he usually did when they saw each other. He had a fondness for dogs, especially Babe. "I'll tell you what's up Speed ... oh hey Ellen, how's it going?" Ike asked, as he looked over and saw her sitting on the leather couch.

Ike always had a kind of crush on Ellen, but she didn't really feel that way about him.

"I'm fine, Ike, how are you?"

"Better, now that I see you here!" he beamed.

"How's your brother doing these days?" Ellen asked Ike.

"He's good, he's working out of town right now ... over in cow-town (Calgary) for now ... making lots and lots of dough!"

"Awesome, tell him I said "hey" when you're talking to him," as she chewed her fingernails.

"Are you okay, Ellen ... you seem a bit anxious or nervous or something ... I'm not making you feel weird or anything am I?" Ike asked, looking concerned.

"No of course not Ike, I just have a bit of a headache going on, and a little buzz from the rum that Sunny gave me," Ellen laughed nervously.

Sunny asked Ike, "so what have you got for me this time, my good man?"

Ike and Sunny were really good buddies. Ellen, Sunny and Ike's older brother Brian, all went to high school together. Sunny met Ike from hanging out with Brian. Whenever Sunny went over to Brian's parents house to drink beer with Brian and shoot pool, little Ike would come down to the rec-room and bug the guys. Sunny didn't care. Brian used to get pissed off sometimes and tell

Ike to get lost, but Sunny would just laugh and tell Brian to chill out. He actually liked little Ike hanging around, showing Sunny how he could pick locks. The kid was amusing and smart as hell! A couple of times, Sunny came to little Ike's rescue, when he was being picked on, down at the park by some bigger kids. Sunny showed up and kicked some ass! He was Ike's personal bodyguard.

As time went on, and as Ike got older, he and Sunny became very close friends, very tight. Ike taught Sunny how to pick locks, all kinds of locks. Sunny became almost as efficient as Ike, when it came to by-passing a lock-set. You just never know when you might lose your key!

"Well, it's not ticking, so I guess you can have it," Ike joked as usual, as he looked over at Ellen and winked. He handed Sunny the small rectangular package, that had arrived earlier in the day for him.

"Great, I've been looking forward to this all week!" Sunny said smiling, as he felt the package and then walked over to his bedroom area and tossed it on the bed. "Want a quick rum and Pepsi, Pic?" Sunny asked.

"Yes, but no, I have to go back to work ... thanks anyway Speed ... see you again sometime Ellen!" Ike said. "Sure, Ike, you take care," Ellen replied.

Ike turned around and sauntered out the door, back to the grind. But he loved his job.

Sunny walked over and locked the steel door, with the two Medeco deadbolts, the ones that Ike had installed for him. They were top of the line security locks, impossible to pick, because of the tumbler mechanism inside. Commercial grade, high tensile steel. Nothing but the best, when it comes to keeping break-and-enter artists out. Sunny always preached, *"in order to beat a crook, you have to think like a crook!"*

"What's in the package, Sunny?" Ellen asked curiously. She wanted to know what that package contained; she was a little nosy sometimes.

"Never mind that right now Elly ... tell me, what did you see?" an over-excited Sunny Kruzik asked.

"I'm pretty sure I got the last three numbers ... of that prick's license plate!" Ellen divulged.

"Seriously ... you're kidding me, right?" Sunny cried.

"No Sunny, it's the straight goods, at first I was like ... in shock, everything happened so fast, it was just a blur, almost like it was a bad dream! I mean I can't be one hundred percent sure, but after I saw him pointing the gun at us, my body went numb and I couldn't move my legs. But I kept looking in the side mirror and I could see past his legs and ... "

"And what? What was it?" Sunny wanted to know.

"Well I think the numbers were 128, I think?" Ellen said unsure.

Sunny closed his eyes for a moment and ran his stocky fingers through his closely cropped hair. He then stretched his arms out, leaned forward and placed his hands on the kitchenette counter and tried to remember, if he could recall any of the details from earlier on that day.

It wasn't a total loss; he remembered the make and color of the car and the guy's sweaty face. He couldn't get that dude's face out of his mind! Never! He would never forget that face. Scruffy, dark, curly hair, unshaven, about forty-five years old with icy-blue piercing eyes! Eyes that were darting back and forth, from Sunny to his trusty dog, Babe; back and forth, back and forth, like he had some kind of nervous disorder! *What a fucking weirdo!*

And that gun, he was pointing at them. A long barreled revolver, maybe a Ruger Blackhawk or a Colt .45

Army model, it was a six shooter pistol, no mistaking that.

Sunny knew about guns. His father Wade, was a hunter and he taught his young son, all there was to know about "how the west was won". Wade often took young Sunny out into the mountains, for target practice or to shoot wild pigeons. They even went on a moose hunt, with some of Wade's work buddies, when young Sunny was only seventeen. Sunny was the only one in the group of "great white hunters" to bag a moose! But that day, Sunny Kruzik, realized that his father's passion for hunting wildlife was not in his own blood! He didn't want to upset his father, but he felt terrible after shooting that beautiful moose with the enormous rack.

It was late October 1992, up in Dawson Creek; Sunny and two other guys from the hunting party were riding off-road motorcycles about ten miles from camp.

Sunny was the first to spot the majestic beast clambering through the open muskeg. The weather was cool with a slight dampness in the air. This was one of the most heavily concentrated areas in British Columbia for *Ursus Arctos Horribilis,* otherwise known as the Grizzly Bear.

They were constantly on the look-out for the man-eaters! Grizzlies are at the top of the food chain and the hunter doesn't want to end up being the hunted.

Sunny jumped off his bike and crouched down into a one-leg kneeling position, while chambering a shell into the breech. The moose was about three hundred yards away, oblivious to the hunters. Sunny set his sights on the neck area of the moose, held his breath, like his father taught him; don't breathe when lining up your target, and squeeze the trigger, don't pull it or you may move the gun off the intended target. Sunny squeezed the trigger on the old, well-worn .303 British Lee Enfield army rifle, that Wade had given him for his twelfth birthday. That rifle was a classic, reconditioned and in great shape; from the second world war. It was a beauty, in the eyes of a young boy.

The moose dropped to it's knees and then slowly got back up, shaking it's large rack, from side to side and then proceeded to stagger away, towards a thicket of pine trees. It disappeared into the dense bush.

The guys rode their trail bikes through the muskeg, over to the thicket and then jumped off their rides, and slowly crept into the grove of jack-pines cautiously.

A twelve hundred pound, wounded bull-moose could easily charge and kill a man if it connected.

The three amigos loaded their rifles, spread out and entered between the trees; they could hear snorting and heavy breathing! The hunters spotted the big hairy beast, laying down, pawing at the ground and swaying his head, slowly side to side. It was as if the moose was trying to get back up, but didn't have the strength. Sunny could see where the bullet hit the neck, dark, red blood was oozing from the bullet wound.

"Finish him off, Sunny!" said Randy.

This was Randy's first big hunting trip too. The other hunter was a fellow named Mike, he was about twenty-four and had more hunting experience than Sunny and Randy.

Sunny looked that poor old bull-moose in the eyes and said sadly, "I'm sorry boy, wished I hadn't injured you, but I can't let you suffer."

Bang! ... Bang! ... Right smack in the forehead, but he wouldn't die, he just kept trying to get up, snorting blood and making awful guttural noises but couldn't move off the ground.

Sunny felt terrible! Bang! ... Bang! ... Bang! The moose let out his last groan and then dropped his head to the side and the mighty rack stuck into the soft ground, with a heavy thud!

Sunny thought to himself, *why did I do that to such a magnificent animal, what a bloody waste of nature, never again!* He felt really bad. It was his last time that he ever hunted animals!

But Sunny knew about guns. The whole family had guns at one time or another. His dad, his uncles, his grandfather and great-grandfathers all had guns. It was just part of the Kruzik clan.

Although, Sunny had a fondness for guns, his real love was knives. All types of knives appealed to him. Pocket knives, fixed blade knives, neck knives, tactical and one-handed openers. Sunny always carried a blade with him, just in case he needed to make a sandwich. His blade of choice was a serrated Dragonfly model, manufactured by Spyderco, with a two inch blade. A very small, concealed, easy-to-carry knife, whom he called "Buddy". He carried this on his belt-loop sideways; very quick for deployment when needed.

The Vancouver City Police Station, located at 312 Main Street downtown, was buzzing with activity, phones ringing, criminals being booked and fingerprinted and fines being paid. The "Station" as it was referred to, by most of the police members, was going "twenty-four seven", nonstop, just like any other big metropolis police station. All in a days work.

But the one big issue, that every member in the place had in common, was having to deal with; the fact, that some deranged monster was killing young children and teenagers on the streets of Vancouver. Many of the clerical workers and officers had kids of their own, so it really hit home!

Detective Kuban was sitting at his desk when his phone rang. "Yes, this is Detective Kuban, how can I help you? Yes, I see ... what's your name?" the policeman asked the caller, as he jotted down some notes. "Can I get your number, where I can get a hold of you?" Mmmm, hmmm, good ... okay, anytime of day at this number, got it! Now, go ahead and tell me what you saw."

Coffee was on the way, as Detective Rhodes was walking towards Kuban's desk, with two medium sized vanilla lattes in her hands. She had a troubled look on her face. No doubt her mind was consumed with the God-awful, horrible thoughts of the murdered children of the Fraser case.

She plopped down the piping hot java, on Kuban's desk and then pulled out a chair and sat down, listening and observing intently, to the responses from the interested detective.

Detective Kuban scribbled more notes on the pad of paper in front of him. "Okay, thanks Mr. Redmond ... I have made note of your information and I will review it with my department, and if I have any more questions, I will call you at the number you gave me. Yes ... we don't know right now ... but everything and anything may help. I may be in touch with you, thank-you, bye now."

Kuban looked at Rhodes with that hopeful look, one gives another when you are hoping for something good to happen, as he reached for his coffee. "Damn that's hot!" as he let go of the latte. "Trying to hurt me?"

Rhodes just smiled and teased him, "don't let the criminals see you do that, tough guy. Sooo, what was all that about Mike? Another tipster?"

"Yeah ... this guy, um ... Frederick Redmond he calls himself," as Kuban looks down at his notes, "claims to have seen a car last night, in the vicinity of the empty lot, where little Randy Dickinson was found!"

"How did he know that there was a murder there, I mean it hasn't even hit the news yet!" exclaimed Rhodes. "Says he lives in the neighborhood and he was walking to the 7-11 store, when he noticed all the people at the crime scene. He said last night, late last night, he was also going to the store and ..."

"He seems to go to the store a lot, eh?" Rhodes quipped sarcastically.

"Kuban continued, "noticed a car stopped at the lot ... kind of backed in with the trunk open. He really didn't think anything of it, until earlier today, when he saw the police cars and firetruck. He talked to someone at the scene and found out about a body lying there, so he thought he should call the police."

"Did he give you a description of the car, Mike?" as she took a sip of her beverage. "God, they make the best lattes," as she cupped both hands around the hot coffee.

"Well ... he really didn't give me much, cause like I said he didn't think too much of it, at the time, and it was also very dark, but he did notice two things," Kuban said.

SIX

Ellen and Sunny waited patiently behind one other couple. The hostess told Ellen, that it would only be a few minutes before they could be seated at a table. It was just after the dinner rush, but The Barking Dog Cafe was such a popular hangout for the East Side crowd. "East Side" was slang for East Vancouver.

"Getting a bite to eat was a great idea Sunny. I need something in my tummy, even though I'm not sure I can eat very much. I'm still nerve wracked from this morning!" Ellen shared.

"I know exactly how you feel Elly, but we needed to step out and eat something and I really didn't feel like cooking tonight. Besides, I have to walk you home after anyway, and this is on your way home."

Ellen lived about seven blocks from Sunny's apartment. When they hung out, they would usually walk to each others place or meet half way at The Barking Dog Cafe (or simply "The Dog" as it is known around the 'hood).

Sunny pulled the odd shift every now-and-then at The Dog, usually as part-time bartender or any general help that was needed at the cafe. It was a fun atmosphere; more of a "neighborhood pub", with pictures and statues of all kinds of dogs, all throughout the place.

DOG WITH A BONE

The family that started The Dog, were Irish; the O'Reilly' clan. Their forefathers were from Belfast and immigrated to Canada in 1910. They were potato farmers back in Ireland, but when they arrived here, they found employment with the railroad and the hotels. Some of the family branched into the liquor industry, working in the pubs, nightclubs and restaurants.

The O'Reilly's came up with the name for the bar, from a bull terrier dog named "Barney" they had owned. He barked anytime someone showed up at their house. Barney lived to the ripe old age of fourteen and then one day had a stroke, so he had to be put down. It was a sad day for the O'Reilly's and everyone else, that came to know Barney. So they named the pub in memory of their "best friend". His picture is on the sign and on all the menus in the bar.

Sunny flipped his "old school" cellphone open and punched in Geena's number and said, "hey sweetheart ... how are you?"

"Doing awesome Sundance, we're having a blast!" Geena replied. *"And how are you and Babe making out, without me there?"*

"Oh I think we can handle it. We're both fine and dandy. Elly and I are just sitting down for a bite at The Dog. Anyway, how's Seattle?"

"Seattle is wonderful!"

"And your sister, how's your sister?"

"Betty is spending lots of cashola, and having a grand ol' time!"

"Great ... okay, say hi to her for me, gotta' go now cupcake, the waitress is seating us! Love you Gee!" chimed Sunny. He closed his phone and stuck it in pocket.

"How's Geena doing, Sunny?" asked Ellen.

"She's good, they're having a blast ... doing lots of shoe shopping and bistro checking. She always wanted to go to Seattle for a few days, she'd never been before," Sunny answered, as they followed the waitress to a waiting table. Geena and Sunny have a total understanding of each other, a kind of open, trusting relationship. Either one, can hang out with the opposite sex, without any jealousy problems arising. Geena and Ellen hit it off, right from the get-go tremendously and Geena knows in her heart, that Ellen is very important to Sunny, because they have been such great friends since school days.

As much as Sunny and Geena loved each other and being together, they both really enjoyed their space as well. She has her own condo over by Granville Island, close to 4th Avenue, where all the funky stores are located. Geena loves to shop, so settling down on the west side of Vancouver in the Kitsilano area seemed to be the place!

After dinner, Sunny walked Ellen home up 41st Avenue, all the way to Sherbrooke Street. It was getting late, about 10:30 pm and the sky was overcast, no moon, dark as a demon's lair!

"I'm scared Sunny, what if that guy knows where I live?" Ellen said fearfully.

"Listen Elly, that idiot, doesn't know where you live, he doesn't know where I live, he doesn't even know who we are! I understand you're afraid, it gave me a good scare as well. If Babe hadn't been in the truck, baring her teeth ... who knows what that guy might have done? Then again, maybe he didn't even have any bullets in the gun."

Ellen started to cry, "I'm sorry Sunny, I ... I ... I'm just worried, that's all. What should we do about it?"

"We aren't going to do anything right now, okay, just trust me Elly, trust me please. I'm going to take care of it!" Ellen wasn't completely sure what Sunny meant by what he just said, *I'm going to take care of it!*

"You're safe ... that was just a random act of craziness. We happened to drive into a weirdo hanging around in the bush, and now we are far away from him," Sunny explained.

"How are you going to take care of it, Sunny?" Ellen asked.

He just smiled and shrugged his shoulders, "trust me, okay ... please? Try and put it out of your mind and get some sleep tonight, okay?" he told her.

"Okay!" Ellen answered, as they entered her apartment building.

Sunny walked her up to her unit on the second floor, gave her a hug and told her not to worry. He said he would be in touch.

Ellen went inside, closed the door behind her and locked it. *I'm going to take care of it,* she thought to herself, *what did he mean by that?* she wondered.

Sunny was the sweetest guy she knew, but Ellen also knew, that you didn't dare push him around or threaten him. He had a lightning-fast temper and she had witnessed him in fights, at school and at the bar, bring down some of the biggest guys.

Ellen brushed her teeth and climbed into bed and lay on her side in the fetal position, closed her eyes and tried to fall asleep, but she kept seeing that psycho with the gun.

Sunny thought he'd take a shortcut home; instead of walking back down 41st Avenue, he figured he would head back along 43rd Avenue and cut through South Memorial Park. There was a slight breeze, blowing through the park and it was still very warm out, but it was pitch black now. He was about half way through the baseball field, when he heard something or someone come running up behind him. He turned around to see what it was and heard something whizz past his head. Narrowly missing his face, the object hit the ground with a dull thud, landing about twenty feet away from him. In the dim light, he could see it was a full bottle of beer, with the cap still on.

Sunny scanned the area quickly, but it was hard to see, because the clouds were blanketing out the moonbeams. He could make out two shadows, maybe three, separating and moving around him about fifteen feet away. Sunny moved back and from the help of the nearby streetlights he caught a glimpse of the dark moving silhouettes.

Street punks! Three for sure, maybe more? No, only three that he could see.

Vancouver had lots of street gangs; some were organized and some were merely kids, who thought they were tough and hung out mainly in the parks. They were known as "park gangs". The only problem nowadays, was that some of these cowardly bastards carried guns, cause they weren't tough at all. That's why they were hanging around in a gang in the first place. They all needed backing from each, in order to beat someone up or rob them!

"Hey fuck! Got a cigarette?" yelled one of the punks. Sunny didn't answer. Talking, expended valuable energy; information his Master had taught him years earlier.

Instead, he reached into his pocket and pulled out his "Kubotan". This was a small pocket-sized item, created solely for self-defense. Sunny learned how to use this neat little weapon, while taking karate. His Master taught him a few great tricks, using it on all the pressure points of the human body. Pressure points, that would disable a person within seconds.

"I asked you a question asshole! You got a fuckin' cigarette? Answer me, NOW!" as the dark silhouette moved towards Sunny.

Sunny charged the mouthy punk. Taking a jump up, to the left side, and while in the air, did a half circle, with the Kubotan tightly clenched in his right hand. In midair, he swung around from behind the guys head and drove the end of the aluminum dowel as hard as he could into the base of the guy's soft neck.

The douche-bag crumpled to the ground, making a wheezing noise, trying to talk, but nothing came out. He was clawing at the ground trying to move his body, but was unable to.

One of the other guys came at Sunny, screaming at him, with his arms flailing recklessly in the air. Sunny put up his fists and stepped to the side slightly. As the attacker got up closer, Sunny dropped down to the ground on one knee and slugged the guy as hard as he was physically able to, right in the "family jewels".

The ruffian let out a screech and fell forward onto the ground, rolling around and holding his nuts, bellowing out intermittent screams of agony. The last wanna-be gang-banger took off running through the park as fast as he could, never looking back.

Sunny stood motionless for a few seconds, taking a good look around the dark park to see if there were anymore trouble makers. None that he could see. He then brushed off his jeans and took a few deep breaths. Sunny slipped the Kubotan into his back pocket ready for action, just in case and then he headed for home through the park.

SEVEN

The morning sun-rays were sneaking through the blinds of the side window of the loft. Babe was nudging Sunny's arm, as she always did at 6:00 am. She needed to have her morning pee and then of course, breakfast!

Labs loved food, any kind of food. Babe's favorites included, carrots, chicken, steak, and even prawn tails, when there were leftovers! But Sunny had her on a certain diet of Pedigree kibbles, mixed with a teaspoon of wet dog food and garnished with a few raw carrot pieces.

The vet told Sunny, that Babe needed to lose a few pounds, so her hips wouldn't bother her as she got older. It was a constant battle for both of them. Babe acted as if she was starving and Sunny couldn't resist those big, brown, sad eyes, so he usually gave in and gave her a Milkbone for dessert. He walked her incessantly, to keep the weight off.

Sunny slipped on his jeans and pulled his worn-out Snoopy t-shirt over his head and took Babe out the back way for a pee. There was a park, just down the alley and around the corner, where she did her business. Babe was a real sniffer. Sometimes Sunny called her "Hound Dog", cause she had to stop and smell every little thing in her path. The tiniest blade of grass and she had to smell what had been there before.

Sunny put the coffee on and then turned on the radio to listen to the seven o'clock news. All the usual negative crap on the morning report. But he did chuckle to himself when he heard the announcer say ...

"Three local teens walking through South Memorial Park, last night about 10:30 pm, were assaulted viciously by an unknown assailant, for no apparent reason. One of the teens had to be hospitalized with severe neck trauma. Police are looking into the matter. Anyone with information can call the Vancouver Police or crimestoppers."

Sunny chuckled again, looked at his dog, and said to her, "those poor boys, hey Babe," as he patted her on the head and then got her breakfast ready. "Just another night in the park and a lesson taught!"

He opened the fridge door and brought out milk, carrots and an apple. Sunny measured out a cup of kibble, cut up part of a carrot into pieces, mixed it into her kibble and put the bowl down beside her water dish. He then made himself some fresh apple and carrot juice and poured the milk over his cereal and garnished with raw almonds.

After breakfast, Sunny opened his Dell laptop which he nicknamed "Della" and turned her on. His first order of business at the coffee table was to check his email. Usually a bunch of jokes and stuff that he quickly deleted. Sometimes a message from one or two of his family members, sister, uncle, nephew, girlfriend, but not his mom or dad. They didn't seem too interested in the new technology. Sunny wasn't really sure why. After all, it was the way the world was going and who wants to be left behind?

He then went to "The Province" newspaper website to check out the news of the day. Staring right at him on the homepage was the headline that read, "FRASER KILLER STRIKES AGAIN".

Sunny took a long sip of his Irish cream coffee. *Man, that coffee tastes good!* He read the article about the young Dickinson boy, and bit his lower lip. *Damn it! That poor kid, just like all the others!* Sunny was following the Fraser murders intently. He was repulsed, that some maggot, was out there torturing and ending their lives, just for his or her own gratification. *And the chopstick! Another bloody fricking chopstick! How sick was this piece of shit?*

Sunny's philosophical assumption on the murders was that, whoever was killing these innocent kids, was nothing more than a bully who had morphed into an evil, vile scum-sucking transgressor, that deserved to die! Sunny could feel his blood run cold and rage starting to buildup inside him!

He closed Della and poured another cup of Joe, stepping out to the front balcony, into the morning sunrise. The air was warm. Sunny took a deep breath of fresh air. As fresh as you can get in the city, that is. He stood there, looking at the sunrise, thinking about those murdered children.

Sunny could hear the pigeons under the overhang of the building. They were building a nest, for their babies. Most landlords or tenants would shoe them away! But not Sunny, he could watch them for hours, going about their business. Birds are one of the most intelligent species on the planet and Sunny figured that they were probably smarter than most people.

He looked down the street, to see the shop keepers getting ready for the busy day. There were produce vendors organizing their fruit and veggies, and the grocery store owner, sweeping the sidewalk off. The young lady that worked at Jimmy's Book Store was washing the front windows. A three-ton delivery truck was parked below Sunny's front windows in front of Black's shop, unloading a safe. Ah, the hustle and bustle of the city.

Time for a morning workout. Sunny went back inside the loft and did some pushups, situps and a few curls with his weights. He liked keeping toned, so he wasn't lifting heavy weights like he did about five years ago. Sunny's arms were as tough as sinew and he's in awesome shape for his age.

Some days he would go for a run around the neighborhood, ride his mountain bike, but usually he would take Babe for a walk. This way she got her exercise too. Babe wasn't much of a runner; just a sniffer and a doddler!

Detective Rhodes' cellphone rang. She was just getting out of the shower, and didn't have time to answer it, so the message went to her voice-mail.

Rhodes dried herself off and ruffled up her squeaky clean hair, trying to avoid tangles. Still dripping, she checked her voice-mail.

"Jane, it's Mike ... I've been thinking all night about the Dickinson case and ... well, call me back ASAP!"

After she dried her silky skin, Rhodes rang Kuban's number, "hey Mike, what's up?"

"I've been thinking, that we should get that witness to come down to the station and give us a statement," Kuban suggested eagerly.

DOG WITH A BONE

"Are you talking about the last guy that phoned yesterday, Frederick Redmond?" Rhodes asked.

"Yes, he sounded ... well, like he was telling the truth, and we need to check every little detail out. I just have a good feeling about his information, even if it's not much." Anytime a crime happens, a serious crime, the police get all kinds of tips, from all kinds of people! Usually, the tipsters have genuinely good intentions, and although they may think, that they are helping out, sometimes they are just bogging down the investigation, with a bunch of misleading tips. But sometimes even the tiniest detail can be the biggest break that the police need in order to solve the case.

With a crime that involves children, it seems to be human nature that everyone wants to help out, but some of those people that want to help are congenital liars, others are delusional and some are just plain crazy!

"I'll call Mr. Redmond and see if he can be down here at 9:00 am, okay Jane? Can you be here by 8:30? My turn to buy coffees," Kuban tempted.

"No problem, see you soon," Rhodes replied as she was checking out her nude, athletic shape in the mirror.

Just as Sunny was pouring his second cup of coffee, there was a long screeching sound and then a huge BANG! Right outside of his apartment. He dropped the coffee onto the counter and ran over to the window and looked down.

A jacked-up Dodge truck broadsided a Nissan Juke. There was steam coming out from under the crumpled hood of the Juke. Sunny could see from the window that the person driving the Nissan was possibly injured. The body of the driver was slumped forward.

Ike and Jim were already at the collision, as well as some of the other shop keepers. The driver of the big truck got out of the cab and jumped down and walked over to the smashed-up "crossover" vehicle. *Big truck, small brain!* Sunny thought to himself. *Those asshole, bully drivers!* "He was on his cellphone, I saw him talking on his cellphone!" cried a lady, who was standing on the corner waiting to cross the street.

"Someone call an ambulance, who has a phone?" said another person on the sidewalk.

Sunny was preparing to call the paramedics, but he could see that almost everyone out on the street had a mobile phone of some sort. He counted about eight people on their phones, so he didn't bother. But that nagging question, always bothered him. *What if they are talking to their friends and everyone else thinks, that someone else already phoned.* So he phoned 911 anyway, just to make sure. Yes, someone had already called. It was all under control.

While Sunny was in the shower, he could hear the wailing of the sirens coming to the accident.

After his shower, he threw on his snug fitting jeans, charcoal gray, v-neck t-shirt and black sneakers. He had about six pairs of sneakers, all different brands and colors. Sunny clipped Buddy onto his belt-loop. He always took his Buddy along for the ride!

"Come on, Babe!" Sunny called as he headed for the exit to the garage.

Down the spiral staircase they went, round and round; Babe right on his heels.

He opened the door to the Accord and she jumped in and sat in the passengers seat, ready to go. Babe loved riding "shotgun" in the car with Sunny. It didn't matter what car they were in, or if it was the truck. As long as she was with Sunny, she was a happy girl.

He clicked the remote and the garage door opened. The black Honda crept out into the alley. Sunny slipped his shades on over his baby-browns. He slid CCR's Greatest Hits into the CD player and turned it up. "Born on the Bayou" spilled out over the speakers. Deadly tunes!

Sunny turned down the opposite way of the accident scene. The tow-truck was still there, loading up the badly mangled Juke, that was now a "Junk". No point in getting caught up in the traffic snarl. Besides, he would read all about it, in the online edition of The Province, tomorrow morning with his coffee. Right now, Babe and Sunny were on a mission! They were heading to Stanley Park for the day.

EIGHT

"I think we need to meet sir ... the sooner the better, for your peace-of-mind."

The voice on the other end of the line was dead silent, for what seemed like five minutes, although it was only a ten second delay, at the most. "Who is this ... and what do you want!?" came the answer.

"You are Dr. Randall Wilson, are you not?" the caller asked.

Again, another long silent pause on the other end, this time with some laboured breathing. "Yes ... yes, I am Dr. Wilson, are you threatening me? Cause I'm ... going to ... hang up now!" the doctor nervously replied.

"No sir, I am not threatening you, please listen ... I read about your wife and I want to help you," the caller said. "This is some sort of a sick joke, isn't it ... and your some kind of a whack job! That's it ... I'm hanging up!" Dr. Wilson said excitedly.

"Please just hear me out!" the caller urged. "Dr. Wilson, do you remember the Marlowe case two years ago, it was all over the news ... you know the lady that was found on the banks of Jericho Beach. It was in all the newspapers and all over the TV."

The doctor didn't hang up, but instead listened to the voice on the other end. He was wondering what this had to do with him. His nervousness subsided a small amount, but he still felt a twinge of uneasiness.

"Yes I remember that murder, it was horrible!" Wilson said.

"Yes indeed, it was horrible, very tragic to say the least," replied the caller. "And do you remember, that the police identified Ms. Marlowe's killer?"

"I do remember that as well ... look, what has that poor lady's death have to do with me or my wife?"

"That crazy psycho was charged with first degree murder and the judge let him walk, because of lack of evidence," said the caller.

"You're right ... who are you, and what's your name?" the doctor asked.

"Burt. I'm the one to help you even the score Doctor!"

Catherine Marlowe's naked body was found on the sandy shoreline of Jericho Beach in the spring of 2010. She was an attractive single woman, in her thirtieth year. Her hands had been bound with zip ties, behind her back and she had a red ball-gag stuffed in her mouth. Catherine had been sexually tortured, cigarette burns all over her chest and buttocks. Her brunette hair had been hacked off and the bottoms of her feet were bruised from some kind of trauma; possibly a form of bastinado.

A jogger and his Irish Setter spotted Catherine from the sidewalk, early in the misty morning.

Given the way she was found, so brutally tortured and tied up, Operations Investigation Section of the Vancouver City Police decided to assign twenty officers to the case. Normally they would only assign five to ten, but they knew they had a real perverted, sadist on the loose and they wanted him caught ASAP.

After two months of pounding the pavement and interviewing witnesses, they got a break in the case. It was revealed that Catherine Marlowe liked to party sometimes. The police had statements from several people that knew her and that had seen her drinking, at the Biltmore Hotel pub on Kingsway, the night before her body was found. According to witnesses, apparently she left the pub with a man in his late twenties. One witness recalled seeing both of them get into a newer red Ford pickup truck with an older Vanguard camper on the back.

"That struck me as very odd," said one witness to the investigating Detective. "The fact, that here's this brand new truck with an old, junky camper ... it just stuck out like a sore thumb! Guess that's why I remembered it."

Global TV and all the other news stations, ran look-a-like pictures of the truck and camper on the morning and evening news. The Province and Vancouver Sun also ran the photos. BINGO! Within a week OIS had over fifty sitings of the vehicle. They checked out each and every lead with a fine tooth comb.

After three weeks and two days, they had their main suspect! A dark haired guy, with a handle-bar mustache. He was twenty-eight year old Jack Phillips from Vancouver Island, and he had been visiting his parents in Burnaby.

The police impounded his truck and camper and sent it to the FIU to have it extensively checked over. Another BINGO! Catherine Marlowe's DNA was all over the camp-er. They even found her brassiere, stuffed in the bottom of the closet, under some fishing gear. The suspect probably kept it as a souvenir. Some of these sick fucks, collect trophy's from their kills. Phillips claimed it was an ex-girlfriend's bra, until the police reminded him that Ms. Marlowe's DNA had been discovered on it.

Jack Phillips confessed to entertaining Catherine Marlowe in the truck and camper, but denied murdering her. He concocted a story and claimed that they picked up a hitch-hiker on the way to the beach. Then the three of them stopped at the liquor store and picked up some more booze and cigarettes.

"What's your name, man?" Jack asked the hitcher.

"Ronald ... what's yours? the hitcher answered with a question.

"I'm Jack and this is ... Cathy ... and we're going to get high tonight, man ... I mean Ronald! A little drink, a little gonja and a whole lotta' sex! You in buddy?"

"Fuckin' rights Jack!" Ronald replied anxiously.

Phillips explained to the packed courtroom, that after the three of them parked in the beach parking lot, they started drinking Old Style Pilsener beer and downing Crown Royal Whisky shooters. Phillips stated that they smoked some high-grade marijuana as well. Then they got to the sex. He said that Catherine wanted to have sex with both of them, but she insisted that they had to treat her rough.

"What are you guys into?" Cathy asked hesitantly.

"I'm game for whatever!" yelled Ronald.

"Me too!" sputtered a drunken Jack.

"I'm into mild bondage, and maybe a little S&M," she submissively answered. "I like to be spanked when I'm a naughty girl!"

They all began taking their clothes off, Jack helping Cathy out of her jeans and then removing her shirt and bra. Within minutes they were all naked and having a menage-a-trois. The camper was a rockin'!

Jack Phillips woke up early, at about five o-clock the next morning. His head was banging, just like it was going to explode! *What the ...* ? He looked down on the floor and gasped ... "Oh my God!"

Catherine Marlowe lay on the camper floor, nude, with her hands secured behind her back. Jack looked around the camper, it was a bloody mess. Beer bottles all over the dirty counter and clothes strewn all over the place. And the ashtray, was over-flowing with cigarette butts and roaches! What a bloody, putrid stink!

Then it dawned on him that Ronald was nowhere to be seen. He crawled down from the overhead bunk to the cluttered floor.

"Cathy, wake up!" Jack shouted with a raspy voice, while giving her a light kick with his foot. "Wake up!"

She didn't budge. Jack bent down to shake her shoulder and then realized that she wasn't breathing. He turned her over and saw that she was starting to turn a bluish color. And those burns, all over her body, those awful cigarette burns! *Christ, she still has that gag in her mouth from last night! What the hell happened?* Jack panicked.

It was still dark outside. Jack opened the camper door and looked around. Ronald was gone for sure. Nobody else was around, so he dragged Catherine's limp, lifeless body out of the camper. She only weighed about one hundred and twenty-five pounds, so Jack dragged her across the parking lot and over the grass, right to the sand. Nervously, he took a deep breath and then dragged her some more, over the sand towards the water's edge. Then he ran back to the camper, scanning the beach and parking lot. Still there was nobody around. *What luck!*

Jack then drove out of the Jericho Beach parking lot and headed towards Kingsway. He followed Kingsway, all the way to Central Park in Burnaby, not too far from his parents place.

Central Park was the biggest park in Burnaby. It also bordered Vancouver. Many would compare it to Central Park in New York City.

Jack pulled into the parking lot, off of Boundary Road and parked at the far end of the lot. Dawn was just starting to break through the night sky above.

He cleaned up the back of the camper, as best he could in his hung-over state. Jack then gathered up all the beer bottles and cigarette butts and threw them into the park waste-bin that was sitting in front of the truck. Then he quickly drove to his parent's house.

The jury bought his story. Jack Phillips was arrested and charged with forcible confinement, rape, torture and first degree murder of Catherine Marlowe. They had his DNA all over the body of Catherine and her DNA was all over the camper. They even had the witness that saw them leave the bar together. What they didn't have was the third party, Ronald! Who was this guy anyway? Did he even exist?

Phillips pleaded "NOT GUILTY" to all counts, as his lawyer had advised him. They used the third party "wildcard". Phillips had insisted, he did not kill Catherine. Yes, they left the bar together and yes, they had wild sex together, but no he did not kill her! This was his confession to the court, the jury and the judge. Phillips testified that after all the drinking and drugs and mild bondage, that he must have blacked out. Ronald had been present for all the wild debauchery, but was nowhere to be seen the next morning. He had just disappeared! And Ms. Marlowe was dead.

Autopsy reports from the B.C. Coroner's Service showed that Catherine Marlowe had been strangled to death. Not from the ball-gag, but from a belt of some sort.

The belt marks on her neck, matched the leather belt that they had found in Phillips' bedroom at his home on Vancouver Island. When he was arrested, the police searched his house for evidence as they normally do with any murder suspect.

The defense lawyer theorized that after his client had passed out, Ronald took Jack's belt and murdered the young lady and then slipped away, before daybreak. It could be possible ... maybe, but not likely, the prosecution argued. A fabricated story to appease the jury, no doubt. There was no trace of any third party's DNA or fingerprints. Circumstantial evidence revealed that, only Jack's and Catherine's DNA and fingerprints were recovered at the crime scene.

The Prosecutor felt that they had a "slam-dunk" case. The jury was out for five days. Not a good sign, when it comes to a horrific murder. It usually means, the members of the jury don't all agree. Usually a guilty verdict will come out on the first day, if all members agree and the evidence is cut and dry.

The evidence all pointed to Jack Phillips, his DNA, his fingerprints, his belt, his confession of being with her and not a single shred of evidence of the man called "Ronald". On the afternoon of the fifth day, the jury found Jack Phillips, "NOT GUILTY" on all charges. They decided among themselves, that there could be "a reasonable doubt". The judge instructed the jury, that they could not convict the defendant, if they felt that he was *probably* guilty, "beyond a reasonable doubt".

Phillips' lawyer was a slime-ball, a parasite, the kind that was able to sway the jury with his bullshit, even though the prosecution had all the evidence they needed to get a conviction. He emphasized the fact to the court, that there was a third person, named Ronald, who had killed Catherine Marlowe, and then left the scene, before Jack Phillips woke up.

He summarized up by telling the jury, "you can't prove that there wasn't a third person, and with that in mind, it would not be constitutional to convict my client, Mr. Jack Phillips, and send him to prison for life ... when there is the possibility, that Ronald murdered Ms. Catherine Marlowe! Please, I ask you ... ladies and gentlemen of the jury, make the right decision and set Mr. Phillips free, so he can continue on with his life."

And the jury bought it! Jack Phillips walked! He was a free man, with a big, sly, shit-eating grin! He beat the system. Well, his lawyer beat the system, like so many other scumbag lawyers that treat the system, as nothing more than an ever growing money-tree.

The justice system doesn't protect the victims or the innocents. It works for the ones employed in the legal system. The lawyers and the judges are the ones it works for! And the politicians are the ones who formulate the laws and hire the judges, so in essence, they are the real reason Canada has one of the worst and most lenient legal systems in the world.

The jury system is outdated, archaic, so to speak! Just think about this analysis:

It takes about six to eight years to become a lawyer in Canada. First, a person has to enroll into a university program, of two to four years and must receive a Bachelor of Laws degree from a recognized law school. The next step is to successfully complete a bar admission course, pass the exam and then to complete a period of articling (training). Again, six to eight years just to become a lawyer.

Now, in order to become a judge, a lawyer needs at least, ten years experience to qualify for a superior provincial court. The superior provincial courts and the Supreme Court of Canada handle all the serious matters, such as murders and rapes. Canadian judges are not elected, but rather appointed, by the Federal Cabinet on recommendation of the Minister of Justice. In present times, it is court protocol, to refer to the judges as "justices". Then there's the jury, a random selection of Canadian citizens. Anyone can be chosen for jury duty, but not all are accepted. After a series of personal questions from the defense lawyer and the prosecution, twelve members are chosen to decide someone's fate! That's right, no law school, no articling, no bar exam, no six to eight years of practicing law, and no ten years experience to become a judge, but they can determine if someone is guilty or not! Right off the street, with zero justice knowledge!

Those twelve jury members can send someone to jail for life or grant them freedom, all depending on which "sales-pitch" they believe, the prosecutor or the defense lawyer. What a bloody crock! No wonder the citizens of the country have lost faith in the justice system and despise the politicians who concoct the laws and appoint the judges to the bench.

"I'm not sure ... I understand ... what you're trying to say, Burt?" queried Dr. Wilson.

"Don't you remember what happened, after Jack Phillips went free?" Burt replied.

"Yes ... I remember ... they found him about two months later on the banks of Jericho Beach, almost at the exact same place where Catherine Marlowe was found. He had been garrotted and he had cigarette burns all over his body ... very similar to the young lady that he killed. I thought that was very strange indeed! Maybe there was ... a third person after all? Thank God he's dead ... whoever did that, saved the taxpayers a lot of money," Wilson said. "Like I said earlier, Dr. Wilson, we need to meet for your peace-of-mind. You are aware, that the the nineteen year-old that murdered your wife is being released next week, are you not?"

"Yes, I'm aware of that, the authorities contacted me last month, to let me know. Are you Ronald? Are you the guy who killed Ms. Marlowe?" the doctor asked with a progressing uneasiness in his voice.

"No Dr. Wilson, I'm not Ronald, I'm Burt, remember?" the caller replied. "I will call you back in a few days."

The caller hung up the receiver and then exited the phone booth. He took off his gloves and put them in his jacket pocket.

Wilson set the phone down slowly, rubbed his chin and then wiped his brow with his sleeve. He looked around his office in a state of shock and then walked over to the water cooler and filled a Styrofoam cup and then sat down and sipped the cold water slowly. Confused, he thought, *oh my God, what just happened here?*

NINE

THREE DAYS LATER – Tuesday

Frederick Redmond had given his statement to the police detectives three days ago. The information he told them, had given them enough evidence to run a mock-up display bulletin, in the newspapers, online with social media, on Global TV news and some of the other stations as well.

Their news release showed a compact car, dark in color, possibly blue or black, with roof-racks on top. The make of the car wasn't exactly known, except that it was an earlier model; possibly late nineties. It wasn't a lot to go on, but at least the police, would hopefully get some tips from the public.

By showing the picture in the news, they felt they may generate some callers to phone in and the police could then follow up any leads that may fit that description. It was a long shot in the dark, but the detectives felt that with all the newer cars on the road, an older, dark colored, compact car with roof-racks might stand out like a beached whale on the sand.

The police were gambling by releasing the bulletin, because the killer could be watching the news also and easily remove the roof-racks, if he or she knew that the police were onto him or her. But nonetheless, if a neighbor or friend of that person, knew about the racks and were to do the right thing and alert the police, it wouldn't matter if the killer removed the racks or not; because the police would most likely find the evidence of scratch marks on top of the roof of the suspect vehicle.

Roof-racks, no matter how gently they are installed and removed, would leave some indication on the paint, that they had actually been there at some point. The only sure way to get rid of the evidence, would be, to have the whole roof repainted, but then the roof wouldn't match the rest of the car.

If the police received any tips about a suspect car, that may have or had, roof-racks previously, they could investigate that particular vehicle. Then, the next shred of evidence for the police would be to match the tires on the car, to the tire tread marks found at the scene of the crimes. The murderer probably wouldn't have enough sense to change the tires, or want to spend the money. The police had not revealed the information about the tire tracks to the press, so in turn it was never released to the public. The investigators felt that if that information had leaked to the public, the killer would have definitely had the tires changed.

Another beautiful, sunny day in Greater Vancouver City! Sunny thought to himself, as he and Babe were walking up Victoria Drive, from Jones Park. Babe loved her walks, she always walked side by side with her master, occasionally stopping for a pee or to sniff something odorous! Sunny loved walking too. When Geena was around and not off, on some faraway adventure, the three of them would walk all around the city.

Vancouver is a big, beautiful city, with so many attractions and fun things to do; places to visit, shop and a plethora of eateries. A person could eat at a different restaurant every day for a year, no problem!

Sunny and Babe stopped at Cookie's Grocery, on the corner of Victoria Drive (or the "Drive" as it was known to the locals) and 43rd Avenue, to pick up a Province newspaper. It was only two blocks from his place. He walked right in with Babe, as she was allowed in to the store, cause the owners had a "pet friendly" policy. Man's "best friend" is always welcome at Cookie's.

The owner and the employees that worked at Cookie's all loved Babe! What wasn't to like about her? She was beautiful, friendly, well-mannered, and those big, brown chestnut eyes could melt a person's heart!

"Ahh, good maw-ning Sunny!" sang Mr. Chan. "How the puppy dog tooday?"

"She' a peach Mr. Chan! Couldn't have picked a better one if I tried," Sunny replied.

"Can I give her Miwk-Bone today?"

"You bet! We just went for a long walk this morning, so she could probably use a snack."

"Here Baby, you have treat!" as the store owner bent over and patted her golden yellow head. Babe's tail is just a waggin', as she crunches the Milk-Bone into smithereens!

"Thanks, Mr. Chan, I'm sure if she could talk, she'd thank you too!" as Sunny picked up a Province paper and grabbed a litre of skim milk from the cooler.

"That it, Sunny?" asked Mr. Chan.

"Yes sir, that's good for now. See you later ... come on Babe, lets go now, say good-bye."

Mr. And Mrs. Chan both smiled and watched Sunny and his dog walk out of the store. They really liked Sunny and Babe. Sunny explained to the Chans', that if they ever had any problems at the store with customers, to phone him and he would take care of the problem. They never forgot that!

The Chans' immigrated to Canada about ten years ago, from Shanghai, China. They brought their two young daughters with them. The Chans' felt their daughters could have a better life in Canada, by studying at a recognized university like Simon Fraser or University of British Columbia, (UBC).

One daughter is presently enrolled in the Bachelor of Dentistry program at UBC and the other daughter is still helping mom and dad with the day-to-day operations in the store. She is planning to eventually become a Certified General Accountant, (CGA) taking her course through correspondence. Her name is May, and she has a crush on Sunny! She is ten years younger than Sunny and knows he has a girlfriend, but she knows she can still dream!

The sweet smell of vanilla wafting from the coffee pot was enough to make a non-coffee drinker, want to have a cup! Sunny poured himself a fresh cup, with a shot of Bailey's Irish Cream, sat down on the well-worn leather couch and dropped the Province paper on the coffee table. He opened up the paper and scanned over the second page.

The heading "POLICE SEEK PUBLIC'S HELP", caught his eye. He read over the short paragraph and studied the photo that was below the article. Sunny sipped on the steaming beverage. The photo showed two smaller type cars, darker in color and both digitally enhanced with roof-racks. Sunny thought to himself, *it can't be, can it?*

This time he took a gulp of coffee and burned his tongue. "Shit!" as he put the coffee down and picked up his phone. He punched in Ellen's phone number. "Hey Elly, how's it goin?" Sunny asked.

"Fine I guess ... how are you doing?" Ellen replied. "Doing okay Elly ... hey did you happen to read The Province paper this morning?" Sunny asked her, as he took another shot of his coffee, carefully this time.

"No, why?" Ellen wondered.

"Well, on the second page, there's an article run by the city police, about those Fraser murders ... and there's also a picture with it ... with two similar, but different cars, and get this ... they both have roof-racks on them."

"Are you shittin' me, Sunny?" Ellen said in disbelief.

"No, Elly, I'm dead serious."

"Are you thinking what I'm thinking?" asked Ellen.

"More than likely! That guy's car had roof-racks on it, remember? You know what else I remember Elly ... now that I'm thinking about it? There was something about those racks that I noticed," Sunny said.

"What was it Sunny?" Ellen asked curiously.

"Those roof-racks were partially wrapped in what looked like black electrician's tape. I mean everything happened so damn quick ... the guy, the gun, the car and those fucking black roof-racks! I'm almost positive they had black shiny tape wrapped around them."

"I'm not sure about that Sunny?" Ellen replied.

"Well I remember now ... *and* it was a smaller car *and* ... wasn't it blue? A darker color, right Elly?" Sunny questioned.

"I don't recall it being darker, I do know that it was a bluish color ... does blue count as a dark color, Sunny?"

"Well, I would say that blue is darker than yellow, white, orange and light blue. It wasn't a pale blue, so maybe it would be considered a darker color," Sunny speculated.

"Maybe we should call the police and tell them what happened to us, it may help them catch the killer, if it's the same vehicle. What do you think Sunny?" Ellen asked.

"No, let's just keep tabs on the news and see what happens. I really don't want to get directly involved Elly. Besides, the police will end up getting dozens of tips from the public. I'm sure it's just a matter of time before they catch him." *And then nothing will happen to him, just like all the other heinous criminals, they all just get a slap on the wrist!* "Look Elly, I have to go, but I'll call you again soon, just be vigilant, okay," Sunny said.

"Okay Sunny, talk soon. Bye."

Sunny closed his cellphone and finished his coffee. It was almost cold by now. Sunny just sat gazing at the newspaper article. He could feel his blood starting to boil as he looked at the photo of the two cars. He couldn't believe it!

Both cars were mid 1990's models. One was a Chevy Corsica, also known as a Pontiac Tempest and the other was a Ford Taurus. They were both very popular compact, four-door sedans, in their heyday. The Corsica was last produced in 1996. The Taurus body design was changed to a more "oval" looking shape in 1997. So the similarities in body design would have been in 1996, as both vehicles body shapes were "squared off". The two cars were quite very similar in looks.

Sunny studied the picture. The more he looked at the image, the more he was sure, that the killer of the Fraser murders, was driving the same car that he and Ellen encountered in the bush four days ago. *Could it be a coincidence? Nah, there can't be more than one freak driving around in a blue 1996 Corsica or Taurus, with roof-racks on it. Besides the common factor was that, this car is a suspect vehicle in the Fraser killings and possibly the same car that was in the bush; when me, Babe and Elly were threatened. It must be the same weirdo!*

But Sunny had one up on the cops. He had the first three numbers from the car's license plate. Obviously, if the cops had that, they would have printed the plate numbers in the newspaper article. He could easily phone the police and give them the "128" numbers off the plate, that Ellen had memorized after seeing them in the truck side-mirror.

And then what? The cops arrest the killer, then thousands of taxpayer's dollars are spent recklessly at a "circus- trial" with an outdated jury system, that are lied to by an unethical scum-sucking lawyer and then the murderer goes free, only to start raping, torturing and murdering all over again!

Not a chance in hell! Sunny sat thinking to himself. *They won't get those numbers, those are MY lovely numbers! Mine!*

TEN

Wednesday

"Thank-you for meeting me here today Dr. Wilson. We really needed to discuss something, and I know just by you showing up, that you are, in fact interested in what I have to say," explained Burt.

The nervous doctor looked around, and rubbed his hands together as if he was trying to warm up his surgery-performing hands. Beads of sweat were forming on the upper and lower sides of the three recessed lines on his well-weathered forehead.

"Sir, I understand your wondering why I'm here. I'm not here to harm you, but we need to walk a little, outside through the parking lot and maybe over to that park, over there," the man told the doctor as he nodded his head towards the exit doors.

It was noon and the food-court was extremely busy. As the two men walked through the main doors of the shopping mall, Burt casually looked all around, just to make sure no one was following them. They walked along the side of the mall and then stepped out across the pavement and on through some parked cars.

Guildford Shopping Center, located in Surrey, had an enormous parking lot. There were hundreds of cars parked every day on the vast ocean of pavement. So many cars in fact, that every day, no less than three cars a day were stolen by car thieves. Burt had witnessed a thief stealing a car from the lot two years earlier. He had been walking into the mall, when he heard a car alarm sound off! He turned around in time to see a guy in a black hoody, breaking through the driver's side window with a heavy metal object. The guy then opened the door and jumped into the car, started it and then drove away with the car alarm still wailing. Had the owner attached a "lock-bar" to the steering wheel, the thief most likely would have by-passed the car.

Burt had called the good doctor, just a half hour earlier, in the hopes that he would show up, and also not to give the doctor any time to alert the police or wear a wiretap. Going for a "walk-and -talk" was a sure way to foil any listening devices, especially through a busy, noisy parking lot.

The man with the blue eyes was an "expert" at his trade! He took no chances. When he had to talk with clients, he was very cautious about his surroundings. Burt did not want to put himself in any circumstances that could land him in jail. After all, if he was in jail, how could he ply his trade?

By the end of the afternoon, the phones were ringing off the hook, down at the Station.

The "tipster" line seemed to be operating on a continual basis. All kinds of information was coming in, ever since the newspaper hit the stores. Also, scads of emails were flooding the inbox of homicide's main computer.

The police knew that running a bulletin with photos of a suspect vehicle, would generate lots of tips. Now came the laborious task of sifting through them. All and any tips could be the critical link to catching the predator.

Every single hint from the public was forwarded to a special team of investigators, who diligently pored through them and prioritized each one, by the amount of information given from each tip.

If a tipster left out any facts, the investigators would drop it down the list and label it as "non sufficient info" and it wouldn't be treated as pertinent, but would still be checked eventually.

Any tips that had a return phone number or email address, were answered personally by the investigating members. This usually consisted of a short series of questions to weed out the crackpots and liars. But still, even a crackpot, could have something that may help the police track down the killer. No information is ever taken for granted or refused and none is ever deleted.

Detectives, Rhodes and Kuban were in a meeting with their boss, Chief Constable Joe Winters and some other homicide detectives. It was a weekly pep talk and time for general information to be discussed only among themselves.

Joe Winters was a hardened, crusty, "old school" cop. He started with the force back in 1978 and was nearing retirement. Joe had seen it all. From working the "beat" in Gastown as a rookie, through all the departments and then right to the top, as head honcho of Investigative Services. He was a so called "tough-nut" and didn't put up with any crap! Back in the day, before the so-called, bullshit Canadian Charter of Rights, brought in by the Trudeau Government, Joe and the boys, could actually manhandle the drug dealers, rapists, thieves, murderers and the other miscreants of society, in a manner that they deserved, without being charged with assault or improper handling. Criminals seem to have too many rights, with the present laws. The laws today, are unbelievably lenient and morally inept, as they are not written to protect the public or innocent; they are written by the bureaucrats, for their own wealth! The lawyers and the judges generate their immense salaries by defending and then releasing the creeps back on the streets. It's a sick rotating, merry-go-round at the expense and lives of the general public.

"Listen up, people ... so what we have here up to-date about the Fraser case is this," as Chief Winters pointed to the list of items on the white board with his red laser pointer. "One, we have the tire tread pattern, left at three of the murder scenes. Two, we have his DNA left on several victims. Three, we have the same type of chopstick used in five of the murders. And four, now we have a fairly good ... well maybe not good, but possible description of the killer's car. We know the car is a domestic compact, possibly a Chevy or Ford with roof-racks, supposedly dark in color.

"We've had our department in touch with the Motor Vehicle Registrar, and are still waiting for a complete list of registered mid-nineties Chevy Corsicas and Ford Tauruses. With this list of vehicles, we can research the owners of the cars ... and then run a search to see if any of them are previous felons. This will greatly help our investigation. We do need to find this ... pardon my Irish ... bastard!"

Forensics had previously tested all the chopsticks, and had revealed that they were all of the same type of material. They were not the wooden kind, but were a straw colored plastic resin, manufactured in China and sold to the Chinese restaurants. This particular brand was not sold in retail stores, they were only available to restaurants from the wholesale suppliers.

OIS had done a check on as many restaurants as they possibly could. It was an exhaustive search, since the Greater Vancouver was home to a large Asian market, and there were literally hundreds of Asian restaurants. It was near impossible to know, which restaurant or restaurants the killer frequented. But the police did believe, that whoever was using the chopsticks in that gruesome manner, had to be getting them from one of those eateries in the city.

"The news bulletin about the suspect's car, only came out this morning in the Province newspaper and, as of, three o'clock this afternoon, we've had over, one hundred and twenty tips ... one hundred and twenty-three to be exact!" as Winters looked down at his notes. "We'll be checking out all of the tips as fast as we humanly can, and I would like all of you to be on twenty-four hour call, and please expect to work some overtime on this case. There will be light at the end of the tunnel, I have my faith in all of you. Any questions?" Winters asked.

Detective Jane Rhodes asked the burly Chief, "What about the possibility of the killer being an employee of one of these restaurants that supply the chopsticks, after all they would have easy access to them?"

"Of course, we've thought that all along, but that is a near impossible task, checking all employees of every single restaurant. Some restaurants have a high employee turn-over rate. That's why it hasn't been easy tracking this guy. It could even be someone ordering "takeout" or home delivery for 'crying out loud'!" as he slammed his large, weathered, open hand on the desk, with a dull thud!

Chief Constable Joe Winters was very pissed off! He wanted to have that suspect brought in, before any other innocent victims were attacked.

"The chopstick clue is very, very, important in this investigation, people ... however, it is almost like a grain of sand on the beach. It leaves a vast amount of possible suspects ... so now that we have the car make and model, as soon as we get that compiled list from the Motor Vehicle Registrar, we will be able to do some background checks and quite possibly find out if any of the registered car owners, are in fact restaurant owners or employees," he said.

Geena had called Sunny on his cellphone, but there was no answer. The robot lady on the other end of the line, gave her usual spiel, *"the caller you are trying to reach is unavailable or away from the phone, please leave a message after the tone"*, BEEP!

"Hey sexy! Where are you? You are hard to get a hold of sometimes, you know that? Anyway, me and my sis are going to stay in Seattle for a few more days ... just a little more shoe shopping and maybe a play, or movie! I don't like talking to a machine, so I'll talk to you later, maybe you can phone me, when you're not so busy! Miss you! Love you!" sang Geena.

Sunny quite often left his cellphone at home if he was walking Babe or going for a run. If he was on the road, sometimes he would just leave it in the car. Sunny hated being a slave to the "cell".

Dr. Wilson and Burt walked a ways through the park, until they came to a wooden park bench, right near a duck pond. Burt and the doctor sat down on the bench. There were ducks and geese wandering around the park and some were swimming in the murky water.

The park was quite active; a group of joggers were cruising by, and some children with their parents were playing on the swings. The doctor still nervous, turned to Burt, looked him square in the eye and said. "I know why your here, Burt. I've figured it out ... you're the fellow who killed that guy ... the guy that murdered Ms. Marlowe," his voice quivering.

Those bright blue eyes just stared at the plastic surgeon. Burt didn't answer yes or no, he just gave a slight grin and slowly blinked his eyelids.

"Of course you're not going to admit something like that to me ... but I'm pretty sure I know what's going on here" Wilson postulated.

"Do you, Dr. Wilson ... do you know why I'm here?" the man with the perfectly manicured mustache asked.

" Yes ... I do, you said before, that you wanted to help me even the score. You want to kill the guy that murdered my wife, right ... that's why your here, isn't it?" the doctor said intently, looking at Burt.

Again, Burt said nothing, he just gave another half-assed smile.

The doctor reached into his jacket pocket as his cellphone rang. He put it to his ear and listened. "Okay, thank-you, I'll be back in about ten minutes." Wilson put the phone back in his pocket and said, "that was my office, I have to get back soon, it's been very busy these last few months, it seems everyone lately, wants a facelift, tummy tuck or big boobs, it never ends!"

"Well that's great that you have a going concern Doctor, it keeps the mind busy, no doubt," Burt noted.

"Yes, it does keep my mind occupied. It's been very hard for me, but more so, for my daughter. She just hasn't been the same since ... my wife was murdered by that psychopath. He took everything away from us. Sometimes life seems so empty. Do you know that my daughter has tried twice, to commit suicide?" Tears were starting to well-up in the good doctor's eyes. "I know it happened over a year-and-a-half ago, but it seems just like this morning and when I wake up ... I'm always hoping that it's just a goddam dream! And then I realize that's it's not and ..."

Dr. Wilson bent his head towards his knees, covered his face with his hands and broke down, snorting and crying like a baby with gas, intermittently trying to catch his breath, between resonating sobs of anguish!

The sounds of the grieving doctor had caught the attention of a few of the park's visitors. An elderly lady feeding the ducks and geese bread crumbs near by, looked over at Burt with a long face and forced a sympathetic, "is your friend okay, deary?"

"He's going to be okay, ma'am, thanks for caring!" Burt called back to the nice lady, while patting the doctor on the back. "Dr. Wilson, nobody can really understand how you're feeling, unless they've experienced a tragedy that you have been through!" Burt said to the sad doctor.

Through blubbering gasps of air, Wilson managed to expel, "I can't believe ... she's gone ... she ... I loved her so much ... I miss her! It doesn't matter ... how much ... money a person makes ... or what they have ... or who they are ... but when you lose ... someone like I lost, so close, a soul-mate for life... well ... the hurting never stops!"

There was a long pause of silence between the two men

"Sometimes I just want to kill myself ... sometimes I just don't want to live anymore ... but then I think of

Melissa ... and ... well ... she needs me ... I mean after-all, she doesn't have her mother anymore ... she needs me now more than ever!" the plastic surgeon managed to spit out.

There was another period of silence between the men, sitting there on that red wooden bench, in the beautiful park, with the sun shining ever-so brightly through the magnificent oak trees, with the birds singing in the background all around them.

Who would ever think, that with all the beauty, mother-nature had to offer everyone, that there would be the doctor's kind of grief and despair running rampant in the world we live in today.

A great percentage of humans roaming the earth fall into the category of the "most despicable and evil species of the animal kingdom that inhabit the planet". Mankind knows no boundaries, when it comes to hurting their fellow brethren. And Dr. Wilson was hurting, hurting real bad!

Finally, Burt broke the silence between the two men, "I followed the case very closely Dr. Wilson, from the moment it was all over the news. I had an obsessive interest with the case."

The doctor wiped away the tears on his jacket sleeve and tried to gain his composure.

After about a minute, Wilson sat up straight and through his bloodshot eyes, he looked straight into Burt's bright, blue eyes and asked, "how much is it going to cost me? How much money Burt? I want that fucker dead!"

"I work by donation, Dr. Wilson ... there is no set price, you pay me what you think the job is worth," whispered Burt, as he casually scanned the park. I will be in touch with you, within a week. Now you go back to work and don't worry, okay."

"Okay!" the doctor replied through sniffled breathing.

The blue eyed, mustachioed Burt and the plastic surgeon both got up off the park bench and started back towards the shopping center.

They strolled through the parking lot, both of them looking straight ahead not saying anything to each other. As they came to the mall doors, Burt and the doctor glanced at each other briefly. The doctor said good-bye and Burt just gave a half grin and nodded. Wilson went through the doors, into the shopping center, and headed for his office.

Burt turned left and walked all the way down the sidewalk, fronting the mall, and then disappeared around the corner.

ELEVEN

Dr. Wilson's young, beautiful wife's life was cut short just over a year-and-a-half ago, by a teenage sexual predator, named William Marcus. William was only seventeen when he did the horrific deed to the doctor's wife.

Stephanie had been out grocery shopping for the family and it was about 8:30 pm when she left the Save-on-Foods store. The store's video surveillance camera had recorded her pushing her shopping cart away from the main doors. She had just finished putting all of her groceries in the family minivan, when she disappeared. The police presumed that she may have been accosted by someone, as there were no witnesses or any clues left at the shopping center parking lot. All they had was the video surveillance of her leaving the store.

Investigating officers from the Integrated Homicide Investigation Team (IHIT), had a strong feeling that she may have been abducted from the parking lot, because her husband explained to the detectives that it was always common practice, for Stephanie to either phone or text him when she was leaving the store.

The Wilson's called it their "buddy system", this way the doctor would know when she would be home safely, in case her vehicle broke down; usually a fifteen minute ride from store to home.

Except that particular night she didn't phone or text. And Stephanie never made it home!

It was about 11:45 pm, that same night, that the Royal Canadian Mounted Police (RCMP) had a roadblock set up on King George Highway in Surrey, in the hopes of catching impaired drivers. But what they found that fateful, windy night was more than they could have ever imagined!

As the minivan entered the roadblock, the officer with the flashlight, took one look at the pimply faced teen and sensed something was wrong. The surprised expression on William Marcus's sweaty face, was a "dead" giveaway.

The veteran police officer projected the beam of light again, over the teen's face, and to his horror, realized that those were not pimples, but actually tiny dried spots of blood!

"Pull over to the side, now!" commanded the officer, as he pulled out his 9mm Smith and Wesson service pistol and raised it to the window of the driver.

The cop stepped back and his partner and another RCMP member also pulled their guns out of their holsters.

The greasy punk edged the vehicle over to the side of the highway slowly.

"Now easy, get out of the van ... easy, now! Keep your hands out front where I can see them!" the policeman ordered, as all three of the cops kept their weapons aimed at the driver of the minivan.

Marcus opened the door and slowly crawled out with his hands out in front.

"Face down on the ground, NOW, do it!" snapped the other constable. "Is there anyone else in the van?"

The teenager didn't answer.

A fourth RCMP member at the scene, ran a check on the license plate number. He was also directing the oncoming cars to proceed ahead.

The constable with the flashlight went down the side of the minivan and shone it into the side window. All he could see were several bags strewn around in the back of the van. Another pass with the flashlight through the windows revealed something on the floor of the passenger seat. It kind of looked like a person hiding!

The policeman motioned for his partner to come over to the side door.

Cautiously, the rookie member side-stepped closer to the minivan door, with his semi-automatic pistol aimed at the shiny red door. Nervously, but quickly, the cop cocked his gun and kept it leveled at the minivan.

Traffic was starting to slow down, as curious onlookers wanted to take in the escapade that was unravelling in front of them.

Police Constable Hart, waiting for the license check from dispatch, kept waving his arm for the cars to keep moving, all the while he kept watching the other policemen, and the teen laying face down, just in case things got unruly and out of hand.

Hart finally received word from dispatch, that the plate number had in fact, been phoned in about 10:00 pm, as a concern from a worried citizen, with the name of Randall Wilson.

The call came in as a possible "missing person" report. A citizen cannot file a missing persons report until at least twenty-four hours after the person goes missing. The information is kept suspended on police files, and then updated after twenty-four hours if the person does not reappear.

Wilson made the phone call to the police, after trying to reach his wife numerous times, because she had failed to show up at at about 9:00 pm. He knew her routine, after shopping for the family groceries. She would call or text him, before the drive home, which was only about fifteen minutes from home. If she had to gas up the minivan or stop somewhere else, she would *always* let him know, that she would be a little later. But on this tragic night, she didn't phone or text him, and he could not reach her, so he felt something was wrong and telephoned the police. His hunch was right!

Constable Perkins, while holding his flashlight grabbed the door handle of the van and slowly pulled it out. The door slid open with a crashing sound. Both cops, jumped to opposite sides of the open door, with their handguns aimed at the person laying on the floor of the passenger area.

"Get up slowly ... and put your hands up in the air! DO IT NOW!" the flashlight cop ordered.

There was no movement from the person laying down.

The cop aimed the flashlight on the body, and to his disbelief, he realized it was a woman with her bare legs sticking out from her skirt. Chills ran up his spine! There was a jacket thrown over her mid-section. She was naked from the waist up.

"Are you okay Miss?" he asked nervously.

There was no answer and no movement from the lady.

The policeman flashed the light around the inside of the van and could see that there wasn't anyone else inside, only about six bags of groceries scattered about.

Perkins told the officers to handcuff the teenager and get him off the ground and into the back of the police cruiser.

Then the constable pulled the jacket back slowly, off of the woman. He gasped. It was the most horrifying situation he had ever witnessed, since being on the police force.

The other two cops came over to the door and looked in and they too were sickened at what they observed.

Stephanie Wilson's forehead was caved in, with some brain matter, oozing out of her skull. Her once beautiful face was caked with dried blood and her silky, smooth auburn hair was matted with gelled blood also. Her delicate face was beyond recognition.

The younger rookie police officer darted over to the edge of the highway, and threw-up his hamburger steak and onions, that he had consumed for dinner two hours earlier.

Constable Hart radioed Surrey headquarters and requested that they send out the IHIT immediately.

Two more RCMP members were dispatched to the crime scene to pickup and escort the skinny, young Marcus back to the police station.

William Marcus was booked in, fingerprinted and interrogated by the homicide detectives, that were called in specially that night. He was placed in a room and seated at a table with only one door, a video camera and a mirror, that was actually a two-way mirror, so all the detectives could observe from the other side.

Homicide Detective Roger Morris, was a hard-core pro when it came to extracting information from suspects brought into the interrogation room or "terror room" as it was known by the members. He had fingers, the size of Dill pickles and a neck as wide as the mighty Fraser River.

Morris laid into the kid hard, right from the get-go. "Tell me exactly, what you did tonight son ... and if you tell me the truth, I'll go easy on you, do you understand? If you don't tell me the whole truth, I'll reach down your skinny little, fuckin' throat and pull all those nasty lies right out! You got that motherfucker?" the hardened Morris blurted out, with his piercing dark brown eyes burning a hole right through Marcus's face!

Almost immediately, the scared shitless teenager started to cry, then broke down and confessed. He confessed everything to Morris, about what he had done. He told the cop, that he had some very strong sexual urges, that he couldn't control and needed to satisfy them and that he was real sorry for his actions.

Marcus explained to Morris, that earlier on, that evening, he had downed a couple of beers and then went into the basement and grabbed a twenty-four ounce framing hammer from the workbench.

He then claimed that he walked to the Save-on-Foods store, with the hammer under his jacket, drinking one more beer on the way. He felt the shopping center would be a good place, to do "his thing", because there was always lots of women at a place like that. Save-on-Foods was surrounded by other smaller stores at the strip mall. The grocery giant was the anchor tenant.

The strapping teenager walked around the strip mall slowly, watching for any unsuspecting females. He saw a few interesting subjects, but those ones were driving small cars. Marcus needed a van to do "his thing".

Back when young William Marcus was attending high school, and not skipping classes, a crime prevention police officer, from the RCMP came to the school and gave a lecture in the auditorium about safety and self-defense. Marcus, remembered the constable, telling the class that women should never pull their car up beside a parked van in a parking lot. "There have been numerous abduction cases across North America because of this, seemingly innocent, but possible fatal mistake," explained the lecturing officer.

The officer went on to explain, "that when the female shopper, comes back to her car with her bags of groceries, she is usually preoccupied with transferring the goods into the car, not noticing that the van's side-door, is being opened and that her abductor is ready to grab her from behind and pull her into the already running vehicle! This criminal method of kidnapping unsuspecting victims is happening all over the world, all the time!" The constable couldn't stress enough, "DO NOT PARK beside a van in a parking lot, ever!"

"What if I park my car between two other cars, when I get to the shopping center, but when I come back to my car ... the car that was beside me is gone and *now* there's a van parked in place of the first car ... what do I do now?" came the question from a young female student.

"Very good question indeed, I'm glad you asked that. If that scenario ever happens ... it will happen and in fact does happen," the officer replied. "You have three life saving choices ... first, you can find a security guard, providing the mall or shopping center employs them, and the guard can escort you to your vehicle, or two, you can enter through the passenger side and keep watch on the van ... and three, I know this step is a bit of an inconvenience, but you can go and get a coffee and wait for the van to leave."

William Marcus never forgot what he learned that day from the RCMP officer. However, with his twisted way of thinking, that lecture did not encourage him to execute that information as a victim. Instead, his overview of the scenario, that the cop described, gave him the ultimate plan to be the attacker. He thought that he would use the information for his own gratification. Yes, he thought, *I can easily grab some unsuspecting bitch that deserves to get raped!*

There was only one problem! Marcus didn't have a van to use. *No problem,* he thought. He would just simply use the victim's van instead.

The demented teenager kept walking around the mall, looking into store windows, pretending to be window shopping, but he was really looking at the reflection of the vehicles in the windows. He could see them all coming and going from the parking lot.

Finally, he spotted a newer, red minivan pull up to the Save-on Foods store. A very attractive Stephanie Wilson exited the van, beeped her remote to lock it and then gracefully headed for the store.

Marcus slowly turned around and watched the doctors wife with anticipation, s*he's the one, I have to have her!* He knew he had to wait for her to finish shopping, so he decided to walk around the strip mall one more time.

This time he lit up a smoke and took some big heavy drags, which gave the stalker a real head rush. He really wasn't much of a smoker and he was getting butterflies in his stomach ... not too sure if he could go through with it. Marcus had never done anything, even remotely like what he was planning. *I have to do this, I need to do this,* he thought to himself. *I can't back out now,* as he took another long drag off the cow-assed cigarette.

Marcus sauntered past the Save-on Foods huge windows and casually glanced in, to see if he could get a quick glimpse of the lady he wanted to "snatch". He couldn't see her anywhere, it was a colossal grocery store.

The teen picked this particular shopping center, cause he knew the mall didn't employ security guards. Some malls had them and some didn't. They weren't required at this mall, because there had been no previous problems. But what he didn't realize, was that there were hidden security cameras installed all around the parking lot.

The troubled Marcus, took one last drag off the burning butt and then flicked it onto the pavement. He walked around the perimeter of the parking lot, checking out the red van from all angles. About forty-five minutes had passed and it was starting to get dark. Marcus started getting agitated, when suddenly, out through the store doors, came the intended target, pushing a shopping cart full of groceries.

William Marcus could feel his heart pounding! It was pounding so hard, he could feel it up in his ears. He thought his chest was going to explode, like a big fat pumpkin being dropped from ten stories up. It was now or never!

Stephanie was heading for her minivan, kind of in a hurry, as there was a slight breeze in the air and she had only a skimpy little sweater over her t-shirt.

The stalker started walking slowly through the parked cars towards the minivan with the utmost caution, glancing all around and over his shoulder. His right foot accidentally kicked a pop-can and it went skidding under a pick-up truck, making a scraping sound. Marcus quickly ducked down, just as Stephanie had looked in the direction of the noise made by the aluminium can. She missed him by seconds.

She turned back and arriving at her vehicle, she clicked her remote and the door locks opened. Stephanie pulled the door latch and slid the van door open. One by one she transferred the bags of merchandise into the van's open area.

Marcus was now moving quicker towards the van, with bursts of adrenaline flowing through his veins like water blasting through a fire-hose! He pushed the handle of the hammer down, between his belt and jeans at the back of his body, underneath his jacket. He had to time his surprise attack perfectly or the whole plan would be a disaster.

Mrs. Wilson closed the sliding door after placing the last bag of goods inside and then opened the driver's door and proceeded to climb into the minivan.

Fumbling around in his pants pocket with his right hand, Marcus pulled out his pocket knife and flicked the blade open. With his left hand, he grabbed the sliding door handle, pulled it out and slid the side-door open, at the exact same moment that Stephanie had started the engine.

She was startled by the door being opened, so she looked in her side-mirror and saw that there was nothing there! The creeper had already jumped into the minivan.

"Don't scream or I'll slash your throat, bitch!" came the harsh but quiet words from Marcus's twisted drooling, ugly mouth.

"Please don't hurt me, what do you ..."

"Shut-up and drive, you stupid bitch, do it now or your dead!" Marcus hissed.

Stephanie drove out of the parking lot.

After the complete investigation by IHIT, and the confession from William Marcus, it was revealed that the minivan was driven by Stephanie to an isolated place in

Bear Creek Park in Surrey. There are several dark areas, that have no lighting within the park and the teen knew his way around the park very well. It was at one of these lonely spots, that the angry young Marcus, tried to have his way with the beautiful doctor's wife.

He ordered her to climb over the seats and into the back of the minivan. He climbed into the back as well. The psycho then yanked her pink sweater up and over her head, then he pulled her t-shirt off as he threatened to slash her if she resisted. Marcus cut her bra off with his knife and then reached under her skirt and ripped her panties off.

Stephanie so badly wanted to struggle, but instinctively knew that he might slash or stab her to death, if she did. *What an awful, painful way to die,* she thought to herself. The scumbag stunk of cigarettes, beer and sweat! He was grabbing at her chest and moaning out loud as he struggled with trying to get his jeans down. Marcus tried to rape her as he held the three inch rusty blade to her slender throat.

Mrs. Wilson was frozen with fear and dared not to say a word to the violent sex offender. She could barely breathe from fear and panic. Thoughts of her husband and daughter were flashing through her mind. Tears were streaming down both sides of her face. Never before, in her whole life did she ever feel so helpless, so scared!

Marcus was calling her a fucking slut that wanted a good pounding! Stephanie didn't move or say a thing, she resisted, hoping he would just get it over with.

But he couldn't get it up ... he couldn't get a hard-on ... *what the fuck ... what was happening? This can't be.*

The sex freak couldn't perform. His whole plan had been foiled! Now he was starting to get angry, he could feel his blood boiling like Mount St. Helen's in Washington State, ready to explode!

The mother of one, could sense the frustration that Marcus was experiencing. Although she did not want to be sexually assaulted by this sicko, she also feared for her life. She felt if she tried to fight back, he would surely kill her.

"You bitch, you fucking BITCH!" he screamed at her, humiliated that he couldn't do the nasty. "I'm not a fucking queer, I'm not ... queer!" as he broke into a hysterical sobbing frenzy.

The twisted, demented William "soft dick" Marcus, reached to the back of his pants that were crumpled below his knees, and grabbed the head of the carpenter's hammer. He manipulated his hand along the wooden handle, until he had a firm grip of the hammer. He brought it forward and high up, in the air above Stephanie's beautiful face.

She could see by the light of the moon, that he had the hammer above her. "Please don't, I beg you, please no, no, I have a young daughter at ..."

"Shut the fuck up!" as he brought the heavy, steely hammer down as hard as he could on to her forehead!

A sickening dull thud, silenced the distraught woman! And as he kept sobbing, he brought the weapon down again and again! Blood splattered everywhere in the minivan! On his face and on the windows of the vehicle.

Stephanie's short life had been "snuffed out" in her very own minivan in the dark park, by a fucked-up product of the devil himself.

After a few minutes of laying there crying, Marcus finally crawled off her lifeless body and threw the bloodied hammer out through the window of the van. He then pulled her body onto the passenger seat floor and covered her with his jacket.

Marcus drove out of the park, dazed and disoriented from the grisly murder he had just committed, not even sure where he was heading, until he landed in the RCMP roadblock.

William Marcus was charged with the kidnapping, attempted rape and first degree murder of Stephanie Wilson. However, before the case went to trial, there was a preliminary hearing ordered, by the judge assigned to the case, to determine if there should be a thirty day psychiatric evaluation of the troubled teenager. Marcus's lawyer provided enough documentation to the judge, to have the psychiatric evaluation deemed necessary.

The prosecution filed a motion to the court, to have William Marcus "tried" as an adult, knowing that as a teenager, he wouldn't receive a long enough sentence. Sentenced as a "young offender" would only warrant ten years or less, under the Youth Criminal Justice Act (YCJA).

The trial judge disagreed with moving the defendant up to adult court. Justice Holmgren felt that since this was Marcus's first offence, even though it was a violent murder, that he should be given a chance at rehabilitation, because of his age of seventeen years at the time of the crime.

The psychiatrists that had evaluated Marcus found that he was borderline manic depressive and had suffered some physical abuse, such as spankings and closed-fist strikes, but no sexual abuse from his step-father while growing up. He did watch his step-father treat his mother rough from time to time as well.

Marcus was considered sane and fit, to stand trial for the kidnapping, attempted rape and first degree murder of Stephanie Wilson.

In court, the defense lawyer, told the judge and jury that when young William was growing up, he had been abused by his step-father and that he had a history of borderline mental illness and in light of these conditions he should not be responsible for his crimes against Mrs. Wilson.

The prosecution argued, that no matter what happened in his past, the killer should pay the consequences and be given the full ten years, the maximum penalty under the YCJA for the heinous, gruesome murder of the young mother and wife.

Most of the evidence produced to the judge and jury during the trial was circumstantial. The abduction, attempted rape and bludgeoning of Mrs. Wilson, were not witnessed by any other person, other than the perpetrator himself.

The only "direct evidence" was William Marcus's own confession of the crimes, to the investigating homicide Detective Roger Morris, and the fact that he was apprehended at the RCMP roadblock in possession of Stephanie Wilson's minivan and her battered lifeless body.

The carpenter's hammer had been located by the homicide officers, the day after the confession from Marcus and displayed in court as Exhibit B as the main murder weapon. His rusty, pocket-knife had been confiscated from the minivan, the night he was pulled over by the police. It was also entered as evidence for the court to examine.

After both lawyers finalized their summations of the case, the Honorable Justice Richard Holmgren, instructed the twelve member jury of their lawful procedure.

DOG WITH A BONE

They could either find William Marcus guilty, beyond a "reasonable doubt" on all three charges or guilty of any one of the three charges, or find Marcus not guilty on all three charges or not guilty of any one of the three charges. As well, they could also find Marcus guilty of the reduced charge of "manslaughter" instead of first degree murder, due to the fact that the Crown must be able to prove "specific intent" (intent to murder the victim) ... and if the Crown is unable to prove this, then manslaughter is the only option.

After five sequestered days of deliberation by the jury, which consisted of seven men and five women, they slowly entered the courtroom one by one, looking exhausted and all sat down, except the jury foreman. He stood facing the judge.

"Has the jury reached a verdict in the case of William Marcus verses the Crown?" asked Justice Holmgren.

"We have your Honor!" proclaimed the foreman.

You could have heard a pin drop on the floor of the "standing room only" courtroom.

"We the jury, find William Marcus ... guilty of kidnapping. We the jury find William Marcus ... guilty of attempted rape. We the jury find William Marcus ... not guilty of first degree murder, but guilty of the reduced charge of manslaughter!" announced the jury foreman.

The silence in the courtroom was broken with loud, mixed emotional sounds. Crying, cheering and grunts and grumbles of disgust!

Dr. Randall Wilson wept uncontrollably!

The judge hit the gavel on the bench and told the court to quiet down!

He then ordered William Marcus to stand and asked him if he understood what the jury foreman had just said.

Marcus nodded his head up and down and meekly answered, "yes, your Honor."

The judge then told the crowded courtroom, that he would reserve sentencing for thirty days. The sobbing teenager was led away and ordered to be held in remand, until his sentencing date.

The jury had reduced the charge from first degree murder to manslaughter because they had reasoned among themselves that the proof to convict, was in fact, not "specific intent".

Marcus's lawyer argued that his client had only intended to rape Stephanie Wilson and not to kill her. He only became enraged when he could not maintain an erection, due to the fact of consuming several beers before the attack. His defense lawyer also explained to the jury that William was caught up in the heat-of-the-moment; that he didn't mean to kill the doctor's wife, only to keep her quiet. This, the lawyer stated would be the charge of "involuntary" manslaughter.

The honorable judge over-ruled the defense lawyer and rejected the term, involuntary. He instructed the jury to understand the difference between involuntary and voluntary.

"Involuntary manslaughter requires no intent to cause death and voluntary manslaughter does include intent at the time of the offence," explained Justice Holmgren.

William Marcus was sentenced to one year in the Burnaby Youth Detention center. Justice Holmgren told the court that due to several of the mitigating factors, a longer sentence wasn't necessary. One, being that William Marcus was only seventeen at the time of the crime, two, he had no previous convictions, three, he had a troubled upbringing, and four, he showed great remorse and may be a good candidate for rehabilitation.

The public was outraged when it hit the "press" and the TV news stations. Another cold-blooded murderer walks free! Response from the public; the Canadian justice system is an international joke!

Dr. Randall Wilson was beside himself. He lost his wife, his soul-mate, the mother of his daughter, to a sick, twisted, psychopath and another fucked-up judge, jury and the Canadian politicians (they make the laws) gave this monster one year in a *detention* house.

William Marcus's conditions after being released were to be as follows:
- Probationary period of two years, reporting to a Probation Officer once a week.
- No drugs or alcohol, during this period.
- No weapons or firearms for ten years.

NOTE: In 1976, the death penalty was completely abolished and the Criminal Code of Canada redefined murder, as either first degree or second degree, both which resulted in life in prison without eligibility for 25 years (first degree) and 10 – 25 years (second degree) respectively.

Canadian law dictates, that young offenders are between the ages of 12 and 17. Under the YCJA , the sentences are not fixed, so it is possible for a young offender to get only one day in custody for murder.

Note: At the time of writing of this novel, the actual above law was in effect.

TWELVE

"So, how's the trip going my little cupcake?" Sunny asked Geena.

"We're having a great time, I wish you were here, Sunny, you'd have so much fun, with us," answered Geena. *What have you been doing ... I phoned earlier, but all I got was your stupid voice-mail!"*

"Oh, I took Babe out for a long walk in Central Park, we walked through all the trails. She chased up a rabbit and man did that sucker run! Now I know where the saying 'ran like a scared rabbit' came from. And I had a couple of other things to do," Sunny replied.

Sunny usually left his phone at home or in the car, when he and his "best friend" were on an outing. He found that the best strolls were usually interrupted by a phone call. He figured, that if it was that important, they would call back.

They talked for a while and then said their good-byes. Geena told Sunny she would be home in two days.

Sunny could feel his stomach telling him it was time for dinner. He had a real hankering for some Chinese food. There were so many Asian restaurants to choose from, but Sunny had some favorites. The one he liked the best was the HoHo Restaurant in Chinatown. Yeah, tonight he would treat himself, "step out" and check the grub at the HoHo.

First, he took Babe down the stairs and out back over to the park, so she could do her "business".

He then went back into the loft and cleaned up a bit, brushed his teeth and threw on a clean t-shirt. Sunny lifted the Van Gogh reprint of "Starry Night" off the wall and then gently removed one of the bricks from the red brick wall and reached inside behind. He pulled out a couple of crisp fifty dollar bills, folded them over twice neatly, and then stuck them in his jeans front pocket.

Very rarely, did Sunny use a credit card or debit card. He felt cash "ruled". Cash was Boss! Sunny's philosophy was that, if everyone used cash, there would be very little debt in the country. His theory was that if you didn't have the cash to buy something, then you simply didn't need it. But with credit, buy anything you want and then have trouble later trying to pay off the interest. It's no wonder that the credit card was invented by a banker in 1958. Besides, Sunny realized that plastic credit cards always left a paper trail.

He kept some of his cash in the brick wall. Nobody would know that there was a hollow spot behind the movable red brick. The rest of his cash he kept in a floor safe, that Ike had installed for him in the garage, where he kept his vehicles, underneath the workbench, covered with an oil drum, out of sight.

Sunny wasn't fond of banks, and besides the interest rate was so pathetically low, he figured why bother.

As Sunny slowly pulled into the HoHo Restaurant parking lot, he scanned all the vehicles that were parked. It was a very busy place at dinner time. The restaurant had an exceptional reputation as being one of the best Chinese restaurants in Chinatown and the whole of Vancouver.

Even celebrities had dined here! Vancouver was known as Hollywood North in the film industry. All kinds of movies have been made in Vancouver. Some well known actors and musicians were born in Vancouver or the lower mainland. Michael J. Fox, Bryan Adams, Pamela Anderson, just to name a few.

It was a warm August night and Sunny was totally wide awake. He was super hungry, but more than that, he was on a mission!

Sunny couldn't get the image of that creep that pulled the gun on him and Elly, out of his mind. That face, that car, those roof-racks, that handgun and the three numbers of the license plate. He had it all. He just needed to find that fucker, before the cops did!

But there were so many restaurants and so little time.

Inside the HoHo, Sunny was seated at a window seat. The place was packed, with all different ethnic groups. The aroma of freshly prepared Chinese food made his mouth salivate.

His waiter came up and gave him a menu and a tall glass of water, and said he'd be back in a few minutes.

Sunny perused the menu, and occasionally glanced around at the other patrons dining. The background noise of chatter was like a dull buzzing sound. It was extremely loud in the place.

The waiter came back to take his order.

"Yes, sir ... do you know what you want?" asked the cheerful server.

"I would like a pot of Chinese tea, a bowl of steamed rice and a plate of beef and broccoli please."

The waiter took the order and five minutes later, returned with the pot of green tea and a cup, a fork, knife and a set of wrapped up chopsticks.

Sunny stared intently at those chopsticks.

He was so disturbed by what those chopsticks reminded him of. Slowly he looked around the restaurant and wondered if, how many of these people eating and using their chopsticks knew, that some sick, ignominious, bastard had hammered a similar eating utensil into some innocent child's ear canal.

The waiter finally brought the steaming hot dishes to Sunny. He savoured the aromatic meal with rapture and finished every last morsel, except two pieces of beef. These, he wrapped up in his napkin, and shoved it in his pocket, to take home as a special treat for Babe. Sunny never forgot about his dog!

While he was sipping his Chinese tea, he was checking out the paper place-mat with the Chinese horoscopes on it and it was at that moment that, something popped into his head. That place-mat gave him an idea! Why didn't he think of that before.

As he ate the last of his meal, the waiter brought the check to the table. Sunny pulled out his cash and gave a fifty to the guy and told him to just bring back a twenty. After the waiter left the table, Sunny slipped the cellophane wrapped chopsticks, into his other front pocket as he stood up.

The waiter brought him, his change. Sunny smiled and thanked him. Homeward bound! He had a plan!

The computer "guru" of the Investigative Services department at 312 Main Street was checking the email inbox from the Motor Vehicle Registrar, when Detective Jane Rhodes sauntered into the office.

"Anything yet, Steven?" she asked the computer guy, as she took a sip from her piping hot vanilla latte.

"Nothing so far ... the first response I got back was just a short email stating that they would most likely have the complete list by tomorrow afternoon," he answered back.

"Christ, I thought computers were supposed to be fast in getting information," Jane grumbled, as she pulled out a chair and sat down.

"Well, they are fast, it's the humans that operate the darn things that are slow. Someone has to actually download the vehicle make and model into the system and then do a search and collect the info. Unfortunately, their offices close at 4:00 pm and nobody works late! So hopefully we'll get it by tomorrow afternoon, or maybe you can arrest them for being tardy!" he laughed.

Rhodes cracked a weak smile and shook her head as she said, "I can't believe the world we live in, Steven! People are given the 'gift of life' and then they willingly take it away from others. Like those poor kids and teenagers. It doesn't make any sense? And then, when we catch those horrible creeps, some slimy lawyer gets them off or some vile judge lets them walk. I don't get it, Steven, do you?"

"No, I've never understood the justice system, Jane. It's just like that saying ... 'it's not the bad people, we need to worry about ... it's the good people, that do nothing about the bad people, we need to worry about', you know what I mean, Jane. It's an unfair world sometimes, void of compassion towards one another," sighed Steven.

"I just want that monster off the streets and locked up in jail!" she added.

"What are you doing here so late, anyway ... shouldn't you be at home watching CSI or playing bridge with the ladies?" teased the computer guru.

Steven Folk was one of the station's computer nerds. He worked on the afternoon shift, and he knew most of the members at 312 Main Street. He was in his mid twenties, and had graduated from Simon Fraser University, with a Master's degree in Computer Science.

His training and degree gave him a career that was "his for the picking". Computer wizards were in big demand in today's job market. Every type of medium to large business or institution relied on computer technicians. They couldn't operate without them.

Folk had many job opportunities offered to him, but in the end, he somehow felt that working for the Vancouver Police Department was his calling. His mother had worked as a dispatch operator for the VPD, when he was younger. But her rheumatoid arthritis got so bad, she had to retire and go on disability leave.

Rhodes always wondered if Folk was gay. He was a little on the feminine side, with his actions and his walk, not to mention his slender build.

"Do you have a girlfriend Steven ... or are you married?" she hesitantly asked.

He started to chuckle, "why, do you want to be my girlfriend, Jane?" Before she could answer him, he added, "I know, you think I play for the same team ... right?"

"No ... no I wasn't wondering that, Steven, I just wondered if you had a partner, and any kids? That's all," as she turned five shades of party pink.

"Jane, you're not the first person to think I'm homosexual, but I'm not, really ... I like women, not men."

She smiled and said, "I'm sorry ... I didn't mean anything by it ... I just wondered ... and just for the record, Steven, I'm not a lesbian, I like men."

He laughed, and so did she.

Steven put his hand in the air, out towards her and said, "give me a high-five, Detective Jane Rhodes."

She put her hand up and they slapped their hands together!

"Well Mr. Folk, I think I will head on home for some shut-eye. I will be looking forward to that list of cars tomorrow!" as she got up out of the comfy chair and stretched up on her tippy toes, and then headed out of the computer room.

"See you tomorrow, Jane," Folk said, as he turned back to the desk of computer monitors.

Babe was wagging her golden otter tail back and forth as Sunny came through the loft door. Her twitchy nose nudged right up against his pants pocket. She knew that papa had a tasty treat for her. The sweet smell of sauteed beef was wafting through the tight cotton weave of Sunny's American Eagle jeans.

"Hey girl, how's my little hound dog? Daddy brought you a snack!" Sunny said. "Here you go girl," as he unwrapped the soy flavored beef and handed it to her. Babe took the treat over to her bed, laid down and gulped the meat down in one swallow. She was a true gourmand through and through.

Sunny kicked off his gray Sketchers and shuffled over to his writing desk, opened up Della and turned her on. The clock on the kitchen stove read 10:35 pm. He clicked on the Internet Explorer icon and then entered Google

Earth into the address bar. Sunny spent the next twenty minutes viewing the Greater Vancouver area maps.

When he was satisfied with the maps, he downloaded them to "Maps" file and then plugged his printer into the laptop. One by one, Sunny printed-off several maps. He wanted all of the subdivisions of the spread-out Vancouver metropolis.

Now a drink was in order. Sunny went over to the fridge and opened the freezer door, pulled out the Sailor Jerry's rum and a couple of ice cubes. He poured a two finger shot of rum and topped it off with diet-Pepsi. Sunny took a swig, then set the drink on the coffee table and went over to the desk. He picked up all the maps that printed off and then grabbed the scissors and Scotch-tape from the writing desk drawer. He jockeyed over to the coffee table and set everything down.

Carefully, he arranged the maps on the table, so they all lined up, street by street. He started taping them together and trimming the edges, so they fit together nicely.

Sunny went back to the writing desk and opened the drawer again, this time picking up both, a red and a black felt-pen, his laptop and the Yellow Pages phone book, then returned back to the coffee table.

He sat Della down, then clicked on the "Speed's Documents" icon. The window opened, so he scrolled down to "FM" and then right clicked, to open the document. It was password protected, so that only he could access the information in the "FM" text document. Sunny typed in his eight digit password.

The document opened with the title "Fraser Murders".

Sunny had been documenting the murders, ever since they had started about fourteen months ago. He was obsessed with the murders so much, that he had kept all the information on file from day one. Sunny, the "Bully

Basher", wanted to find this killer, and teach him a lesson.

Now, more than ever, he was positive, the killer that had murdered those innocent kids, was the same creep that confronted him and Ellen in the bush a week ago.

Sunny read through the articles and wrote down on a pad of paper, all the locations around Vancouver, where each body had been found. He then carefully, made a small "x" on the map, at each location with the red felt pen. Then with the red felt, he joined each location with a straight line.

Sunny sat back and took another swig from the half full glass of rum and diet-Pepsi, and studied the map. Strange! He found himself staring at what seemed to be an almost perfect, elongated rectangle shape.

Sunny opened up the Yellow Pages and thumbed through to the restaurant section. He jotted down on the pad of paper, all the Asian restaurants, within the oblong shape that was sketched out, on the map in front of him.

He knew it was a "shot in the dark", but he had a suspicion, that maybe, just maybe, the killer dined at one of the Chinese restaurants that was located within the rectangle.

How could he fall asleep, when he knew the car model, three license plate numbers and all the locations of the dead body locations! Not to mention the fact, that he knew exactly what the killer looked like.

Sunny took the black felt pen and made a dot on the map for each of the restaurants, that he had jotted down on the pad of paper.

He then went over to the kitchen counter and picked up his small black Canon digital camera and came back to the map with all the red x's and black dots on it. He focused the view-finder on the coffee table and took a picture of the map he had created. He checked to make sure it was a crystal clear image. Sunny then pulled out the SD chip from the camera, and inserted it into the laptop. He then downloaded the picture into the password protected FM file. When it was securely loaded into the file, he deleted the map image from his camera.

Sunny picked up the scissors and began to cut up the map into pieces. He pulled the list of body locations and restaurants off the pad of paper and took the list and the map pieces over to his writing desk. He then fed the hungry paper shredder, that was sitting to the right of his desk, all the evidence. *No point in leaving a paper trail for someone to find,* he thought to himself.

Back to the coffee table, he picked up his empty glass and headed for the fridge. He poured himself another drink. Sunny took his nightcap back to the coffee table and reopened the FM file and clicked on the image of the map, that he had just downloaded into the file. He sat there studying the picture on the computer screen, sipping his beverage.

When Sunny was twenty-three years old, he worked as a courier driver, delivering parcels for a stationary company situated in the downtown area. He had an awesome memory of all the streets and stores in Vancouver.

Just by looking at the image of the map on the laptop screen, he could picture almost all of the Chinese restaurants in his mind.

Sunny glanced at the kitchen clock, it was 11:15 pm. Too late tonight, all eateries would certainly be closed, but tomorrow was a new day!

THIRTEEN

Thursday

The Burnaby Youth Detention center was home to literally hundreds of troubled teenagers. It was designed for two hundred inmates, but actually housed closer to three hundred and twenty, give or take a few. The age acceptance at the outdated facility, was thirteen to seventeen. If the offender was admitted at seventeen, but had to serve any time past that age, they were then transferred to a separate wing, where they housed the eighteen and nineteen year-old's. Also, there was a smaller wing adjoined to the main structure, that the bad girls stayed in. Usually, only about twenty or so, naughty girls were living at the "dorm" as it was referred to.

The detention center had been William Marcus's home for the last year. He was not considered a "model" inmate, as he would not participate in volunteer programs, such as self-help, anger management, sexual therapy or any other programs offered by the institution.

Inmates were not forced to participate, because it was their, so-called "charter of rights" to be themselves, without being forced to do anything against their will.

However, if they didn't get involved or participate willingly, it would go on their progress report that was to be sent to their parole or probation officer, depending on who they had to report to. This would be a "red flag" on their record. By having this red flag, the press and the police would usually alert the general public, upon their release date, about the possibility of the convict, being "high-risk" and possibly re-offending again.

Marcus was definetly labelled high-risk to re-offend. He was also nineteen now, and considered an adult, by the justice system. His picture and release date were published in the Province and Vancouver Sun newspapers, in print and online, two weeks before his scheduled release date. The story also ran on Global TV news and all the other local stations.

It was also standard practice, to inform the victims of the perpetrator, of their impending release date. Dr. Randall Wilson had been notified about a month prior to Marcus's release date.

The newspaper reporter stated in the article, that *"William Marcus was a 'high-risk, violent sex-offender, that has every bell and whistle to re-offend again".*

Readers of the newspapers responded with emails to the editors, about their disgust with the justice system and "what about the safety of society". Another killer walks out to freedom, again to wreak havoc on yet, another unsuspecting innocent victim. The crazy merry-go-round of the Canadian justice system!

The famous "Snoopy Dance" ring-tone was barely audible, over the whirring sound of the Breville juicer. Sunny just barely caught the tail-end of the jingle. He turned the juicer off and answered his cellphone. "Yel...low!" he joked.

"Sunny? It's Lola ... just wondering if you were available today? One of the girls called in sick. It would only be a four hour shift?"

"Hey Lola, how's business?" he asked the bar manager.

"It's been busy Sunny ... do you think you can come in today?" Lola wondered.

"I wouldn't be able to show up until noon, that okay?"

"You're a lifesaver Sunny, see you then!" she said with relief in her raspy voice.

"Later, waiter!" as he shut off his phone and left it on the kitchen counter.

He then went over to the juicer and grabbed a glass from the cupboard. He poured the carrot and apple juice mixture into the six ounce glass and stirred it with a teaspoon. Sunny washed all his vitamins down with the healthy concoction. He was a huge believer in fresh carrot juice, cause it was loaded with Beta-Carotene, one of the major protectors against cancer. Years ago, Sunny read about the "Juiceman" a.k.a. Jay Kordich, who had been diagnosed with bladder problems at the young age of twenty-two. At the time, the doctors told Jay that there was no cure, but instead of giving up, he saw a German doctor, who instructed him to drink carrot juice every day. Jay is now in his nineties and believed that the carrot juice may have been his saviour! The drink is known as the "Champ"!

Lola is the full time bar manager at The Dog and pretty much runs the whole daytime show. She is a divorced mother of two and has worked in bars or nightclubs most of her life. Whenever, they were short staffed, they would call Sunny on a whim, hoping he could show up to tend the bar or throw some unruly customer out. There aren't too many problems at The Barking Dog Cafe, because the East Side crowd usually takes care of the problems themselves. They are a tough bunch and don't put up with any bullshit or gang activity. Sunny loathes gang-bangers with a passion!

The ten o'clock sun was shining brightly at the front gates of the Burnaby Youth Detention center (BYDC). It's William Marcus's big day today! It's his release day. He's very, very happy to be getting out but he's also a little bit nervous.

After all, he read some of the reader responses in the newspaper after he was only sentenced for one year. The reader's were not too happy, to say the least.

Fuck them! I did my time! Besides the government owes me, they all fuckin' owe me. And if they piss me off, I just might do it again, he thought to himself as he checked out through the front gates of the long standing, red brick building.

"Stay out of trouble Marcus, or next time it will be the "big-house" that you'll be doing your time at!" the check-out guard said to him as he left.

"Yeah, I don't think so," he replied.

Marcus walked down the cement stairs, that led from the detention center, squinting into the beautiful August sunshine. He strutted across the freshly cut lawn, instead of using the sidewalk, towards his mother's worn-out car, parked at the curbside.

His mother opened her car door and exited. She walked towards her son and opened her arms wide, for a hug. He approached her and told her to quit being so emotional. He declined the embrace, by circling around her and climbed into the passenger side of the car. In his hostile state of ungratefulness, Marcus failed to notice the car on the opposite side of the street, with the man sitting inside, donning sunglasses, drinking a coffee and reading a book.

Mrs. Marcus started her car, fastened her seat-belt, turned her left signal on and pulled away from the curb.

The coffee drinker put his book down and started his car engine. He poured the cold coffee out the window and looked in his drivers side mirror. He waited about thirty seconds, until the Marcus's car was at the end of the street and then pulled a u-turn in the middle of the road and followed at a fair distance.

"Mrs. Harrington is on the phone, Dr. Wilson ... she says that one of her breasts is leaking a little bit of clear fluid from the incision," the receptionist relayed to the doctor.

"Which one is it, the right or the left?" he queried.

"She says, it's the right one."

"Tell her, a small amount of leakage is normal, it's caused by the swelling from the operation. The bodily fluids are finding an escape route. Some gets absorbed by the body tissue and a little bit may weep from the healing, sutured area," the doctor explained, as he looked high above the receptionist's head.

She relayed the information to the client on the other end of the phone line and then hung up. "Are you okay, Dr. Wilson? You seem a little stressed lately," she asked him.

"I'm fine Ginney, I just need a little more sleep, I suppose. Thanks for asking though. You know, anytime a woman enlarges her breasts from an "A cup" to a "D cup", there is always going to be some fluid leaking out from the nipple incision. I mean, that's a big jump! I try and reason with these ladies about only up-sizing, two cups sizes, at the most, but they always want to go larger.

Most of them are not satisfied, unless they are the size of Texas!" he joked.

She giggled, as the good doctor walked into the lunchroom. Dr. Wilson went over to the coffee pot and poured himself a cup of coffee. He mixed in some sweetener and cream and put the steaming cup of coffee to his lips.

"Oww, shit!" as he burned the tip of his tongue. He set the cup down on the counter, closed his weary eyes and thought deeply, *what the devil am I doing? I could go to jail for the rest of my life. How do I know, that Burt isn't an undercover cop? He could be setting me up! No, why would they want to harass me, when a prick like Marcus is getting out of jail, only a year later. Hell, the police at the trial, were just as pissed at the judge and jury, as I was. Besides, the guy that murdered Catherine Marlowe, was taken out by a ...vigilante? And he wasn't the only one. What about the man that slit his wife's throat ... he was found with his throat slit, only one month after he was out on parole! And then there were the other two strange cases of retribution, last year ... murderers that had been murdered in the same way, that they had killed their victims. Burt?*

Dr. Wilson opened his eyes to see his work partner, Dr. Rebekah Mills standing there, looking at him.

"I think Ginney was right, you are stressed aren't you Randall?" Dr. Mills asked, with her hands on her hips.

"No Rebekah, I'm not stressed ... I just miss my wife, that's all. I was having a moment, I ... I ... was seeing her, in my mind's eye, how beautiful she was. It's hard, it's very difficult to know that she's gone and I'll never see her again and that despicable bastard is being released today! It's just not fair! Now I know for sure, Rebekah, that there is no bloody God!

"I believe in "karma", Randall. That no-good, "waste-of-skin" will get his one day! There maybe no God, but I do believe, karma will get him!" the lady doctor reassured him.

"Any word yet from the Motor Vehicle Registrar, about the list of cars we need, Mike?" Detective Rhodes asked her partner.

"Not yet, Jane, looks like later today for sure though. An email came through, stating that, this afternoon the list should be compiled. Wouldn't hold your breath though, you know how the workforce is today ... except the police, that is," chuckled Kuban.

"You know when you're waiting for something important, it always seems to take forever, and when you could care less, it's instant. Why is life like that, Mike?"

"Because if it wasn't like that, then we would have nothing to bitch about, I guess," he said. "You know, the "big cheese" is really cheesed off!"

"I don't blame him Mike, I'm upset too, why can't we nab this guy?" Rhodes sighed.

"We will, we'll get him, it's just a matter of time Jane, but what bothers me, is that he'll only get twenty-five short ones! Twenty-five years is not very long for taking a life, never mind eight lives and maybe more, that we don't even know about! An asshole like that, has probably been killing for a longer period than we realize," he said with disgust. "By the time most serial killers are caught, they have already racked up a long list of victims. Especially, killers that are past the age of thirty years. They never confess to all their killings, they only usually confess to the ones, where the bodies are found by the authorities," Kuban reasoned.

"What do you think makes a person become a serial killer, Mike?" Rhodes asked.

"I don't believe, somebody wakes up one morning and decides they want to be a serial killer ... honestly, I believe it's genetics, Jane, something they are born with ... you know it's like a "genetic code", in their brain, made up of various nucleic acids, that are localized in their cell nuclei."

"You mean it's like a congenital blueprint already mapped out in their brain?" she wondered, as she fidgeted with her shiny hair.

"Exactly right! No one decides, they want to be gay, or a lesbian, or a pedophile, or a serial killer. It's the cards that they are dealt at birth. But that doesn't mean that it's not their fault, because they were born that way ... that a killer can not be responsible for his or her crimes. We live in a civilized world with man-made laws, that society must abide by. That's why we have prisons ... for the lawbreakers that cannot control their inner urges," explained Kuban.

"Makes sense, except for the prison part. The killers don't go to jail for life, they just get a slap on the wrist. I praise the American justice system, at least when an American judge sentences a murderer to "life in jail", it's normally forty to sixty years. Now that's justice!" she said with a smile.

"Yes, that's justice!" Kuban agreed. Now let's go and get a coffee, I believe it's break time."

"Blenz or Starbuck's?" Rhodes asked.

"Blenz of course!" he answered quickly. "We can check back this afternoon, about the MVR list."

Mrs. Marcus turned right onto Willingdon Road, heading south. After a couple of miles she came to a main intersection and then turned left onto Canada Way.

Neither, Mrs. Marcus or her troubled son, William, noticed the car following them. Once on Canada Way, she travelled approximately five miles, before turning left onto 10th Avenue.

William had the car radio tuned on to 99.3 FM rock station. He was singing along to a Guns and Roses song. Mrs. Marcus, who's first name is Mary, asked her son to turn down the volume a little, so she could talk to him, but he ignored her and just kept singing to the music.

Mary kept following 10th Avenue, still unaware of the vehicle, about four cars behind hers. 10th Avenue is the main street that acts as the boundary separating the municipalities of Burnaby and New Westminster. Rounding the bend, changing into McBride Boulevard, from 10th, they were heading to the Pattullo Bridge, which crosses the mighty Fraser River, and into Surrey.

Mary was taking young William home, to stay with her temporarily, until he could find a job and get back on his feet. She loved her son and hoped that everything would work out with him coming back home. At the same time, she had an uneasy feeling, after all, her son was a convicted murderer.

Mrs. Marcus had separated from her husband and filed for divorce, while William was in the detention center. It was a longtime coming, and she felt that it was the right thing to do, since he was mean to both her and her son, and she didn't love the man anymore. He was a drunken deadbeat, and a shitty step-dad to William. She hoped by giving the old crud, the "boot", that her and her son would be able to bond closely as mother and son, without any interference.

DOG WITH A BONE

The Marcus's old car rattled over the antiquated bridge, high above the muddy Fraser. The river was about a mile wide and one quarter mile deep. It would have been a great place for Mary to stop and push her ill son off.

The great river has swallowed many bridge jumpers, since the day it was built. Committing suicide from this bridge wouldn't be too difficult. One hundred and fifty feet high from the center of the span. If the long fall didn't do a person some harm, surely the cold, dark, murky, turbulent waters below, would certainly finish them off!

The Pattullo Bridge was built in the nineteen thirties. The construction of the bridge was started in 1935 and it was completed two years later. The bridge was officially opened on November 15th, 1937 by Premier Thomas Dufferin "Duff" Pattullo. The four lane bridge cost four million dollars to build, is two thousand two hundred and eighty-six metres in length and has thirty-one piers. The Pattullo Bridge was also the first bridge in Canada to be illuminated by sodium vapour lamps, just like the San Francisco-Oakland and Golden Gate bridges in the United States.

The municipality of Surrey was mainly farmland, in the "dirty thirties", right up until the nineteen seventies. As the City of Vancouver became more populated, real estate values increased and in turn, forced young families looking to get into the housing market, out to the outer lying areas or "suburbs" such as Surrey, Delta or Richmond, which were generally more affordable. This attracted lower income families, such as single parent families and such. In the earlier years of Surrey's development, the crime factor was high, because of the broken families and the lower income class.

FOURTEEN

As she slowed down her vehicle, Mary Marcus put her right turn-signal on. She then wheeled the older, white Ford Fairlane into the driveway of the small rancher-style house and drove the rusty car into the rundown carport.

The house, about forty years of age had definitely seen rosier days in it's life. Construction of that style of house, seemed to be the norm, for that era. It was very typical of builders in the nineteen seventies, to build smaller, two bedroom rancher style homes. These kinds of dwellings were cheap and quick to build. The contractors could slap them up in a few months.

Surrey and other outer lying areas of the Greater Vancouver district had affordable land and so builders and real estate developers jumped on the opportunities, available to them.

It was evident, that Mrs. Marcus was falling behind with her cosmetic duties on the old house. Living with a drunkard for a husband, probably didn't help getting the maintenance around the house done. The faded light blue paint on the cedar siding was peeling off, leaving a light gray color of the original wood showing through. The asphalt shingles on the roof were curling and some had obviously been blown off by the wind. Streaks on the windows, suggested that, they hadn't been washed for half a year or more. The yard was another story. The grass was long overdue for a cut, and the flower bed, up along the front bay window, was full of weeds. The carport was full of junk and her car barely fit in between all the crap piled up in there.

William and his mother opened the car doors and squeezed out from the vehicle and walked towards the back of the car. She opened the trunk to retrieve his bag and some groceries she had picked up earlier.

Neither one of them had noticed the vehicle that had been following them. It had slowed down and stopped in the shadows, of the big oak tree's leafy branches on the opposite side of the street.

The Marcus's headed for the backdoor of the house, out through the dilapidated carport. Mary fumbled with her keys until she found the right one. She opened the weather- beaten backdoor and pushed it open with her left foot. In she went, with William following behind. He closed the squeaky door behind him.

The man in the sunglasses, on the far side of the street, sat with his car idling and watched mother and son disappear into the house. He made a careful, complete observation of the surrounding houses. Then he pulled away from the curb and drove off down the street.

The lunch crowd at the The Barking Dog was starting to shuffle in. It was 11:40 am, when Sunny showed up, just in time to start the noon shift.

"Hey, Sunny ... you walk to work?" Lola asked him as he entered the bar.

"Yeah, figured I needed the exercise," as he patted his firm stomach and winked at her.

"Sure Sunny, you really need to lose some weight!" she kidded him.

"So Lola, what have you got for me today?" he asked.

"Can you help Dixie out on the bar for me please, Sunny?" Lola asked.

"Sure thing, sweetness!" Sunny sang out.

The lunch crowd was noisy, but you could still hear the music from the jukebox playing in the background. The sound of Bruce Springsteen's, "Born in the USA" was rambling out from the ceiling-hung Bose speakers.

There were always the regulars that worked in the area, who came in for their lunch breaks and the staff at The Dog, knew most of them. Some of the customers would phone ahead and place their lunch order with the kitchen. The cafe also sold beer and coffee mugs and t-shirts with the logo of Barney imprinted on them; these items were a big hit with the tourists.

Dixie and Sunny were brewing up a storm. As fast as he could draw the draft beer from the puncheon, the suds were taken away by the bubbly waitresses. The two behind the bar worked great as a team, Dixie concocting a multitude of exotic cocktails and hi-balls and Sunny lining up the "brown pops". The Dog was a fun and friendly atmosphere.

Celina, one of the younger waitresses, came up to Lola and told her, "over by the pool table, there are three dudes sitting there, and one of them has a hunting knife on his belt. I don't feel comfortable serving them, Lola."

"That's not acceptable. They can't stay, come with me and we will tell them, that they have to leave," Lola said to Celina.

The ladies approached the young men and politely asked them to leave, informing the three, that it was forbidden to bring a weapon into the cafe.

"It's not a weapon, lady, it's a tool, I use it in my trade," the guy arrogantly replied, as he looked at his buddies and smirked.

"Whatever ... you can't stay, I asked you politely and now I'm telling you. You have to leave, now!" Lola demanded.

"It's a free fuckin' world, we only came here to have lunch and a beer for shit's sake! Why don't you put up a fucking sign on the entrance, "No Tools Allowed!" the guy argued loudly.

"Yeah, well that would mean you then, wouldn't it? Celina, go get Sunny please!" Lola ordered.

"Sunny, what kind of a girlie name is that ... hahaha Sunnneeee. Oooh, I'm scared!" the guy with the knife laughed.

The other two guys sitting at the table fidgeted nervously and one of them said to the others, "maybe we should go Fred, people are starting to stare at us."

"Fuckem! We have every right to be here Jimmy, we're not doing anybody any harm. It's not illegal to carry a knife around on your side, it's not concealed, so what the fuck?"

Sunny was cruising through the bar straight to the table of three. As he approached the table, he quickly scanned the surrounding tables and patrons around him.

"The nice lady asked you guys politely, to leave the premises!" he told them, as his brown eyes started turning to a charcoal black. He could feel his blood turning cold.

"We haven't done anything wrong buddy! We just want lunch and a beer, Sunnneee! Is that your name?" Fred with the knife, taunted. "Besides, you don't look very big, to be telling me what to do anyway!"

"Last chance, goof! (Get Out Or Fight)!" Sunny ordered, with his fists ready for action.

"GOOF! Who you calling a GOOF, ASSHOLE!" Fred screamed at Sunny, as he started to get up from the table, while reaching at his side for the hunting knife.

Sunny moved in quick towards Fred and grabbed his hair as he was almost out of his seat. With both hands full of hair, he pulled the guys head downwards and smashed his face into the hard edge of the table. There was a loud cracking sound, like someone snapping a dry piece of kindling. Blood squirted from the side of Fred's fat face. Sunny broke his nose. Fred frantically tried to grab at his knife, as Sunny slammed his face into the table again and again. Fat fucking Fred slumped to the floor. A patron at the next table grabbed the hunting knife from the sheath on his belt and handed it to Lola, for safe keeping.

By now the other two guys had gotten up from the table. Sunny let go of Fred and went into his defensive stance. Jimmy came at Sunny. Sunny right jabbed him, as hard as he possibly could, smack right in the throat. The attacker was gasping for air and clutching his neck. Sunny moved in, and drilled him, right, left, and another right, this time in both temples. Jimmy went down hard and hit the floor with a heavy thud!

Sunny looked at the last man standing and said, "you can leave 'em or join 'em!"

The third member of the trio backed up slowly and then turned and quickly walked out of The Barking Dog Cafe.

The pub patrons clapped vehemently and cheered loudly as the melee ended.

"Big Bob" came over and patted Sunny on the back and told him, "I had your back Sunny, but it looks like you didn't need any help, that was a fast fight, if I ever seen one! No wonder they call you 'Speed'."

Big Bob was a paltry three hundred and forty pounds and stood about six foot four! He drank at The Dog on a regular basis. Big Bob the friendly giant! The big man was not a fighter, but his mere presence, when he stood up, was enough to make a rhinoceros turn tail and run! He was buddies with most of the regulars. A real character, he always had a joke ready and was always in a good mood. He grew up in the projects, just down from Sunny's childhood house.

Sunny and Robert (his birth name) went to different high-schools, so they never really knew each other, growing up.

The two men, met one night at The Dog, when a table of out-of-town railroaders started getting intoxicated and causing a disturbance. Big Bob, his lady-friend and another guy were sitting at the table having dinner, when one of the railroaders bumped the table that Big Bob and his friends were sitting at. Drinks on the table were spilled, so Big Bob stood up and asked the guy to take it easy!

"No you take it easy, fatso!" was the reply.

The other four railroaders got up from their table, once they saw the size of Big Bob. They started to move in behind their mouthy friend. Big Bob was feeling his adrenaline start to rush through his veins, like fire through a balsa-wood factory. He knew he was alone on this account, cause his buddy he was with, had a bad back from a car accident four years ago.

Although he was as big as a cruise ship, he knew his fighting skills "sucked" because he never had many fights in his life. Most big guys don't get the opportunity to "scrap" as often as smaller guys, because usually their size, scares the opponent off. And of course, the smaller guys always have to try harder, so they become more adept at "kicking ass"!

But Big Bob knew, not to show any fear, it was better to stand your ground and bluff your way out, or it would sure as shit, be suicide.

"Why don't you pick on someone your own size?" came the voice from behind the railroaders.

They all turned around to see Sunny standing there, with his fists clenched by his sides. What they didn't see, were the plexiglass knuckles on both of Sunny's fists.

Glass "knucks" were Sunny's own invention. They were not available anywhere. You could buy brass knuckles on the black market, which were not actually brass, but some metal alloy, such as aluminum and tin. Or you could sometimes locate steel knuckles, which were cast out of iron and steel. These types of knucks were heavy and cumbersome to swing through the air. But if you connected with the intended target, they were bloody deadly! That's the main reason Canada outlawed brass knuckles. They were classed as a prohibited weapon by the government.

Plexiglass wasn't even half as heavy as steel or brass, so they wouldn't usually kill a person, when they came in contact. Although they would normally warrant a knock-out, knockdown or cut up flesh. And since they are ultra lightweight to use, swinging a punch is swift! Because plexiglass is clear, the knucks are damn-near invisible on the hand.

Sunny had made his own glass knuckles out of three-quarter inch thick plexiglass, that he ordered from a hobby shop. Merick lent him the shop one night, cause Sunny told Ike that he had a little project he wanted to complete and he needed to use some of their tools. Black's Lock Shop had almost every tool under the sun.

"Mind your own business shorty!" came the response from the drunken train worker.

"Shorty" was the *one* word that many guys paid dearly, for saying. Sunny had heard the word shorty his whole life, and was was sick and tired of hearing it. "You are my business!" Sunny explained, as he kicked an empty beer bottle laying on the floor, off to the side with his foot.

As he pointed to Big Bob, one of the five guys said, "look, we don't want no trouble, but the big guy here, thinks he can tell us what to do!"

"Leave now!" Sunny ordered.

The red-headed railroader, charged Sunny with all his might. Sunny grabbed the back of one of the spruce barchairs and swung it into the carrot-top's path. The angry guy crashed through the chair and slipped and fell. One of the other four, grabbed a bottle of beer and went to throw it at Sunny. Big Bob reached for the attacker's arm and pulled him backwards and with all his weight, pushed the enemy into the wall and broke the guy's arm.

Sunny went for the "mouthpiece" who called him shorty, and had started the whole fight. Speed raised both fists and waited for the dude to respond. He did, so Sunny used his face as a punching bag. He drove both sets of those glass knuckles into his ugly, bearded, railroad scowl. Sunny pummeled the guy's flesh-tone into a bright cherry red color. The remaining three guys jumped Sunny from behind.

Big Bob ambled over and grabbed one of the attackers by the throat with both of his mammoth hands. As he pulled the guy off Sunny's back, the railroader almost ripped Sunny's t-shirt right off. Sunny turned quickly around and elbowed the opponent in the side of the face. Then he smoked the guy repeatedly with his plexiglass covered fists! That sickly, squishing noise, echoed with every impact of those glass knuckles. The guy fell hard into a table and then dropped to the floor. He was hurt badly!

Sunny slid the glass knucks off quickly and handed them to one of the waitresses, who was standing by. Then he gave her the "nod" to leave. She left immediately and went around the bar and into the kitchen and threw them into the garbage can.

The police and ambulance were dispatched to The Barking Dog Cafe to pick up the pieces. Three of the five men were taken to the hospital and the other two were hauled off to the 312 Main Street police station, downtown and were charged with; "disturbing the peace by fighting" and "being drunk and disorderly in a public place".

No charges were laid against Big Bob, Sunny or the bar. There were plenty of witnesses who claimed that the group of five started the fight and Big Bob and Sunny acted in self defense. The railroaders never returned to the bar after that ordeal. Sunny and Big Bob remained friends since that night and always had each others back, whenever it was necessary.

It was about 3:20 pm, when the email came through, from the Motor Vehicle Registrar to the Investigative Services department at the police station. Steven Folk had come into work earlier, rather than starting his usual shift at six o'clock. He knew the cop shop was buzzing with anticipation for the arrival of the list of cars, to search for the suspect vehicle, that was wanted in the Fraser murders.

Folk "red flagged" the email with the list attached and called Chief Constable Joe Winters into the computer room. He had already printed the list off. Folk handed it to Chief Winters.

"Thanks Steven!" Winters said as he plucked his reading glasses from from his shirt pocket and studied the list intently. He grumbled a few times and cleared his throat once or twice as well. After a few minutes, he looked at the young computer nerd and said, "looks like we better call everyone in for a rendezvous! Steven, send out a text message to all members to report here at 5:00 pm today, ASAP! I'll inform dispatch also, to call everyone in ... okay let's get on it son!"

Sunny was just finishing his four o'clock shift. The police had come and gone, after the bar brawl with the three hoods sitting by the pool table. Fred and Jimmy, the ones that got their asses kicked by Sunny, were escorted down to the station and held for a few hours, then released without being charged. Lola and Sunny didn't want to press charges, they figured that the beating might have taught them a lesson.

The police warned the trouble makers however, that if they set foot in The Barking Dog again, that they would arrest them for trespassing.

Lola thanked Sunny for coming and doing a shift and said she would let him know when he was needed again.

Sunny liked the sporadic shift work; he was not suited to a nine to five job, and Lola understood that, but she sometimes wondered how he could make ends meet, especially in today's costly world. *Must be a good saver,* she thought.

Babe was at the door, snuffling along the crack at the bottom of the door, just like pigs do when rooting around on the ground for morsels of food. She knew Sunny was on the other side. As he opened the door, she was swinging her tail so hard, that her whole back-end was swaying back and forth.

"Hey Babe!" he said as he pushed the door open and patted her golden, white head. "Dinner time girl, let's get you some chow," as he headed for the kitchen to fix up her bowl of goodies; some dry kibble, mixed with some chicken pieces and carrot slices. He put the bowl down and filled her water dish with fresh water from the water cooler.

Sunny never drank tap water or gave it to his dog, because it contained fluoride, a known cancer causing chemical. The bottled water was fluoride-free! *Hell, if you're going to drink tap water, you may as well smoke!* Those were his thoughts about water. It was the only thing all humans had in common; consuming water, maybe that was one reason for all the cancer in the civilized world. Fluoridated water? Cavity-free teeth, look great, but the trade-off may be some form of cancer. Flip a coin!

Sunny opened up the fridge and grabbed an apple. He was going to pass on dinner tonight, cause he had sampled some chicken fingers and a salad at The Dog. A quick glass of water and some bites from the shiny red Gala apple, because tonight, he was on a mission. A restaurant drive-by, surveillance mission.

Babe finished up her bowl of chow and drank about a pint of water. Sunny knew it was time to take her out, to do her business.

They headed outside and over to the park, that Babe had claimed as her personal toilet. Sunny always picked up after her. "If you're going to own a dog, you better walk it and be prepared to clean up it's poop! Otherwise, don't get a dog, get a cat!" Sunny would tell people.

Back inside the loft, Sunny gave Babe a rawhide chew. She trotted over to her fluffy, round bed and did a couple of circles on top and then settled in, to work-over the tough piece of leather. That rawhide would keep her occupied for some time.

Sunny left his cellphone on the counter, but grabbed his pocket-size binoculars, and headed for the garage. He jumped into the Accord, hit the remote and then backed out of the garage.

He cruised down Victoria Drive towards Kingsway. The traffic wasn't too busy on the "Drive", just the typical idiots that must have got their drivers license in a raffle.

Some young kid with his "N" sticker (New driver) on the back of the car, went speeding past Sunny. He often wondered how these new, young drivers passed the road test, with bad habits like that. *I guess I probably drove like "there was no tomorrow" when I was that age too,* he thought, as he slid Rod Stewart's, A Night On The Town CD into the car stereo. "Tonight's The Night" lyrics erupted from the speakers. *How fitting, "tonight's the night",* as he smiled to himself.

When Sunny came to Kingsway, he turned right. He was heading back towards the direction where he and Ellen were accosted by the freak in the bush. There were a multitude of Asian restaurants along Kingsway alone, never mind the rest of the city.

Sunny had a mental image of some of the restaurants, from when he worked as a courier driver. But that was quite a spell ago and he knew, that since that period of time, some restaurants would have closed their doors and new ones opened. So he was going to just motor around in his ride, with the mellow tunes of "Rod the Mod" and check out each place, one at a time.

As he cruised southeast on Kingsway, he started to take note of all the types of businesses along the major route. Kingsway is one of the longest four lane streets, running diagonal, right through the center of the eastern side of Vancouver. Starting at Main Street, in the Mt. Pleasant area, the thoroughfare stretches about four miles to Boundary Road. Boundary Road is the border between Vancouver and Burnaby. Kingsway carries on from Boundary Road, right past Central Park, the largest park in Burnaby and keeps on going another four miles through Burnaby and then stops at 10th Avenue, the border of Burnaby and New Westminster.

Sunny was backtracking to Central Park along Kingsway for two reasons. The first one being that the park was at the farthest, eastern end of the elongated rectangle, on the map that he had put together the night before; not even half a mile from where one of the murder victims was found. The second reason was, Central Park lay right across the way from the location that Ellen, Sunny and Babe had bumped into the suspected Fraser Case murderer.

What was that guy doing in the bush in the first place? He didn't know we were coming in there and he was sweating excessively. Maybe he was doing something physical to create the perspiration, like maybe dumping and burying a body? But that's not his "modus operandi". Why would he go to the trouble of digging a shallow grave for his victim, when he has been dumping them all over the streets for the cops to find? Something doesn't fit.

Sunny's mind was racing as he drove along the busy four lane street. The Chop Suey House was coming up on the right side of the street. He slowed down and wheeled into the parking lot. The place was packed. Why not, after all it was Thursday evening and it was the dinner hour. He had never dined at this place, but heard through the grapevine that the food was superb!

Lots of cars, small cars, big cars, but no Ford Taurus or Chevy Corsica. *What if the guy changed cars? Nah, those kind of scumbags only own one car. They don't even work!*

It was a known fact among law enforcement agencies and investigative profilers, that about ninety-five percent of serial killers could not hold down a steady job. This is due to their insatiable appetite to hunt down and execute unsuspecting victims. So obsessed with finding their next victim, they are unable to concentrate on working at a career. The only deed, a true serial killer can focus on is murder!

Canadian authorities believe, that at any given time, there is a minimum of forty serial killers roaming the countryside looking for humans to prey on! Every seven minutes, in North America, a person goes missing and sadly, most of them are never found.

Sunny had passed about six Chinese food restaurants by the time he had reached Boundary Road. The parking lot of each eatery, had almost no vacancies, but there was no sign of the suspect vehicle.

As he neared Boundary, he clicked his right turn signal on, and then headed south, down Boundary Road. He had an uneasy urge to drive past the area that the killer had cornered Ellen and himself. Sunny didn't plan to visit the site just yet, but figured, since he was in the vicinity, he may as well do a drive by.

Sunny could feel his adrenaline starting to formulate, as if each molecule in his bloodstream were hundreds of tiny soldiers, being pushed from behind, by hundreds of more tiny soldiers, waiting impatiently to attack the enemy! His heart started pounding, faster, pounding harder, so fucking hard and fast, that he could feel it in his eardrums.

He was approaching 48th Avenue. Sunny slowed the car down and "HONK, HONK, HONK"! Quickly he looked in his rear-view mirror. The impatient driver behind, was blasting his horn and giving the "one finger salute"! It was now obvious that Sunny had been driving too slow, thinking about that scary day in the bush.

Instantaneously he snapped out of his momentary lapse of driving skills and flicked his right turn signal on, and then wheeled the Accord onto 48th Avenue. The angry driver behind Sunny, honked a couple more times and then sped off down Boundary Road.

Sunny drove about fifty yards and then pulled the vehicle over to the side of the road. He turned the motor off and slowly inhaled, deep into his lungs as he glanced across the street, over towards the unmarked dirt road entrance, that led to *that* wooded area. He then exhaled. Sunny sat there in his car for about five minutes, just staring at the entry to *that* place.

Sunny could feel shivers run up and down his thirty-eight year old spine! He had goose pimples all over his muscular arms. *That was a close call! My life could have ended right there, with Babe and Ellen, just like those poor kids. If Babe hadn't behaved the way she did, baring her teeth and growling and barking at that prick, he may have shot me, while I was talking to him, face to face! Then, what would he have done to Elly and my dog? Pounded chopsticks into their ear canals? That sick fuck!*

Sunny's goose bumps gradually started disappearing and he could feel his inner fear emotion, start changing into his angry "S" emotion. He could feel his Irish/Croatian mixed blood starting to boil into a molten fury! *That son-of-a-bitch! How fucking dare he, pull a gun on Elly, Babe and me! A psychotic lunatic ... killing innocent children and teenagers! I will find you, and when I do, you better hope the devil has mercy on you, cause I won't!*

The boardroom at the police station was filling up. Detectives, Mike Kuban and Jane Rhodes were in the corner discussing some notes with a couple of other homicide detectives. So far, about nine members had arrived. It was already ten past five o'clock. Twenty police members had been assigned to the Fraser case. Chief Joe Winters knew it was short notice to assemble his army by five o'clock, but he was a demanding fellow and he knew, that they all wanted the child killer caught, so of course, the army would show up as quick as humanly possible.

Winters looked at his watch. It read five fifteen. *Time for a big dump! The "motley crew" won't be here for another twenty minutes,* he thought.

Winters headed for the can, to do his business. He could sit down for a minute and call his wife, to let her know that he would be home a little later for dinner.

The meeting room was almost full now that it was five forty-five. Only two more members to go, that would bring the total to eighteen. Two officers had called in to say, they wouldn't make it in, on time. The two were in the middle of some undercover drug surveillance at the very moment, and were ready to bust a crack dealer, down on the corner of Hastings and Main Street.

Winters appeared at the doorway, looked into the room full of cops and then checked his watch again. "Hey Sparky, everyone here?" Winters asked one of the long-haired undercover detectives.

"We're still waiting for Robinson and MacDuff, they should be here any minute ... Burton and Williams won't make it in, they're doin' a bust!" Sparky replied.

"Shit, it's almost six o'clock for shits sake! Okay, anyone need coffee, go and get it now, while we're waiting for Robinson and MacDuff," Winters ordered, looking at his watch again.

Only seven members left the room, to go get java.

"Listen up everyone, while we're waiting for the last two, here's a copy of the list of vehicles from the Motor Vehicle Registrar. Look it over for a few minutes," Winters said with a tired look on his weathered face.

Just as he handed out the last two copies, his cellphone buzzed. Winters answered his phone. "Oh my God, tell me it's not true!" he gasped as he put his hand to his forehead and turned around, with his back to the group of members sitting in their chairs. "Holy shit ... shit, son-of-a-bitch!"

Detective Mike Kuban and another homicide detective named Darrell Ford walked over to Winters. Ford put his hand on the Chief's shoulder and asked him if everything was okay.

"MacDuff's been killed in a shootout during a botched bank robbery over on East Broadway, just minutes ago. That's why they're not here ... goddammit! Robinson's okay, apparently he killed the holdup guy, but the guy driving the getaway car disappeared," Winters explained to the room full of shocked and saddened police, with a look of disbelief. "I can't fucking believe it ... MacDuff is gone? It doesn't make sense, sometimes this job doesn't make any sense at all!"

There was silence in the room. You could have heard a feather hit the floor. No one said a word after Winters quit talking. They all just looked at one another with blank, hollow stares. A few of the members, looked down at the floor.

All police officers know the dangers and risks that go with the career. They learn the potential fatalities that they may incur when being trained as a peace officer upholding the law, but no one expects to die or have a partner or associate get killed in the line of duty. It's just not a realization, until it actually happens. And when it does happen, it's unbelievable, just too surreal!

Finally, the Chief broke the silence, "this is going to be difficult for everyone, if anyone needs time off to reflect on what just happened, I understand completely! It's tragic, such a tragedy! MacDuff was a great person and a well respected police officer ... we will miss him greatly. In light of the circumstances, I will make this meeting as brief as I possibly can. You all have a list of the possible suspect vehicles in front of you. There is a total of four hundred and sixty-nine Chevy Corsicas and Ford Tauruses from the mid nineties, still registered and on the road in B.C. We need to narrow this list down, by focusing on the vehicles that are registered here, on the lower mainland first."

"What about the possibility of a registered owner, from the interior or even further up north, that has moved to the lower mainland and not updated his or her address?" interrupted one of the members, sitting at the back of the room.

"Well, you didn't let me finish! Of course that's a possibility, like I was saying we focus on the lower mainland

FIRST and then we look at the rest of the province. Nothing is overlooked, nothing is left out, nothing is forgotten! We need to arrest this demonic individual, before he strikes again and by the dead body count in fourteen months, it seems like he's just getting started!" Chief Winters expressed to the Fraser case division. "Two of you are going to categorize the list, into municipalities, and then starting with the Greater Vancouver district, we will do a background search on all of the car's registered owners. From there, we will move east and north into the remaining municipalities of the province. Chances are that this individual, lives close by. Most of these assholes, have no money, no job and so they probably haven't traveled from very far away!"

Forensic profilers have determined from past criminal cases, that over ninety-percent of serial killers are white males between the ages of twenty-five and thirty-five. They generally have IQ's in the intelligent range, but do poorly in school and have trouble keeping a job. This is usually due to the fact that they are are always preoccupied with perverted thoughts about finding their next victim. Most of them are unemployed or work periodically as unskilled laborers. Serial killers almost always have a special hatred for their mothers and fathers. Sixty-percent of them, had wet their beds beyond the age of twelve and another interesting fact is that, most serial killers have blue eyes!

"So listen up comrades! I need two volunteers to organize this list, so we can start checking all these potential vehicles," Winters said.

Half a dozen members put their hands up. Winters pointed to two, and said, "good , let's get on it, I'll talk to you guys after we're done here. Once we categorize the list, I'll assign everyone, their own municipality, so you can get busy investigating the possible suspect vehicles. Any questions?"

Nobody raised a hand, they all knew their protocol.

Sunny wasn't ready to go back into *that* place just yet. He pulled a "u-turn" on 48th Avenue and pointed the Accord back towards Kingsway. Sunny wasn't finished doing his restaurant surveillance.

Going north on Boundary, Sunny was destined for Broadway, a few miles away. Broadway is home to a multitude of shops and restaurants. It is also close to the northern perimeter of the oblong rectangle of the unsolved Fraser case murders.

It was still peak time for the dinner rush, although Sunny didn't really count on a serial killer wanting to dine and hobnob with too many other diners. He had to do it though, in order to satisfy himself, by checking out as many restaurants as he possibly could.

Only a few minutes after six o'clock now and Sunny was approaching Broadway. He put his left turn-signal on as he approached the busy intersection and then hung a left on Broadway.

A fine night for hunting, he thought to himself. Sunny was driven by an intense underlying passion of vengeance!

FIFTEEN

The blistering sun was slowly sinking into the rooftops of the neighborhood houses, as the sluggish car, coming down the gradual dusky street, veered into the curbside.

The headlights darkened as the motor shut down. No one exited the car. The man inside the vehicle sat there, staring intently at the person walking down the empty, quiet street.

A young woman by the name of Jenny, only nineteen years old, with a slender build, weighing about one hundred and five pounds was on her way home from work. She had got off the bus and had to walk a short distance to her parents house. Her dynamic iPod in-ear headphones were snuggled into her petite ears, just like a fresh marshmallow wedged inside a toilet-paper tube. The superior noise-isolating design of the headphones, blocked out all ambient sounds. She was merrily singing along with her deafening tunes, oblivious to anything around her.

"Oh my God!" she yelled, jumping backwards and clutching her chest as a black cat darted out in front of her from a juniper bush. She started to laugh a nervous laugh, as she thought, *how ridiculous, afraid of a stupid ol' cat!*

DOG WITH A BONE

Jenny's heart was thumping hard, as she watched the cat skedaddle across the gloomy street, over the sidewalk and disappear into the darkness of an overgrown cedar hedge. She stopped for a few seconds to adjust her backpack. It had shifted over to one side of her body, when she had jumped backwards, from the scare of the black cat.

The young lady was so busy repositioning her pack and checking her headphones, that she didn't notice the man slip out of the passenger side of his car, on the other side of the street.

He crouched down below the roof line of his car quickly. Leaning, with his hands on the side of the car, he peered through the darkened windows of his vehicle, at the pretty young girl across the street.

Jenny was still fumbling with her pack, but was walking at the same time, trying to get comfortable with the weight on her back. As she passed by the man's car, he inched down a little bit more, so that only his nose and eyes were visible in the moonlit windows.

The day's sun had been swallowed up by the night and replaced by a dry moon. The street was vacant, except for a few cars, here and there, parked along the sides of the dark, eerily quiet road.

Nervously, Jenny kept walking, but picking up the pace, as she felt a weird uneasiness come over her. She kept her music going, as if to keep her mind off the dark street. Glancing around from side to side, she kept moving, a little quicker than before.

Shadows, they're just shadows from the trees and bushes. The moon is casting shadows on the trees! I should have called my dad to pick me up. He did offer, after-all! Why didn't I call him for fuck's sake? Jenny's mind was now racing! Her heart was pounding so hard that she couldn't hear her music clearly. She put both of her hands in her purple hoody and kept moving. The leafy shapes cast on the sidewalk from the light of the moon were starting to freak her out! *Maybe I should start to run. Home is only two more blocks away. No, I'm overreacting. Don't be stupid ... grow up, there's nothing to be afraid of!*

The hunched-over, shadowy figure moved out slowly, from behind the car and then in a crouching posture, quickly jetted across the street. He was only about seventy-five feet directly behind Jenny.

Sunny had scoped out, over twenty-five Chinese food restaurants, and not a sign of the suspect vehicle. It was getting to be about nine-thirty and he had to get home to let Babe out.

He had done the "circuit" within his homemade oblong rectangular map, that was burned into the memory bank of his brain. *It's possible that the killer, doesn't even eat at any of these restaurants. Maybe he orders in! Nah, a true serial killer wouldn't want anyone to know where he lived, of course he eats out,* thought Sunny.

The quest was finished, for now. Sunny had been all over Vancouver, the east side, west side, Chinatown and downtown. No sign of any nineties Taurus, Corsicas or Tempests. *But that's okay, a real true "Bully Basher" never gives up! Time to go home and feed the dog.*

Babe was doing her usual tail wagging and sniffing at the bottom of the door as she heard her master, coming up the spiral staircase from the garage. As he turned the key, she started talking to him in her doggie-growl voice.

"Hey girl ... no luck today," he said to her, as she cocked her head on an angle, like she completely understood what he had just said. "Come on, let's go outside for a pee," as Sunny grabbed her leash. Out the door they went.

William Marcus was arguing with his mother about him cleaning up his room, putting away the dishes and the mess he created around the house.

"Will, why can't you please clean up after yourself?" his mother pleaded. "I'm not asking for much ... as an adult you should be able to put things away, after you have used them."

"Why are you always telling me what to do? I can't stand it when you keep bitching at me! Just shut-up!" William screamed at his mother.

Mary Marcus was deathly afraid of her psychopathic son. She didn't want to get him all riled up, but at the same time she needed to keep the house in order. Getting him to "pull his weight" was going to be a task. Sometimes she wished, he had never been born!

A mother's natural instinct is to protect and love her son, no matter what "trials and tribulations" he is faced with in life. But Mary had her doubts about the natural instinct bullshit. *My son is a sick individual, with sadistic and violent tendencies and he doesn't treat me with any respect! How can I trust him? How can I fall asleep at night and hope that he doesn't come in my bedroom and harm me, like other children have done to their own mothers and fathers,* she thought.

William stormed out of the kitchen and went into his bedroom and slammed the door. Inside his bedroom, he turned up his stereo, with some heavy metal headbanging noise. He stayed in his bedroom most of the night. Every now and then, he would come out of the messy room for a drink or some snacks.

Mary was watching a movie in the front room. She asked her son if he would like to join her and maybe they could order a pizza. "Will! Would you like to get a pizza delivered? We could order a large Hawaiian or maybe a pepperoni and cheese," she asked.

"You just don't get it, do you? I don't want no damn pizza, why are you trying to be nice to me, what's the catch? Huh? Everyone in jail treated me like shit! You don't know what I went through in there. They can all go to hell, and you too!" William yelled back at her.

Mary was terrified! She could feel herself trembling inside. She was on the verge of tears. Desperately, she wanted to help her only son, but didn't know where to start or what to say to him. It seemed anything, that came out of her mouth was the wrong thing to say to him. "I'm sorry Will, I won't bother you again tonight," she quietly told him.

He stormed back into his room and slammed the door. She went back to watching her program on television, and thought to herself, *tomorrow I will phone the police and ask them what I should do. He's very unstable. I can't live like this! The Canadian justice system is a goddamn joke! He's my son, but he should be locked up for life!* Mary kept the phone by her side all night.

Jenny was only about a block away from home and it now seemed darker out than ever.

Suddenly, without any warning she could feel her backpack being pulled away from her body. As she tried to turn around, she could feel something covering her mouth. Hands! But those hands didn't feel like skin, they kind of felt like and smelled like rubber. Jenny panicked! Her mind was racing!

She tried to scream, but only muffled, poor attempts of would-be sounds came from her covered mouth.

Those rubber encased hands were large, very strong and fast moving. Her pretty, delicate face was being rubbed and mushed with those terrible rubber gloves. It felt as though her skin was being pulled from her skull. The pain was unbearable for the horrified girl.

Jenny was panic stricken and could barely get enough oxygen into her lungs, from between the attacker's fingers. She almost passed out from the lack of air, but the will to survive overcame her.

Immense fear charged up her adrenaline supply and she instinctively started to kick backwards at the legs of the creeper. Her headphones finally fell out of her ears from the rough rubber "face washing" she was receiving.

Now she could hear heavy breathing in her ears, from behind. And that potent onion stench of B.O. and cigar smoke was invading her nostrils. The assailant was very strong. He kept mashing her face with those rough rubber gloves!

Jenny was sobbing and trying to scream, but she couldn't get the breath out of her lungs to formulate a proper scream.

The stalker slammed the side of her head with his fist! He hit her so hard, she fell to the ground. She landed on her hands and knees, and tried to crawl away. Then the attacker kicked her in the ribs. Jenny let out a gasp! She could barely breathe. The asshole had knocked the wind out of her. He kicked her again and again! She rolled over on her back and was crying. He then dropped his rubber gloves on the sidewalk.

The creeper grabbed her by her limp ankles and dragged her over to an overhanging hedge that was shadowed in the dim moonlight. He straddled her torso, like he was sitting on a horse. He slapped her across the face as hard as he could. She didn't move. He slapped her hard, one more time. Still no movement. She was in a state of semi-consciousness.

Looking up the street, and then back down the street, the violent offender, started to rip her t-shirt open. He ripped it all the way down to her navel. Then in a hurried frenzy, he reached for her belt buckle and frantically tried to undo it. The assailant was getting frustrated, trying hard to get the buckle open.

Jenny started to move a little. The attacker wound up and slapped her hard, right across her face. Blood spurted from her tiny nose. She coughed and had trouble breathing. His weight on her slight frame was too much for her to hold. Jenny's breathing pattern was becoming erratic from the pressure of the heaviness over her.

The maniac was breathing heavier now and getting more and more aroused each time he slapped her. He was jerking her tight jeans down bit by bit. Jenny's eyes were closed, but she was now conscious. She was too afraid too move, for the fear of being beaten to death!

She thought about her family, her mom, her dad, her little sister and her two cats. She wasn't ready to die. What about her boyfriend, and her grandparents? *I can't die like this! I have to fight back. Why can't someone come along and help me!*

Her jeans were at her ankles now, and the would-be rapist, grabbed her pink thong and tore it off her cream colored hips. He was anxiously undoing his jeans button and fly with trembling fingers.

Jenny, ever-so-slightly opened her eyes up to the narrowest slits she could manage, in order to see the attacker, without him noticing her, looking at him. With him busy, trying to pull his pecker out, she remembered what she had in her hoody pocket. She knew it was now or never!

Slow and easy, she lifted her hand and put it in her right-side pocket. Gently, she wrapped her delicate hand around the small cylinder, and with her thumb, rotated the top of the cylinder until it stopped. She didn't move another muscle.

The sick pervert had his manhood in one hand and attempted to guide it into Jenny's private domain. He was winding up with the other hand, to slap her again.

Jenny's right hand came shooting out of her hoody pocket! She aimed the tiny canister at the rapist's face and squeezed down on the top, just mere seconds before the creep could assault her. The liquid spray showered his ugly face. He let out a high pitched, blood curdling scream! His erection turned to mush! He fell off of Jenny, clutching at his eyes, rolling on the ground. The capsaicin in the pepper spray was no match for his delicate eyeballs!

Jenny cried for help as loud as she could. She managed to crawl to the edge of the road, underneath the streetlight. She was unable to stand. Dizziness and shortness of breath, kept her from getting up. Jenny managed to pull her jeans back up, but didn't have the strength to button them closed.

A few front porch lights came on, and one elderly man came walking down his front stairs with his terrier. Jenny kept calling out for help.

The assailant was wiping his eyes and trying to get his pants up at the same time, while staggering back down the street towards his car. He stumbled and fell, but got back up and kept on hobbling away. The sheer will, of not getting caught, for what he just did to Jenny, kept him going, even with blurry, burning eyes. He finally made it to his vehicle, but not without a witness or two, observing him.

Across the street from the elderly man, a middle aged couple had heard cries for help. They had been watching television, but the woman thought she had heard "HELP ME" pleas, coming from outside. The man left his comfy chair to look out the window and was horrified to see, young Jenny crawling on the front boulevard across the street. Both of them hurried outside to see what was going on.

The old man's terrier went charging over to Jenny, wagging his tail and sniffing her all over. Jenny started to cry happy tears. She couldn't believe she was alive and was able to pet the little dog's head. The old man gasped when he saw what his pooch was sniffing at. He turned and looked down the street at the attacker, getting into his car. He quickly shuffled over to Jenny as fast as his seventy-five year old body would allow him.

"Oh my Lord, honey are you okay?" the senior asked as he bent over her.

"No ... no, I'm not okay," she replied between sobs, as she collapsed on the grass. "I ... I ... was attacked, by someone, he tried ... to ... rape me!"

The middle aged man and woman, ran from across the street, over to Jenny and the old man. The husband took off down the street in the direction of the would-be rapist, but he was seconds to late, as the car sped away from the curbside, squealing it's tires.

Another woman, a few doors down, had left the comfort of her warm house to venture out into the night to see what the hell was going on!

The wife of the couple, ran back across the street, to their house, so she could grab her cellphone to call 911.

As Jenny lay on the ground, the older gent, took off his sweater and asked her if she could turn over. She turned over on her back very slowly. The concerned man, rolled up his sweater and neatly tucked it under Jenny's head for a makeshift pillow. He told her not to move.

"Just relax, dear ... the nice lady across the street has called the police and an ambulance. They should be here soon!" the woman from a few doors down said to her in a comforting voice.

"Please ... get my parents ... please ... they just live at the end of the block ... second house from the ... corner, brown house, with white trim ... please get them for me," Jenny begged slowly, from her bruised mouth.

It was about 10:35 pm, when William Marcus stepped outside for a smoke. The shrill chirping of crickets could be heard in the night air, as he sat on the back porch stairs and lit up a cigarette. William inhaled that cigarette smoke like it was his last one. He dragged on that fag, till he had sucked the life out of it, then flicked it into the long grass.

Up into the dark sky he peered, checking out all the stars. Then into his shirt pocket he fished out his pack of smokes and sparked up another one. That one too, he smoked to death!

By the light of the moon, he noticed a neighbor's cat walking along the top of the wooden fence, dividing their two properties.

William got up off his lazy ass, and walked over to the overgrown garden and picked up one of the larger ornamental white stones. He made a sucking noise through his fat, ugly lips. The feline stopped in her tracks and glanced toward the disgusting sucking noise.

The troubled ex-con wound up and pitched the boulder as hard as he could at the curious cat. The big rock whizzed past the cats body, missing it ever so slightly, causing the furry nocturnal mouser to disappear over the fence!

Laughing hysterically to himself out loud and mumbling "stupid fuckin' cat" he didn't notice the dark silhouette standing in the carport on the far side of his mother's car, watching him. The figure was motionless and invisible to the young William.

William walked around the yard, looking up at the sky, filled with stars and occasionally kicking at the overgrown grass blades. He booted an old rusty pail that was laying in the yard. He kicked it again and again, denting it real good.

The black silhouette wasn't so motionless now, as it was moving through the carport, around the family car and towards the open gate of the back yard.

Suddenly, the dilapidated back door swung open, and Mary stuck her head out! "Will, are you out here, your Uncle Ted is on the phone!" yelled his mother.

"Yes, I'm out here, where else would I be for fuck's sake!" he screamed back at her. "I'll be right there!"

The shadowy figure stopped "on a dime" and observed William from the shelter of the dark, cluttered carport.

Young William gave the pail one more boot and then headed for the door. It seemed to be his "lucky" night!

DOG WITH A BONE

The wailing sound of the ambulance's siren could be heard getting closer, in the darkness of the night.

Jenny's mom and dad had run as fast as they could, down the dark street to see their daughter lying on the ground, on her back with several neighbors attending to her.

Her mother burst out crying and fell to her knees. She reached for her daughters hand; at the same time stroking her forehead with her other hand, and asking her what happened. Her distraught mother looked up at the concerned onlookers and asked, "what is going on here?"

The elderly gent replied, "your daughter was brutally attacked by a man, who had been following her. He beat her and tried to rape her, but your daughter fought him off! I ... we heard her calling out for help, and found her this way, ma'am."

"Where is this guy now, where did he go? Does anyone know ... did anyone see him, I mean ..." Jenny's dad angrily asked the neighbors.

"He ran back down the street sir, back that way and jumped into a blue car," the husband from across the street offered.

"Did you get his license number?" asked Jenny's dad.

"I tried, but his car was quite a distance down the road and it was too dark to see the numbers," replied the husband.

"The police and ambulance are on their way!" reported the wife, who lived across the street.

"Don't move sweetheart, just relax and take it easy, the paramedics will be here soon," Jenny's mom said, comforting her.

Her dad was seriously fucking pissed! "Sick, sick world we live in! I'd like to get my hands on that lowlife bastard! Did anyone see what he looked like? How old of a guy ... young, old what ...?" Jenny's dad was infuriated! He wanted to kill someone!

"Rick, please calm down, getting angry isn't going to help your heart. Please be calm!" Jenny's mom said to her husband.

"Mom ... I just want to go home, I don't want to go away in an ambulance, please ... just take me home," she pleaded with her mother.

"Jenny, you need them to check you over, we'll see if you need to go to the hospital or not. You've had a life threatening experience and we need to wait for the police and the paramedics. Thank God, you're okay. I wished you had phoned us to come and pick you up!" she said as she wiped her tears away.

The first police cruiser on the scene pulled into the curb on an angle. Moments later, two more police cars came from the opposite end of the street, with lights flashing. One minute after the cops arrived, the ambulance made a grand entrance, with lights flashing and the siren screaming. And then the siren was abruptly silenced!

The emergency response team attended to the bruised and battered young lady on the ground, while one of the police officers questioned the onlookers, about what they had witnessed.

Another officer radioed for one more squad car, as they needed to block off both ends of the street, so no traffic could get through, until they were finished their investigation.

One of the constables scoured the ground area with her flashlight. She checked all over the boulevards and up and down the sidewalk. The yellow rubber gloves were on the sidewalk about thirty feet, from where Jenny was found.

The constable told the neighbors to move onto the road and away from the injured girl and the paramedics.

"Thank-you for your co-operation people. We need to get a statement from each of you; of what you know about this awful incident, and please do not touch the rubber gloves or anything else that may be laying on the ground. We want to make sure that any evidence we find is not altered," commanded the senior officer.

Jenny was fitted with a neck-brace and then lifted onto a gurney. She was crying and telling the paramedics, that she just wanted to go home with her mom and dad.

Her mom told her, "honey, it's going to be okay, dad and I will go with you in the ambulance. You need to go to the hospital to make sure your neck isn't fractured and that you don't have a concussion." Then she whispered in her daughter's ear, *"he didn't rape you, did he honey?"*

Tears ran down the each side of her face, as she slowly nodded her head back and forth. Her mom wept too!

The paramedics loaded the gurney into the back of the ambulance. Her upset mom and dad climbed in with her. The ambulance started up and headed off to the emergency ward at St. Paul's Hospital.

"Hey Ryan! Come over here and check this out!" the female constable named Denise, yelled to the senior officer.

The senior officer walked down the sidewalk a ways, toward Denise. It was in the same direction as the attacker had escaped. About thirty yards from where the assault took place, she pointed her flashlight beam on the grass. There in the cut grass was a straw colored object about eight inches long.

"A chopstick! I don't believe it! Another freakin' chopstick! It's our guy, for crying-out-loud! Shit, this guy is way out of control!" cried Ryan. "Call the station Denise, and tell dispatch to put out an APB on any, and all blue colored Chevy Corsicas and Ford Tauruses within a ten mile radius of this location, pronto! I'll put a call into Investigative Services and have forensics come out here. We have to tape off the area. This is obviously a damn botched Fraser murder attempt!"

SIXTEEN

Friday

"Yellow!" Sunny answered on his cellphone.

"Hi loverboy! I'm almost home and I can't wait to see you!" Geena said.

"Same here cupcake," he replied. "Babe and I are doing a walk right now. So, if you'll be home around noon, pop over to the loft when you get back and I'll make you lunch. Okay?"

"Okay sweetheart, see you then!"

It was only seven o'clock Friday morning, and already Babe and Sunny had walked to Kingsway and back; about five miles. They were up at sunrise, Sunny had showered, ate breakfast, fed Babe and out the door they went. Walking was a sure way to keep fit, and the way Sunny saw it, it was free and it was right out the back door. He figured that if everyone walked more, there would be less obesity and less air pollution from vehicles.

Man and dog entered the loft. Babe checked out her water dish and drank it dry. Sunny filled her dish up to the brim a second time. "You're like a bloody camel Babe, you know that?" he chuckled.

She looked at him and wagged her thick otter tail, as if to say, *"I'm much more cuter than a camel!"*

Sunny went over to the kitchen and put the coffee on. He then picked up his laptop from his writing desk, set

Della on the coffee table, opened her up and turned her on.

He Googled The Province newspaper, like he usually did when he was home in the morning. As he waited for all of the morning news to download onto the computer screen, he moseyed over to the coffee pot and poured himself a steaming cup of java with an ounce of Bailey's Irish Cream added.

Sunny glanced over at Babe as he sauntered back to the couch to check out the news-worthy information on Della. Babe was already sound asleep and snoring from the five mile stroll. He set the coffee on the table and stared at the computer screen.

"Son-of-a-bitch!" Sunny shouted aloud as he read the morning news. "Damn him!"

Babe woke up from Sunny's booming voice and peered over at her master.

Sunny could feel his blood start to boil! Rage was filling his brain, his pulse was starting to accelerate, exactly like a quarter-mile race car going from zero to sixty in seven seconds!

Splashed across the cover page of The Province online news, the headliner in big bold letters read:

FRASER MURDER SUSPECT STRIKES AGAIN!

"The Vancouver City Police have confirmed an attempted sexual assault and violent beating of a nineteen year old woman walking home at approximately 9:00 pm, Thursday night, in the Killarney area of McKinnon and Waverly Streets. Clues left at the scene of the crime and witnesses to the attack, who came forward to the police indicate it may be the same person responsible for the other eight murders of children and young adults. The

police are warning citizens to be extra vigilante when walking alone. Any information about this crime, can be forwarded to the Vancouver City Police or Crimestoppers. Remember, tipsters remain anonymous!"

Sunny picked up his cup of Joe and pressed it to his lips, and very slowly tilted his favorite ceramic mug imprinted with Snoopy and Woodstock on it; staring at the headliner, sipping his coffee and seething! He kept the coffee mug to his mouth and kept sipping on it, the whole time just glaring at the disturbing news on the coffee table.

Finally he scrolled down the page and read the rest of the news. On page two he read another disturbing article. It was written about an animal abuser. A man in Burnaby had beaten his rottweiler dog to death with a shovel.

The news story stated that:

Man's "Best Friend" Beaten To Death

"Police were called to Cottonwood Manor at 212 Bonneville Drive in Burnaby, after neighbors living in the apartment complex had heard what they thought was an animal screaming and loud thumping, on the floors and walls. The screaming lasted about twenty minutes and then total silence. After the initial investigation, the police discovered a dead rottweiler in the back alley behind the apartment. Upon further investigation, the police determined that one of the residents had owned such a dog. A search of the tenant's unit turned up a bloody shovel with a broken handle and a blood soaked carpet, with dog feces and urine all throughout the rooms. Charges are pending against the owner of the apartment unit. The Burnaby SPCA are also investigating the alleged animal abuse."

Sunny was sickened by the gruesome story! He shed a tear for the deceased "rotty", looking over at his own dog and wondering how anyone could hurt man's best friend. *What the hell is wrong with our society today? That fucker will get off "Scot-free" knowing our Canadian laws!*

Then he closed his laptop and sat for a minute thinking. He hated reading all the negative, disturbing crap in the news every day. But Sunny had a job to do! Now it was time for a shower.

From the four hundred sixty-nine possible suspect vehicles registered to their owners in British Columbia, the two officers in charge of organizing the list into the municipalities, came up with eleven districts.

Chief Joe Winters wanted to start with Vancouver, then Burnaby, New Westminster and so on, all the way to the east and then northward. He wanted to get a grasp on anything remotely close and use the "process of elimination". Eliminating one municipality at a time. The only obstacle was that, the Vancouver City Police would have to work with the RCMP in order to interview any possible suspects outside of metro Vancouver. Winters' concern was that, this could slow down the investigation, because of all the "red tape" and bureaucracy between the districts.

Winters had an uncanny sixth sense; being that the person responsible didn't travel from too far away, due to the lack of funds. Of course he knew the "exception to the fact" of a serial killer not holding down a job, also gave them free range to travel, in order to them keep from getting caught.

Most serial killers are divided into two classes, the "homebody" type and the "nomadic or drifter" type.

DOG WITH A BONE

The serial killer that stays in one certain area or region is commonly known as a homebody killer. These types of subhumans generally want to "show off" their handywork. Proud of what they have done, so to speak! They "get-off" on leaving bodies out where they are found by citizens or the police. Some of the homebody types are so mentally messed up, they think of it as kind of a cat and mouse game. It's the old adage, "catch me if you can"!

There have been cases of serial killers, taunting the police, by phoning them and leaving twisted messages and/or sending disturbing letters to the police as well as the press.

The "Zodiac Killer" from San Francisco, back in the late sixties and early seventies, taunted the public and the police by sending a series of letters and cryptograms to the newspapers. Seven people were murdered by gun and by knife. The Zodiac was a "spree" killer, just killing random innocent victims for fun.

The case was never cracked, although the authorities had several suspects in mind. One person the police thought to be a suspect in the Zodiac killings was Theodore John "Ted" Kaczynski; the same person identified as the "Unabomber" many years later, between 1978 and 1995. Kaczynski was arrested in April of 1996, at his primitive cabin in rural Montana.

Kaczynski was not a spree killer. His reason for killing was to attract attention to the "erosion" of wildlife; the devastation of human freedom by increased development, around his rural home. His sick way of attracting attention was to plant or mail home-made bombs to computer store owners, universities and one airline. Of all the bombs sent, three people were killed and twenty-three injured, some severely injured.

Ted Kaczynski also wrote several letters to the newspapers and promised to stop the bombings if *The New York Times* or *The Washington Post* published his thirty-five thousand word type-written manifesto, "Industrial Society and it's Future" (also called the "Unabomber Manifesto").

The FBI insisted on having the "Manifesto" published out of concern for public safety, in hopes that a reader would be able to identify the writer.

Kaczynski was tipped off to the FBI, by his own brother, after the brother was encouraged by his wife to read the manifesto. The brother browsed through old family papers and discovered old letters, from the 1970's, that were written by Ted, that had been sent to newspapers, protesting the misuse of technology and also contained similar statements used in the Unabomber Manifesto.

This discovery of similarities, led Ted's brother to inform the FBI of the suspected Unabomber, of being his own brother.

Ted Kaczynski's own belligerence, led the authorities to his capture!

Police Chief Joe Winters pegged the "Fraser Case" murderer as a "homebody" serial killer. He felt strongly about this, since all the killings had taken place in the metro Vancouver area, and that the killer was leaving the bodies out in the open to be found by the public or authorities.

The other type of serial killer, known as the "nomadic or drifter" breed, moves around; across the province, state or country. They usually stay on the move, picking up odd jobs here and there or freeloading from food banks, missions and hostels. Panhandling and stealing are also a way of the nomadic serial killer.

One example of this kind of behaviour was Henry Lee Lucas and Ottis Toole. These two travelled from state to state in the United States leaving a trail of bodies along the way. Their evil, sick minds let them befriend unsuspecting victims into having a beer, or smoking a joint with them and then killing them, before they went on their merry way!

Lucas was only charged with eleven murders, but he claimed that he had killed plenty more. Up to six hundred, he told the authorities, that he had murdered; although, the Texas based "Lucas Task Force" didn't believe that amount of victims had been killed by him. Maybe half that number, but they had no proof. Lucas also claimed that Toole helped him kill one hundred and eight people.

Lucas was apprehended by the authorities in 1983 and sentenced to death, but his sentence was commuted to life in prison in 1998 by Governor George W. Bush. Henry Lee Lucas died in prison of natural causes.

Another example of the nomadic serial killer type is the unsolved murders and disappearances of eighteen young women, in northern British Columbia, known as the "Highway of Tears". The five hundred mile (800 km) stretch of Highway 16, runs from Prince George to Prince Rupert.

Bobby Jack Fowler was identified through DNA samples as the killer in one case and a strong suspect in two more. However, he has since passed away, but authorities believe he was responsible for about ten more murders.

Police investigators believe, more than one killer is working Highway 16. The murders and disappearances started back in 1969 and have kept happening up to present day. The police do have persons of interest in the case, but not enough evidence to lay charges.

The Fraser case list, of possible suspect vehicles in the Vancouver area, totalled one hundred eighty-three. Not all registered cars were insured, according to the Insurance Corporation of British Columbia (ICBC). The other two hundred eighty-six, were scattered all throughout the rest of the province.

Taking time to review all the 1990's, Chevy Corsicas and Ford Tauruses would be a huge gamble!

After all, the only people who witnessed the suspect vehicle, were Frederick Redmond who saw the car with it's trunk open, on his way to the 7/11 store and the few neighbors that came to the aid of young Jenny being attacked. Redmond only saw that the car was a darker color, possibly blue or black and that it had roof racks. He had stated that he really wasn't sure of the make or model, except that it was most likely a 1990's model, compact in size. The other witnesses attending Jenny, watched the assailant jump into his car, down the street, but the night was so dark, that they couldn't get the license numbers or reveal the brand of vehicle; only that it was darker in color and mid-size.

It was a "crap shoot"! The police didn't have the exact make or model of the suspect's car. They only assumed it was a Corsica or Taurus from the descriptions of the only witnesses. But at least it was something! It was better than no vehicle siting at all.

From the Vancouver list, of one hundred eighty-three; forty-seven cars were listed on the registration documents as the basic body color blue. Twenty-one of the listed blue cars, did not have up-to-date insurance. That meant that only twenty-six possible suspect vehicles were insured and on the streets of Vancouver.

DOG WITH A BONE

The narrowed down inventory of Corsicas and Tauruses would be the first cars to be investigated by Winters' detectives.

As the detectives showed up at the station, they were all summoned into the meeting room for a quick briefing by the Chief of police. "Good morning everyone!" he said with a solemn grin. "Enjoy that cup of coffee, cause today is going to be a busy day for all of us. We have the breakdown of municipalities for each and every one of you."

Winters pointed to the white board with his red laser pointer and said, "I want you and your partner, listed on this here board, to do your homework first. We will all have to work with the RCMP, intensively and extensively through each jurisdiction of each municipality outside of Vancouver. God knows this won't be any easy task! Some of those members, for whatever reason, believe they are above our heads. If anyone of you, find any kind of resistance, abuse or any other bullshit from these guys, I want to know about it immediately. Understood!"

On the white board, were the names of the detectives with the municipality, that they were assigned to. Detectives Mike Kuban, Jane Rhodes and two other detectives were assigned to the Vancouver list.

"Take your document with the registered owners, male and female and do a background search, in depth. Know this! Our killer is most likely a male, but just because the vehicle may be registered to a woman, doesn't mean her boyfriend or brother hasn't borrowed the car to go out and murder someone!" Winters explained.

The Chief inhaled a long, deep breath, then reached for his coffee and took a sip. He put the coffee down on the desk, wiped his mouth with his sleeve and then carried on, "do your background check online, first, this morning, and then visit their residence and check them out. Prioritize the felons first. Even though the suspects DNA isn't in the system, doesn't mean he has never been arrested for a petty crime. And, if you can view the top of the vehicle, check for marks, left from the roof-racks. I'm sure the creep has removed the racks from the roof already. And don't get too pushy with anyone! We don't want to screw anything up with the courts or the judges, due to some bullshit technicality! Any questions?" Winters asked.

No one raised a hand. They were all experienced homicide detectives and knew the job well. Raising a hand was frowned upon. It made the Chief look bad, if questions were asked. It made him seem like he didn't explain things properly.

"No? ... Okay then, let's get to work comrades!" he said. "One more thing ... John MacDuff's funeral will be next Thursday, one week from now! I would really expect to see everyone there!" Winters added.

There was a sharp knock on Sunny's back balcony door. Babe trotted over to the steel reinforced door and sniffed along the bottom crack as she usually does.

Sunny was in the kitchen, getting brunch ready for Geena and himself. He put down the spoon that he was stirring the pot with and headed over to the knocking sound.

Babe was doing her tongue rolling, growling talk, the kind of dog-talk she does, when she knows who's there.

Sunny put his eye up to the spy hole and then unlocked the door. "Hey sweetheart, welcome back!" he said lovingly to his girl, Geena.

DOG WITH A BONE

As she entered the room with two shopping bags full to the brim, she said, "I sure missed you Sunny ... and something smells delicious! What are you making us for brunch my hunky man?" she asked as she placed the bags on the dining table. "Oh yes, Babe, I see you girl, I see you! Yes, I missed you too!"

The portly yellow lab was all over Geena's legs. Rubbing her nose and snorting, waiting to be petted and loved up by the buxom, black haired beauty. She bent over and gave the excited dog a good head rubbing.

Standing five foot eight, with the greenest jade colored eyes, known to mankind, Geena's thirty-two years of life was a sight to behold!

"Come here you devil!" she told Sunny with her open arms reaching forward for a hug.

Sunny and Geena embraced each other tightly and then kissed with a deep passionate lip workout! Holding one another and kissing, was too much for Babe to bear! She nuzzled between the couple's legs, forcing them apart, while whining a deep guttural whine, and wagging her tail.

"Babe, come on, you've had him all to yourself, let me have him for awhile," Geena told the dog jokingly.

"So the trip was everything you thought it would be?" Sunny wanted to know.

"It was a fun time, Sundance. We must have bought all the stores out, I think. Those are your presents over on the coffee table. You can check them out after we eat, cause I'm starving! What are we having?" she asked.

"We're having Sunny's homemade soup with wholewheat buns and cheese! Potato and chicken chunk soup. Protein for your little muscles!" he chuckled.

"Soup for brunch?" Geena asked with a puzzled look.

"Why not? What book of rules states we can't have soup for brunch? It's going to be damn good!" he said with a big smile from ear to ear.

Sunny started stirring the gourmet concoction in the big pot and sprinkled in a few spices for added flavor. He was never afraid to try new dishes, but his most favorite dish of all, was good old fashioned homemade soup, just like his mother's, mother used to make.

His grandmother used to collect her herbs and vegetables, fresh, right out of her garden. She had the biggest garden on the block, full of nutritious wonders.

Fresh peas were Sunny's favorite. When he was a very young boy, his mom's mother or "Gramma" as he used to call her, would let him wander through the neatly planted rows of vegetables and pick the peas off of the vines to eat, right on the spot! Nothing tastier than plump, garden fresh peas right from the vine. Sunny's Gramma always told him, "eat lots of fruit and vegetables son, because your health is the most important thing in the world. Without it, nothing else matters!"

Those were "words of wisdom" from his Gramma and Sunny has never forgotten them. Her words, were what set the groundwork and put him on his health conscious regime, of carrot juice, vitamins and working out. His grandmother lived to the ripe old age of eighty-eight.

While Sunny was serving the soup into bowls and cutting the cheese for the buns, Geena was walking around the loft, looking at things, straightening up the pillows on the couch and glancing out the front street windows. On her way back to the kitchen, she passed Sunny's bedroom, and had a quick peek into his lair. His bedroom area was usually neat and tidy, except for a few clothes on the floor. She glanced over at his dresser and noticed a brown package sitting on top.

"Is that a present for me?" Geena asked.

"What's that?" he asked, over the noisy whirring of the kitchenette exhaust fan.

She slunk over towards him and asked again, "I said ... is that a present for me? The package on your dresser ... did you get me something?"

Shit! I forgot to put that damn thing under the bed! He hesitated for a moment and then replied, "no cupcake, it's not for you, it's ..."

"Is it for your other girlfriend?" she laughed. "How is Ellen, anyway?"

"Ellen is okay, she is doing fine ... and no, it's not for her either, and no, she isn't my other girlfriend. She is my 'girl friend'," Sunny remarked.

"I know that silly! I'm just giving you a hard time!"

"If you want to give me a HARD time, I can show you another way to do it," Sunny said with a glint in his eye.

"Is that a threat or a promise?" Geena answered back.

"Soup *'a la Sunny'* is now being served my little cupcake!" as he brought the aromatic lunch over to the dark stained oak table.

Babe's wet twitching nose was high in the air, as her nasal, sensory preceptors welcomed the wafting, delicious smell of basil and chicken! Not to mention, that one of her favorite snacks was cheese! Dogs love cheese. She always managed to get a sample from her master, just by looking at him with those big, brown eyes!

As they sat down to the brunch style meal; once again, Geena asked, "so what's in the package, Sundance?"

Sundance was Geena's personal nickname for Sunny, her own pet name for him.

"You are the nosiest person I know, Gee," Sunny told her as he ripped off a piece of his soft bun, to dip into the piping hot soup.

Gee was Sunny's pet name for her. She didn't really appreciate the fact that he called her a name, that her mother had called her growing up, but it seemed to fit. So she was okay with it. But she preferred being called cupcake, as he sometimes called her as well.

"Well what is it?" Geena asked again.

"It's nothing ... maybe it's your Christmas present!"

They ate their meal, and what a great meal it was! After lunch, Geena showered Sunny with the souvenirs and gifts she had brought back from the U.S. As he tried on the t-shirts and cologne and sampled some of the candies, she couldn't help but wonder, *what's in that darn package?*

"I have one more surprise for you honey," Geena teased seductively.

"Oh yeah? What would that be?" he asked curiously.

She snickered and said, "it's on my body ... but you're going to have to find it, big boy!" as she gently took his hand in hers, and led him around and behind the bamboo dividers, into the bedroom.

"How are you feeling dear?" asked the nurse, as she set down the tray of lunch for young Jenny.

"Not very ... good, I have a ... severe headache. My head keeps ... throbbing, and it's hard to ... breathe, my ribs hurt," Jenny slowly answered the RN.

"Do you feel okay enough to talk, because there are two police officers here, that would like to ask you some questions about what happened to you last night. If you're too sore, I can tell them to come back later," said the thirty-something nurse.

Jenny paused for a moment before she answered, as a few tears rolled down her bruised and blackened face.

"Jenny, it's okay sweetie ... you don't have to talk to the police right now, if it's too hard to, but if you can honey, it may help them to catch the man that hurt you," her mother offered.

Both parents were sitting by her bedside. They had stayed there all night. Neither one of them had caught any sleep. Who could sleep under the circumstances? Visibly shaken, by what had happened to their eldest daughter, they were most anxious to have the police catch the bad guy! Jenny's parents had already been informed by the police, earlier this morning, that the suspect who had attacked their daughter last night, may be the person responsible for the Fraser murders.

Jenny's face was black and blue, from being slapped and punched by the assailant. The flesh around her blue eyes was swollen and made it very difficult for her to see and cry. She had an extremely hard time breathing, from the repeated kicking she received on her delicate ribcage. Her luscious lips had been split in two places and required twelve sutures. The dried blood around her lips was caked in and around the sutures. She couldn't hold back the tears, when she went to the bathroom and saw her appearance in the mirror. Jenny, her mom and dad all wept together.

"It's okay mom ... I can talk ... to them. It'll be fine," she told her mom and dad.

The RN smiled at Jenny and then turned to her parents and shook her head up and down slowly and said, "I'll go and get the police then, if you all feel okay with it."

"That would be great," said her dad, with a laboured look on his tired, unshaven face.

The nurse disappeared for a moment and then returned with two police officers, a man and a woman.

"Hi Jenny, I'm Detective Rhodes and this is Detective Kuban. We're very sorry about what happened to you last night. I know you're not feeling well, so we won't take too much of your time, but we would like to ask you a few questions, if that would be okay?" Rhodes asked the young lady.

"We believe the man who attacked you, may be responsible for other attacks as well," Kuban added as he turned to look at Jenny's parents. "Jenny did you get a good look at the man's face, or did you notice anything about him that may help us catch him?"

She nodded her tender face up and down slowly and quietly said, "yes," and then started to cry again softly.

As her mom started to cry also, Jenny's dad put his arm around her, rubbed her back gently and told her, "it's okay now Beverly, she's safe and we're going to put this bastard behind bars!"

Rhodes looked over at the parents and reassured the two of them, "we ARE going to get this guy, with your daughter's help, I promise! We have some very substantial clues and leads on him, and last night's attack on Jenny gave us even more to go on."

"What do you remember about that man, Jenny?" Rhodes asked her quietly.

Jenny hesitated and then slowly and softly replied, "he was about ... forty-four ... to maybe ... fifty years old ... he had, bad ... body odor and ... smelled like a cigar ... his hair was ... very short but ... curly ... he had beard stubble ... on his face ..."

"You mean like, he hadn't shaved the day before, type of thing?" Kuban asked the sensitive girl.

"Yes, that's right. Also ... in the streetlight ... I could see his eyes ... they were ... light blue ... almost an eerie ... color blue," Jenny explained.

"Did he say anything to you Jenny? Could you hear his voice at all?" Rhodes asked.

"He was breathing ... real heavy like ...he did say something. He said ... I was nine? Then he ... screamed ... real crazy like ... when I pepper sprayed him ... in the face."

Kuban was jotting down notes as they spoke to her. He then asked, "is there anything else you can remember, that you can tell us Jenny?"

"No ... I don't remember ... anything more ... than what I told you ... already," Jenny replied, while looking at her parents.

"Okay Jenny, that's really good, I know it's been very difficult for you to talk about this, but you've helped us tremendously. Detective Kuban and myself, really want you to get better soon. We are going to do our very best to catch and arrest this individual," Rhodes assured her.

"Why would he have said she was nine, he must have known she was older than that?" Jenny's mom asked the detectives.

Kuban looked at Rhodes and then back to the parents and asked, "can I talk to both of you out there?" as he motioned with his thumb, pointing to the hospital hallway.

Mom and dad followed the detectives out into the hallway, as Kuban turned to them and whispered, "your daughter is a very lucky girl indeed. This may come as a shock to both of you, but that psycho wasn't referring to her age. He was informing her, that she was going to be his ninth murder victim."

"Oh my God!" the police did tell us this morning, that he may be the same person that killed others, but I didn't believe it. It doesn't seem real!" Beverly exclaimed.

"I don't know if you have been following the news, but there have been eight murders. Eight children and teenagers combined, stalked and murdered by a serial killer, on the streets of Vancouver. We believe it is the same individual responsible, by the clues and evidence left behind at all the crime scenes," continued Kuban.

"You need to catch that fucker and send him to hell!" Jenny's dad fumed.

"Rick! Please keep your voice down!" Beverly said to her husband.

"Sir, I understand how you feel, we want him to burn in hell too! We know we are getting closer, we have twenty detectives actively working on this case, around the clock, twenty-four seven!" reported Kuban.

"Our team of investigators will be interviewing a list of possible suspects all week long, Mr. Piper. We are getting closer, like Detective Kuban explained. I know it's very frustrating, but these things take time, unless we actually catch the perpetrator in the act. Your daughter's assault was the closest, that anyone has come to catching him in the act. Jenny has given us a very good description of what he looks like. We have other eye witnesses, that have given us descriptions of the kind of car he may be driving. Our investigative team is fairly confident, that it will only be a matter of time before we bring him in," Rhodes added, "here's my card, if Jenny can remember anything else, please give us a call, and if anything else comes to light, on our end, we will definitely contact you. Thanks for your time."

The two detectives turned and walked down the hospital hallway, smiling at the nurses on their way out.

"That was unbelievable Sundance!" Geena remarked as she lay naked, just like the day she was born, staring up at the ceiling, breathing deeply.

"You were pretty awesome yourself, little darlin'!" Sunny quipped, also nude, gently running his fingers over her hipbone, where her brand new tattoo was.

"Why a four leaf clover, Gee?" Sunny asked.

"Because, it's a symbol for 'good luck' and I guess it really does work ... cause I just got lucky, didn't I?" Geena snickered.

"I guess you did at that. I guess we both got lucky."

"Are you going to get Stone to do any more work on your back Sunny?" Geena wanted to know.

"When I get some time, I will. I want to keep adding until it's finished. It's a big project."

Sunny had about half of his back tattooed by a well known Vancouver tattoo artist named Stone. The theme on Sunny's back displays a Japanese style mural in the works. Stone had already inked about twenty hours of vibrant colors, depicting a Samurai warrior, fighting a red dragon, with two-tone blue wind swirls, gray clouds and streaks of yellow and white lightning. The artwork was a masterpiece, or as Stone would declare, a *"Magnum Opus"*; Latin for the meaning:*"Great Achievement"*!

Stone Walls, a forty-two year old homegrown, Vancouver East Sider owns and operates a tattoo parlor, called Inkredible Tats, in downtown Vancouver, located near the intersection of Beach Avenue and Jervis Street. Stone's parents had decided that since their surname was Walls, that "Stone" only made perfect sense. Solid as a rock!

Inkredible Tats is a very busy shop that specializes in tattooing only. Lots of the other shops around town offer other services combined with the tattoo trade, such as body piercing, body modification and branding.

Stone's philosophy is quite simple; if you are going to excel at something in life, then you should concentrate on that one particular thing, and that one thing only! Combining other trades with the dermagraphic profession would only clutter the smoothness of the "inking" productivity. Besides poking holes through peoples flesh, wasn't Stone's calling. Tattooing his artwork all over their flesh was his real passion. Learning to draw and color from an early age, made Stone Walls the accomplished tattoo artist, that he is today.

Sunny would usually have to book in advance with Stone, in order to get an hour or two of color and pain! Tattoos are immensely popular today and setting an appointment is normally the only way in. Although, Inkredible Tats also does walk-ins, with no appointment necessary, but it is very rare to land a spot in the "chair" from a walk-in. Stone's shop is one of the busier shops in the city, employing another full-time artist besides himself, an apprentice named Dolly and a receptionist.

Sunny walked from the bed to the kitchenette nude, as Geena turned on her side, to have another glance at that white tight butt.

He poured a big glass of water from the water cooler, added three ice-cubes and headed back to the bedroom. Sunny offered the cold drink to Geena. She took a few sips and then handed it back. He finished it off. "Damn! Brain freeze," he yelled, as he held his hand firmly against his forehead.

"What's your plan for today Sundance? I have to go home and do some banking and other chores, but maybe you and I can hook-up later for dinner or catch a movie or something," Geena wondered.

"I have some things to do and also and I need to walk Babe, but maybe later we can meet up again, I'll call you and let you know what's up, okay?" Sunny replied, while he was really thinking; *I have to hunt a bully today, honey.*

Sunny didn't want to tell her about the bad incident, that had happened to him and Ellen a week ago. Geena didn't live in the real world sometimes, quite often she pretended, that stuff like that didn't exist or happen. She wouldn't even watch scary movies, cause it gave her nightmares and made her feel uneasy. Sunny never forced her to watch horror movies with him; if he had the urge to watch a gruesome movie, he would watch it by himself, usually when Geena was away travelling with a girlfriend or visiting her sister.

If he did explain to her, that someone had pulled a gun on him in the woods, he would never hear the end of it. She would worry constantly and that wouldn't be healthy for either one of them. He had told Ellen, not to mention it to Geena either, for that exact reason. Sunny didn't want to lie to Geena, so instead he just neglected to tell her about the incident. He felt that what she didn't know, wouldn't hurt her.

Sunny's cellphone rang. "Yellow!" he answered.

"Sunny, it's Lola. I was wondering if you could come in today for a few hours?"

"No, I can't Lola, it's a little short notice. I have a few appointments booked today, I'm sorry about that," Sunny said.

"Are you sure you can't Sunny? Another waitress called in sick, I don't know what's wrong with this new generation, they want the money, but don't want to work for it!" Lola complained to Sunny with utter disgust in her voice.

"I know Lola, they're a pathetic bunch, living at home with mommy and daddy. Their parents are probably still wiping their asses!" Sunny laughed. "Did you try calling Burton? He always needs the money."

"Well I guess, I will have to call him if you won't come in ... it's just that the girls enjoy working with you more than him, you're fun to work with and he's so boring. You're sure you can't come in ... pretty please with sugar on top."

"You sure know how to make a guy feel bad Lola, but really I can't make it in today, sorry about that, sweetness," Sunny replied.

"Fine then, we'll just have to make it without you today. Hope your appointments are really, important," Lola chuckled.

"Oh they are Lola, trust me, they are! Bye," Sunny said to her.

"She wanted you bad, eh baby?" Geena asked.

"I guess," Sunny sighed.

Sunny and Geena showered together, got dressed and then she left for home.

Sunny glanced at his clock on the kitchenette stove. It read 11:30 am. *Time to head out!*

He took Babe outback for a pee at the park, and then brought her back inside the loft and gave her a rawhide bone to gnaw on.

"See ya later girl," as he patted her soft, golden head.

SEVENTEEN

Another beautiful, bright day in the bustling city of Vancouver and life is great! Cruising down Kingsway with "hair straight back"! Sunny loved life. He had his health, a beautiful girlfriend, loving parents, a sister he loved and of course his beloved companion, Babe! It couldn't get any better. Or could it? *If I could just locate that scum sucking pig that pulled the gun on me and Elly, that would complete my day,* he daydreamed.

Mr. Sunny Kruzik had an appointment all right; an appointment with the devil! Being on time for his appointment might prove to be a bit of a challenge though; but he was a fighter. No sir, Sunny would not give up easy. He was "old school" stuff! East Side tough stuff!

The need to satisfy his own mental state of well-being and to seek retributive justice for the murdered children and teenagers, drove Sunny to locate the killer, before the cops did.

Some relaxing music was in order, while scouting out the lunchtime crowds at the Chinese food restaurants along his predetermined mental mind-map. Van Morrison's, Moondance CD was the ticket. Sunny plunked it into the CD player and hummed along with the crystal clear lyrics.

He knew the route he would take today. Rechecking some of the eateries that he had checked last time and some new ones were on the agenda. There was no shortage of restaurants or hungry customers. Most places were very busy at lunchtime and the busier restaurants usually had an "all-you- can-eat" buffet.

This time Sunny drove all the way to the end of Kingsway, through Burnaby and on towards New Westminster. He had passed all the same restaurants that he had driven by the night before. Carefully "scoping out" every single car, in every parking lot, of every Chinese and Asian restaurants, that he drove by, Sunny still came up empty handed. He knew it wouldn't be an easy task, but sheer determination kept him going.

This time, he decided to check out the New Westminster eateries.

Just blocks, before the Burnaby and New Westminster boundary, Sunny decided to turn left, while still in Burnaby. He stopped at the extremely busy four-lane intersection of Kingsway and Edmonds Street; waiting for the red light to turn green.

While he was waiting in the three car lineup to turn left, he decided to change the tunes. He pressed the eject button, popped out the Van Morrison CD and then slid it back into the plastic case. Sunny flipped through his selection of music and picked out the "Greatest Hits of the Sixties" CD. He inserted the disc into the player and pressed the track selection button until he came to "Ninety-Six Tears" by the Mysterions.

The traffic started to move through the intersection. As his black shiny Accord inched into the center of the intersection, something caught Sunny's attention from the corner of his eye. Traffic was fairly heavy at the lunchtime hour and it was bumper to bumper, no less. Keeping his eyes trained on the road, and on the car in front of him was distracting him from glancing over to the opposite side of the bustling street.

What the ... is that what I think it is? No it can't be!

As Sunny wheeled his car left onto Edmonds Street, he had a flash of what looked like an older blue Pontiac sedan, sitting in the Tim Hortons, parking lot. Instinctively, he shut the stereo off.

Sunny could feel his pulse racing and his heart starting to pound.

He was in the left-hand lane and there were cars beside him in the right-hand lane, so it was impossible to get into the turning lane, to enter the parking lot of the donut shop.

As he was forced against his will, to follow the procession of traffic left, onto Edmonds Street and along; past the Tim Hortons and beyond, he quickly made another glance over his shoulder towards the busy parking lot. *Damn it! I can't see the car anymore. The traffic is blocking my view!*

Turning his head back to look where he was driving, he slammed on his brakes! SCREEECH! ... *"SHIT! Damn it!"* he shouted.

The traffic had slowed down in front of Sunny and the car in front of him, had almost come to a complete stop. He was only inches away from rear-ending the Mazda 3 with two small children in the back seat. One of the kids looked back at Sunny and stuck out his tongue. The young woman driving the Mazda, looked in her rear-view mirror with disgust. Sunny shrugged his shoulders and mouthed the words, "I'm sorry." *Keep cool Sunny boy! You almost got in a frickin' accident. Stay calm,* he told himself.

The vehicles started to move again. Sunny put his right-hand turn signal on and kept moving along. It was about a block-and-a-half before some nice motorist let him into the right lane.

It seemed like hours to Sunny, but it had only been about five minutes, from the time he had turned off of Kingsway onto Edmonds Street. The first side street he came to, was Humphries Avenue. He made a quick right and booted it down the short side street. Then another fast right turn at Hubert Street.

Within minutes, Sunny was back at Kingsway, waiting impatiently at the stop sign, to turn right again. *Come on! Come onnnn! Stay cool! You almost had one accident already,* he thought to himself as he waited for the line of steady vehicles to diminish. *It never fails. When you are in a hurry, the traffic never ends!*

Finally, the last car zipped past the front end of Sunny's Accord. He pulled out, onto the busy street and gunned it! In less than a minute, Sunny Kruzik was wheeling towards the front entrance of the lively Tim Hortons restaurant.

Tim Hortons is the largest and most recognized donut-shop chain in Canada. There are over one thousand stores to date. Almost every Tim Hortons donut shops are constantly busy, at anytime of the day or night. Lineups are the norm, whether walking into the store or going through the drive-thru express lane.

Sunny turned into the restaurant parking lot slowly and intently scanned the vehicles. Over by the southeast corner of the lot, parked between a pickup truck and a Ford Escape was the blue vehicle that he spotted earlier as he drove past. Sunny turned right and eased the pearl black Accord over towards the blue car. It was definitely a blue Pontiac Tempest, but without roof-racks! The car was parked with the front-end facing Kingsway. Sunny could only see the back of the car from where he was sitting. He pulled up behind the Tempest, and then backed his car into a vacant spot, two parking spaces over from the blue Pontiac. He turned off his motor and sat staring at the back of the suspect vehicle.

Something didn't feel quite right. He studied the license plate numbers FLA 851. *Those aren't the right numbers! And no roof-racks. This can't be the right car. Sure, there's more than one fucking Pontiac Tempest on the streets! Damn it!*

Sunny's excitement had fizzled just as fast as his adrenaline had kicked in about eight minutes earlier, when he had first spotted the Tempest, sitting in the parking lot. While he sat there for a few minutes, studying the car and the surroundings of the parking lot, an RCMP cruiser pulled into the lot and parked right beside Sunny's Accord.

Sunny felt a nervous twinge run up the back of his neck. Even though he wasn't doing anything wrong, he still encountered that sense of nervousness that most people feel when they see a cop. *Yeah, I'm not doing anything wrong; I'm only tracking a maniacal serial killer by myself, instead of alerting the authorities! There's nothing wrong with that at all! I don't even have a coffee or a donut in my hand. I need to either go inside or leave. I can't just sit here looking stupid!*

Sunny turned his head toward the police car and then leaned over, as if to get something out of his glove compartment. He quickly glanced at the two RCMP officers and realized that they were more interested in getting out of the car and into the donut shop, than they were with him.

I'm over reacting for crying-out-loud! They don't give a hoot about what I'm doing.

As the officers headed for the door of the donut shop, Sunny started up his engine, still debating if he should check out the crowd in the Tim Hortons. *Nah, it's not the right license numbers, why waste time? Must keep looking, time is running out. The cops might find him first, if I waste time.*

Just as Sunny was pulling out of the parking space that he was in, a Ford pickup drove up blocking the way out. So he turned left instead, and drove past about six parked cars and trucks, when he suddenly realized, there was no exit at that end of the parking lot. He put the tranny in reverse, and backed up past the spot he had been at, and then pulled forward into the same parking spot, he had been sitting in, just a few minutes earlier. This way, he could turn his car around and exit the way he came in.

As he backed out of the parking spot, he looked both ways for cars and pedestrians. Sunny checked his rear-view mirror and side mirrors as well. One can never be too sure, when backing up. Always trust your mirrors.

Sunny took one more panoramic view at that blue Pontiac Tempest in his rear-view mirror as he was backing out. He swung the Accord's back-end out to the right and then shifted into first gear and rolled toward the exit leading to Edmonds Street. As he was waiting to merge into the busy street, he had a quick flashback of the rear-end of the blue Tempest. There was something strange about that license plate!

Detectives Mike Kuban and Jane Rhodes split the list of twenty-six possible suspects with two other long standing members of the force; Detectives, Johnson Fong and

Bernard Drake. Both men have been working in the homicide department for the last decade. Fong has been a police member for eighteen years and Drake at least twenty-one years. Tough cops! They have been partners in crime for the duration of the Fraser murders.

"Bernard and I can take the west side of the city, and you two take the east!" Fong told the fellow cops, standing by the water cooler. "If you're cool with that?"

"Sure, give us the bad side of town," Rhodes said sarcastically. "You know those east-siders!"

"Yeah, a crazy bunch of neanderthals!" Kuban added as he sipped his coffee.

With glee in her middle-aged eyes, one of the dispatch operators, walked up to the four detectives, and excitedly chimed, "did you hear the great news? The getaway driver in MacDuff's death has turned himself in, only about an hour ago!"

All four of the investigators gave a "high-five" and hugged each other.

"Hope that fucker fries!" Drake chanted.

"Yeah, like that's not gonna happen, not with our system!" Kuban confirmed with disappointment.

"Especially since he turned himself in. Some hotshot lawyer will plead his sad case to some self-centerd judge, and he'll get a reduced sentence and *walk* in a couple of months. Our justice system is such bullshit!" Rhodes said with bitter disgust in her voice.

"What are the details, Angie, do you know?" Fong asked the dispatch operator.

"Well, all I know, from what I heard ... is that the guy is eighteen years old and he is a repeat offender. He has been involved in other armed robberies. Apparently he has a fairly lengthy rap sheet from doing mom and pop corner stores, at an early age and then graduating to banks," Angie quickly answered.

"Was he the shooter who killed MacDuff, Angie?" asked Drake.

"I didn't hear all of the info, but I don't believe so. What I did hear was that, the holdup guy shot MacDuff, coming out of the bank and that Robinson, shot and killed the holdup dude, while he was running to the getaway car."

"Even if the creep did shoot MacDuff, he would never admit to that anyway ... sure as shit, he would blame it on his dead buddy. That way he gets a lessor charge. Robbery, not murder," said Drake.

"He is still, theoretically, an accomplice to MacDuff's murder, Bernie," Rhodes added.

"True enough, but those misfit defense lawyers and judges always seem to let those assholes back out on the street!" Drake said with burning anger in his deep voice. "You know, sometimes I just want to quit the force ... just retire ... just quit. It's frustrating! We work hard to bring these scummy, slimy, lowlifes in, and the lawyers and the judges let them go! It's not about protecting the public; it's all about 'the almighty dollar'. The judges and lawyers are getting rich off of, the pathetic Canadian justice system."

"If you can call it a system," Fong said. "At least the guy came forward, that's a load off everyone's minds. It's a relief and I'm sure MacDuff's family will be glad to hear the news. It will be a large funeral ... MacDuff was an awesome person and had lots of friends. Now let's get this crazy child killer off the streets!"

"Hi Mrs. Kruzik, you're either needing a key cut or looking for your son?" Ike pondered, as he was cutting a key for a customer.

"Hi Ike. Well you got one of those questions right. I am looking for my son. Have you seen him lately?" Annie asked the pro lock picker.

"Just the other day, as a matter of fact," Ike replied.

"I know he's been busy, and he doesn't carry his phone with him all the time. I was going to take him for lunch, but I guess that isn't going to happen today," Annie said.

"I haven't had lunch yet," Ike joked.

"Nice try Ike," she said as she fumbled around in her purse. "Actually, I do have a key, I need a copy for," as she placed a copper colored key on the counter.

Ike finished with the customer ahead of Sunny's mom and bade him a pleasant "good day". The big man turned around and smiled at Annie, on his way out.

"Aren't you Harvey Smith?" she asked the man who smiled at her.

He stopped short of exiting the locksmith shop, "Yes I am, you look familiar ... but I can't place where I know you from," answered the portly Smith. "Do you work nearby?"

"No, I don't ... but I remember you from Carleton Secondary School; over on Kingsway and Rupert Street," Annie said.

"Yes, that makes sense. You hung out with Wade Kruzik and his buddies?"

"Yes I did, and I ended up marrying him after highschool," Annie told Harvey while waiting for Ike to finish cutting the key copy. "How about you, what are you doing these days, Harvey?"

"Well, I married a gal named Linda Murchie ... she didn't go to Carleton, she went to Gladstone Secondary

School, but after ten years, we ended up getting divorced. Now I'm on my second marriage," Smith said.

"Any kids?" Annie asked.

"No I never had kids, I guess I forgot to have them," he laughed. "How about you?"

"Yes, we have two ... one of each. My daughter lives on Vancouver Island and my son, well he actually lives above this store. I came by to take him out for lunch, but he's not home, I guess I should have phoned first," Annie remarked.

Ike smiled at both of them, thinking, *yes you should have phoned first, cause Sunny is always on the go, "heaven knows where"*. He had finished cutting the key and placed it on the counter, waiting patiently for the two to end their conversation.

Finally, Annie said, " It was good to see you after all these years, Harvey. You have a nice day and maybe we'll bump into each other again."

"Likewise Annie, take care!" Harvey replied, as he pushed open the door to leave.

She turned to Ike and rummaged through her purse for her wallet and said, "he's a nice man, but I didn't think he was going to quit talking."

"He's probably lonely," Ike assumed. He shook his head from side to side, as he watched Sunny's mom pull her wallet out of her purse. "No, it's on me Mrs. Kruzik."

"Don't be silly, Ike ... you can't give stuff away, that's not good for the business!" Annie said.

"No, I'm serious, I don't want your money. Besides it's only a couple of bucks, it's no big deal!" Ike insisted. "You may not realize, but your son has done a lot for us. For one thing; just him living above the store, makes it like we have twenty-four hour security. Also, if we need a hand moving anything large, like a heavy safe, he will always give us a hand."

"Are you sure?" Annie asked.

"Positive!" Ike returned.

"My son has been hard to get a hold of lately, if you happen to see him, can you get him to get in touch with me?" Annie asked.

"I certainly will," Ike reassured the attractive Mrs. Kruzik, as she strolled out the door into the sunshine.

The break in the busy traffic, gave Sunny the opportunity to "bust out" onto Edmonds Street. As he was driving down Edmonds, towards New Westminster, he couldn't get the image of the back-end, from the blue Tempest out of his mind. It was gnawing at his nerves like a dog with a bone, all smothered in homemade gravy. He ran it through his mind, over and over, like an obsessive, compulsive crazy man!

Something about that license plate! What was it? FLA 851 ... FLA 851? Damn it! What the fu ...! FLA 851, Elly only saw three numbers on the plate, she saw 128. She said she saw them in the mirror. 128 in the mirror! That's it! HOLY SHIT! 128 in the mirror is 851! ... "Son-of-a-bitch! That's the damn car ... that's the killer's car!" Sunny said out loud to himself, as he stomped on the accelerator.

He had to get back to that donut shop ASAP! But he had already passed Humphries Avenue, so he would have to take the next street and circle around again, like he did before.

"Come on! Come on!" Sunny cursed, as the cars ahead of his were slowing down. *Gotta get back there fast! Before that fucker leaves,* he thought to himself.

The next side street coming up was Mary Avenue. Sunny signalled right, and turned the corner like a madman. Down Mary Avenue like a rocket-ship through the milky-way! Then another hard right, back onto Hubert Street. He raced to the end of Hubert and hit the brakes hard at the stop sign. *No cars coming! Perfect!* Sunny fishtailed onto Kingsway and put the "pedal to the metal".

As he neared the Tim Hortons parking lot, he couldn't believe his eyes. The blue Pontiac was gone! *Shit! No way! He can't be gone, he can't be!*

Frantically, Sunny scanned the vehicles in front of the restaurant, as he neared the entryway that led off of Kingsway, back into the parking lot. Sunny turned the Accord into the active eatery's property and pulled over to the side. Expeditiously and thoroughly, he checked the remaining vehicles that were parked and couldn't see the blue Pontiac Tempest anywhere.

As he glanced toward the building, he noticed the two RCMP police officers looking right at him through the massive plate glass windows. Sunny casually looked away and proceeded to drive through the parking lot. As he looked in his rear-view mirror, he spotted the back-end of the blue Tempest driving out of the opposite end of the parking lot, onto Edmonds Street.

The driver of the Pontiac turned left and headed towards Kingsway going southwest.

Sunny had to keep his "cool". Knowing that those cops were sitting there, having coffee and munching on greasy donuts, was reason enough to stay calm. He knew that they didn't have a clue, what he was up to. It's a "mind thing", when a person may break the law and the police are near by; getting nervous is natural, but not let-

DOG WITH A BONE

ting the police know your nervous is the key to being aloof!

Sunny pulled the car forward into one of the empty parking spaces and then backed out so he could swing the car around and follow the Pontiac. The cops were still watching him as he commandeered the Honda forth and back. *I must look like an idiot to those guys,* he thought. *But I need to get out of this damn parking lot and follow that killer! Just take it easy, those cops are probably still watching.*

As Sunny exited the Tim Hortons, he made a left-hand turn and watched the suspect killer's car stop for the red light at the intersection of Kingsway and Edmonds. Sunny was six cars behind the blue Pontiac Tempest. He looked over to his left and could see the two policemen walking out to their cruiser. One of the RCMP officers faced the direction of Sunny, as he clambered into the police car.

He's not looking AT me, it's just a coincidence, he's merely looking at the traffic, that's all, Sunny reassured himself.

The red light turned jade green. The backed up traffic snaked it's way through the lively intersection. Sunny kept his eyes on the suspect car ahead of him. On through the crossroads the vehicles rolled. The blue Tempest drove straight across Kingsway, through the traffic lights and onward down Edmonds Street. Three of the cars ahead of Sunny turned off of Edmonds, so now there were only three cars between Sunny and the Pontiac. Sunny looked in his rear-view mirror. He wanted to make sure those policemen were not behind him. But to his horror, they were! Only five cars behind his.

Several news reporters had congregated outside of 212 Bonneville Drive in Burnaby, at the Cottonwood Manor; the building where the rottweiler dog had been savagely beaten. Since the news of the tragic animal abuse had aired earlier in the day, the feelings of the general public was harsh bitter outrage!

Phone calls and emails were flooding the local radio and TV stations calling for the perpetrator to turn himself in to the authorities.

Police had not yet made an arrest, as the investigation was still in the early stages and any evidence available was presently being determined. The police were not yet, able to make contact with the individual whom they believe was responsible for the heinous deed. The person of interest was not at home when the police were called to the scene of the crime.

Most of the residents that lived in the low-income apartment building were too apprehensive to say anything to the RCMP. The ones that did, asked for complete anonymity, for the fear of retribution, by the culprit.

Everyone that resided in the old building, knew all too well who had actually owned the friendly canine named Rex. The dog was always wagging his "scut" when he encountered one of the tenants. Rex's owner, Justin Fairchild, was a twenty-nine-year-old, "wanna-be gangbanger". He dressed and walked, like he shit his pants; big baggy jeans hanging down by his crotch, baseball hat turned sideways and big ugly, cheap-looking silver chains hanging around his neck. He swaggered like he owned the block. Justin was a drug dealing lowlife that had the same kind of lowlife associates hanging around his stinky, dirty little apartment unit.

These assholes would come and go at all hours of the night, buying dope from Fairchild. Pot, crack, cocaine

DOG WITH A BONE

and ecstasy were all available on the menu, for the addicted!

Some of the neighbors complained to the landlord, about the comings and goings of the troublesome so-called men, on the third floor. At first, the landlord ignored the complaints of the other residents, but as the complaints kept coming, he had no other choice, but to confront the young drug dealer.

It wasn't a pleasant meeting with Mr. Fairchild. The Hong Kong immigrant landlord, explained to Justin, that various complaints had been brought forward about the late night visitors and the loud music, which could be heard throughout the halls of the apartment. Fairchild "freaked out" and threatened the Asian property owner. Fairchild told the landlord that he had rights; that he had the Canadian Charter of Rights, in his favor. He rambled on that, he was born here and that the Asian landlord was not; that he was an immigrant, and that if he hassled him, maybe the authorities would deport his ass out of Canada!

The Chinese apartment owner backed down and asked him to "please, just turn it down a little" and that there would be no further problems. It seems the landlord didn't want to deal with the intimidating prick!

Fairchild walked Rex sometimes around the neighborhood, but usually he would take him for rides in his car away from the apartment building. When he didn't walk him or take him for rides, he would merely escort the big warmhearted dog outside of the apartments and let him do his doggy "business" on the grassy boulevard. The angry punk never picked up the poop, that big Rex left behind. More than once, a passing pedestrian or tenant from the apartment would make a comment, that it was in fact, a city bylaw to pick up, after ones dog. That just angered the wanna-be gangster even more!

"Fuck You!" was always the response.

Nobody in the building could understand, why Fairchild or anyone for that matter, could harm a lovable, friendly pooch and then beat it to death with a shovel.

Speculation among the dwellers ranged from Fairchild being "whacked out" on drugs, to him owning a dog that was just plain ol' great with people, instead of being some ferocious guard dog on steroids, protecting his booty of drugs. Embarrassment and failure of his canine to be mean, may have provoked him to act in such a cowardly way.

The reporters came from Global TV, CTV and a couple of the local newspapers, the New West Weekly and the Coquitlam This Week.

Two volunteer members from the Vancouver SPCA and two from the Burnaby SPCA were also on hand.

The small group of reporters were there to interview the tenants in the building and to talk to the suspect, in order to highlight the story for the six o'clock news and the weekly papers.

The earlier report from the police, to the media that ran in the morning Province newspaper, indicated the address of the building in Burnaby, but did not disclose the actual apartment unit number. The media hounds were hoping to discover exactly where the animal abuser lived.

A few of the residents had gathered outside with the SPCA members and the reporters and were talking to them. The twenty something reporter from the New West Weekly had brought a box of donuts and coffees for the group.

DOG WITH A BONE

"The more I work in this field, the more I realize how fucked-up the world really is!" exclaimed the woman reporter from CTV, as she glanced at her smart phone.

"It does make you wonder, doesn't it," Frank Reynolds, the camera-man from Global TV replied.

"Do you know which unit, Justin Fairchild lives in sir?" the reporter from Global TV asked an elderly man, as Reynolds aimed the oversized camera at him.

The old man shook his head up and down, and looked around and then quietly said, "no, not really." Then he shuffled away from the camera.

"I know which unit that bastard lives in, he's in number thirty-one on the third floor. I heard noises from that apartment, thumping, banging and high-pitched screams from that poor dog!" said a red-haired, middle-aged woman, as she waved her arms around and started to cry. "Something needs ... (sob) ... to be done (sob) about that ... poor excuse of a man!"

Other residents came forward to the press, and also indicated, that the police should do something, cause the landlord is too afraid to do anything.

The red-haired lady let all the reporters through the main doors into the secure building, so that they could get up to the third floor. The media had lots of questions for the alleged animal abuser. One by one they entered the elevator, until it was full. A few of them had to use the stairs.

The Global TV reporter knocked on unit number thirty-ones' door as the small group waited in the hallway quietly for a response. There was intermittent hushed murmuring between themselves, as the news person knocked again.

No answer. They all waited patiently. A different reporter knocked again. Still no answer. It was obvious that the tenant was either home and wouldn't answer the knocking on the worn door, or he wasn't home.

The camera-men from CTV and Global TV, simultaneously pointed their cameras at the door, displaying the tarnished brass numbers of the three and the one, which were loosely attached by screws to the laminated wooden door. The whole world would know at six o'clock tonight, exactly where the dog killer hangs his hat!

The reporters decided among themselves that they would wait together for at least another hour, to see if Justin Fairchild would show up. The SPCA volunteer members also decided to wait for a bit longer. Several residents of the building were also hanging around in the dingy hallway of the third floor.

The red-haired lady and two other tenants were being interviewed by the media staff, with the cameras rolling!

"I live on the second floor, right below Mr. Fairchild, and I could hear awful, awful sounds coming from above me. Heavy thuds and scratching noises, like ... like something or someone trying to crawl away, and the loud cries and whimpering! My God, I couldn't stand it any longer. I had to phone the police. It sounded like ... like ... someone being murdered!" explained a man in his forties, with tears in his eyes. "I felt helpless ... what could I do. We all know what goes on in that apartment, the drugs and the booze, but that banging and screaming! Enough is enough! I don't care if he knows what I am telling you. He is a sick man!"

"Everyone loved Rex! He was such a gentle giant of a dog!" said the red-haired lady with sadness in her voice and a Kleenex pressed against her nose. "I feel so bad for him, he died a terrible death ... and none of us could help him."

One of the SPCA volunteers put an arm around the red-haired lady, to comfort her, and told her, "we are going to make sure that he is prosecuted to the fullest extent of the law!"

"When this airs later tonight, you can bet your last nickel, that there will be a ground-swell of public outrage," reassured one of the news hounds.

EIGHTEEN

"I would like to make a cash withdrawal please," Dr. Randall Wilson told the female bank teller, as he fidgeted with his reading glasses.

"How much did you want to withdraw Mr. ... ?"

"Mr. Wilson, it's Mr. Wilson, thank-you," he said kind of nervously.

"Well Mr. Wilson, just insert your client card into the debit machine," as she pointed to the small black machine on the counter in front of the doctor, "and enter the amount you want to withdraw," said the pretty teller.

"I don't think that will work ... I need more than a thousand dollars," he whispered quietly.

"Oh, I see. How much are you requesting then, Mr. Wilson?" the teller asked.

"Twenty-five large ones," Wilson replied.

"Pardon me sir?" she asked.

"Twenty-five thousand."

"For that amount, Mr. Wilson, we will need to give you a certified cashiers check," the teller explained.

"I don't want a cashiers check ... um ... Ruby," Wilson said as he quickly glanced at her name tag. "I need to withdraw MY cash out, not a check," he replied with a raised voice and an obvious sample of frustration.

"But Mr. Wilson, you know that nowadays, with Interact and direct deposits and such, that it's much safer to take a cashiers check than to walk around with that amount of cash," explained Ruby.

Taking a deep breath and slowly replying, the plastic surgeon said to the nice lady, "I understand my dear, I do understand, but you see, I come from a time when cash money talks and B.S. walks!" As she raised her eyebrows, he continued, "I want to purchase a car privately, and I want to receive the best deal I can possibly get. The only way to do this, is to have cash money ready available to the seller! Believe me, it works like a 'hot-damn'! I realize that you are working in your career at a time, when everything is now electronic, but when you want the best deal, in life, when buying anything, you pay with cold, hard cash! Now can you give me my withdrawal please," Wilson said with overdue patience.

"There is one more thing Mr. Wilson, any amount over ten thousand *large ones*, as you call them," with a hint of humour in her voice and a smile on her youthful face, "we have to order that amount in, and it takes twenty-four hours," as she shrugged her slender shoulders.

"Oh for Christ sakes," he said as he caught himself losing it. "It's ... it's not your fault, I know ... I'm sorry, I apologize, but it is rather frustrating, that I can't even withdraw my own money when I want it," Wilson said shaking his head.

"I know Mr. Wilson, it's just the Canadian banking system nowadays. We actually don't keep very much money in the vault. For safety reasons, I'm sure you can understand?"

"Well to be quite honest, no I don't understand, but that's fine, I will be back tomorrow ... wait tomorrow is Saturday, you ARE open tomorrow aren't you?"

"Yes we are, but we close early on Saturdays, we close at 3:00 pm. The money will be here by 1:00 pm. I will put the order in right away Mr. Wilson," Ruby told him. "Just sign here Mr. Wilson and we can get the ball rolling."

"Thank-you Ruby, I will be back tomorrow."

Randall Wilson turned and walked away, shaking his head and muttering to himself, *what a bunch of crap!*

Sunny kept an eye on the RCMP in his mirror, only five cars behind him, as well as the blue Tempest, three cars in front of him. It was like doing the rumba shuffle! The line of cars came to the three-way traffic lights at Edmonds and Rumble Street. A couple of cars in front of the suspect killer's car turned left at the lights. The rest of the lineup turned right, onto Rumble Street heading west.

Sunny looked in his rear-view mirror. The cops turned right also. *Shit!*

The car in front of his, had it's right-hand turn signal on; it slowed down and then turned the corner. The suspect car was getting further and further away.

Sunny couldn't speed up and risk having the police stop him and then lose sight of the Tempest. The two cars in front of the cop car, turned off. Now, only two vehicles separated Sunny from the RCMP and the blue Pontiac Tempest, front and rear.

It was like the hunter, being hunted by the hunter, being hunted!

The procession of vehicles made their way down Rumble Street. Sunny kept looking in his rear-view mirror. The cops were still behind two cars; everyone doing the speed limit. To Sunny it seemed like everything was in slow motion! Seven cars parading down the street, with the suspect killer's car leading the way, like an engine on a freight train, the RCMP at the end, like the caboose, and Sunny was the the freight in the middle.

What a bloody predicament to be in, he thought to himself. *Just keep calm and stay focused! Those cops can't be following me. I haven't done anything wrong yet!*

Rrrrrrrrooooooowwwww! Without warning, the police siren wailed hysterically!

Sunny's heart skipped a beat, maybe even two or three! He checked his rear-view mirror and saw the bright flashing red and blue strobe-lights dancing haphazardly on the roof of the cop cruiser.

Be cool, be coooool! Sunny thought to himself.

The RCMP quickly pulled out to the left and around the cars in front of them. Upon hearing the ear piercing, deafening sound of the siren, all six drivers pulled their cars over to the curbside.

Sunny's adrenaline started building. He sat in his car, watching his driver's side mirror, as the cops neared. Within seconds, they flew right past Sunny's Accord. He wondered if they were after the blue Tempest as he watched intently while they approached the suspect's car. No, they sped on by the suspect's car, and kept on motoring down Rumble Street as their siren became less and less audible.

Must have been dispatched to some accident or maybe one of the cops has a bad case of diarrhea, Sunny chuckled to himself, with a tremendous sense of relief.

The vehicles at the curbside started pulling back out onto the road. The car behind Sunny pulled out fast and passed him, and then hung a quick left onto the first sidestreet. Sunny could see up ahead, about a hundred yards, that the blue Tempest was already edging out onto the pavement. He had to keep that car in his sights. One by one the drivers resumed their positions on Rumble Street.

The blue Tempest drove through the green light at the intersection of Rumble and Royal Oak Avenue. The car behind the Tempest slowed down with it's left turn signal blinking, waiting for the oncoming cars to end. The light changed to amber and the Nissan directly in front of Sunny slowed down. Sunny was still about ninety feet behind the Nissan.

"Shit! Go through the light you idiot!" Sunny said out loud to himself.

The Nissan slowed to a dead stop. Sunny hammered the gas pedal and swerved around the car and ran the now, red light. Traffic from the right side on Royal Oak, proceeding through the intersection were blasting their horns at the crazy fool in the black Honda Accord, running the red light.

Sunny could care less. He was on a mission! He wasn't about to lose that psycho suspect killer's car. *Good thing that bloody cop wasn't behind me!*

Sunny Kruzik was feeling real fucking fine right about now. It was a clear, beautiful day and he had that blue Tempest in his sights. He was gaining on it, but he had to make sure that he was far enough back, so the guy wouldn't know he was being followed. He stayed back about seventy-five feet, equivalent to seven car lengths.

The Pontiac drove about another six blocks and then slowed down with the right-hand signal flashing. The car turned right onto Sussex Avenue and then headed north. Sunny followed. He kept his distance of approximately seventy-five feet. The suspect killer passed four sidestreets, and then crossed the active Imperial Street. Sunny had to wait for a break in the traffic at Imperial, all the while, watching the blue car on the other side, getting further away. He could see the brake lights on the Tempest in the distance, shine a bright red. The car was slowing down.

Finally, a break in the continuous traffic. Sunny smoked it across Imperial Street. Three hundred yards ahead, he could see the tail-end of the suspect car turning left, into the underground parkade of an older style, apartment building.

With his adrenaline starting to flow, he drove on and pushed his "Panama Jack" shades back up over his nose a bit. His sunglasses had slid down a ways, from when the cops were behind him; he must have released a sweat gland or two.

As he neared the parkade he wondered, *should I drive by or should I drive in? If I drive by, I won't see who's driving that car. So I need to drive in, right now. I have my sunglasses on, so he won't remember me and I was in my truck, not this car. Besides, for all he knows, maybe I live here.*

Without hesitation, Sunny turned into the underground parking lot and down the concrete ramp. It seemed extra dark with his shades on. He could see brake lights over by the far right, against the wall between two other vehicles. He made a sharp left and spied three empty spaces on the far side of the parkade. Sunny pulled into the center spot and threw the gear shifter into neutral, but kept the engine running, just in case. *Last time, that fucker pulled a gun on me!* In his rear-view mirror Sunny is watching and waiting!

Out of the blue car, stepped a woman, with long, shoulder length, dirty blond hair. She swung her head around, to throw her hair behind her, as she flipped the shoulder strap of her black leather purse over her left shoulder. Then she slammed the car door and walked to the back of the car and opened the trunk. The lady picked up a plastic bag, full of what looked to be groceries and then shut the trunk. She was kind of a "plain Jane", dressed in blue-jeans, a red and black checkered blouse and white sneakers. Sunny figured her to be about forty-two years old. *Is it the right car? Is she borrowing the dude's car? Is it his wife? Something doesn't add up!*

A thousand thoughts were running through Sunny's brain-box! He watched her walk over to the elevator, press a button, and twenty seconds later as the elevator door opened, she stepped in and disappeared. Sunny shut his motor off. He waited a few minutes, processing some of his thoughts. Then he took off his shades, so he could see better in the dimly lit underground parkade. *A freakin' woman! That just beats all! Now what?*

Sunny waited another minute, dropped his Panama Jacks back over his chestnut brown orbs and then opened the car door and got out. The first thing he did, nonchalantly, was scan the inside of the cement underground parking lot for security cameras. He walked slowly towards the elevator door, just in case someone entered the parkade, that way it would seem like he was heading to the elevator.

Looking up at the surrounding ceiling, he dropped his car keys on the ground purposely, so he could bend down and turn around in a circle to check the complete circumference of the parkade's ceiling. *No security cameras!* More than likely, because it's an older building; built sometime around the nineteen seventies, before security cameras were an issue.

Sunny sidestepped over to the blue Tempest. He raised his sunglasses slightly, with his left hand and peered through the windows of the vehicle. There was nothing out of the ordinary inside the car. A Tim Hortons coffee cup and napkin on the front seat and a pillow on the back seat.

Sunny visually inspected the roof edges of the car, carefully not to touch. *Hmmm, slight scratches! Two of them about three feet apart, directly above the windows, on the the outer edge of the roof.* He quickly walked around the back of the car, to the other side and checked out the paint on the roof. *The same as the other side! Marks from roof-racks? I need to be sure!*

Straightening his solid frame and scrutinizing the concrete compound, Sunny noticed a door approximately fifty feet away, along the same wall as the elevator entrance. The sign on the dark brown door read "STORAGE" in white letters.

He walked past the car situated on the right side of the Tempest, and over to the next two open parking spaces, and saw the bright yellow painted numbers on the cement floor. *Parking space numbers, seven and eight. So that means that the suspect killer's car is in parking space number ten!*

Sunny went back to his Honda and opened the passenger-side door. He pressed the chrome button on the console compartment lid and it popped open. He pulled out his tight fitting, black "Mechanix" gloves and slipped them on his strong, stocky fingers. Then he rummaged through the glove box and located his lock-pick tools that Ike had given him on his thirtieth birthday.

Like a shadow in the windy dark, he drifted over to the storage room door and immediately went to work on the dead-bolt lock. Sunny inserted the torsion-bar with his left hand and employed ever so-slight pressure. Inserting the tiny hook into the key-way, he "raked" the pins in the tumbler, while putting gentle strain on the torsion-bar, just the way Ike had taught him. Sunny had it down to a science. It wasn't his first time! Within twenty seconds, CLICK! The dead-bolt slid open. Sunny stuffed the pick-set into his front pocket and then opened the door and entered the storage room.

William Marcus was sitting on his front couch watching the television, when the door bell rang. Brrriiiinnnggg! He got up, off his lazy ass and sauntered over to the front door and opened it.

"Hi Uncle Ted, what are you doing here?" William asked somewhat surprised.

"It's so fuckin' nice to see ya too, Willy!" came the reply from the burly uncle. "I came here to talk with you, cause you don't seem to have very much respect for yore momma, now do ya?"

"Why do you say that, Uncle Ted?" William asked.

"Don't give me no backtalk boy. You know damn well, what I'm talking about! You got any beer in the fridge kid?" Uncle Ted questioned, as he made his way to the kitchen. He opened the fridge door and grabbed a Budweiser. He twisted the cap off, took a big hearty swig and then let out a stinking belch. "Brraaapppp!" Uncle Ted set the beer on the table, then turned and looked at William, who was now standing in the doorway with an axe.

"Watch ya think yore gonna do with that thing you stupid fuck?" the burly uncle growled.

"I don't want you hurting me anymore!" the scared young killer pleaded with his uncle.

"Don't be stupid kid, I came over to talk to you ... nothing else. Put that thing down, so's we can figger thins' out."

"I'm not puttin' nothing down, till you get out of this house! You always treated me like shit and I ain't takin' it anymore," William demanded.

"Listen Willy, you kilt a woman and yore lucky you only got small time man! They coulda locked you away a lot longer," Uncle Ted said.

"That bitch got what she deserved. She didn't deserve to live. I'm glad I killed her, and I'll kill you too if you don't get out of this house, right now!" William shouted at his fat uncle as he raised the axe with both hands.

"Easy boy, take it easy ... okay, I'm leaving, put that there axe down," Uncle Ted said as he placed his bottle of beer on the kitchen table. "Yore goin' to end up in the 'big-house' if you don't change yore habits Willy boy. Where's yore momma right now anyway?"

"She went shopping. Now GET OUT."

As the two relatives stood their ground, Mary Marcus pulled into the carport and started unloading her goods. She lugged the bags through the yard, to the back door and then turned the doorknob. She opened the old door and was shocked to see the big back of her brother, in front of her and her deranged son standing in the doorway of the kitchen and the hallway.

"For God's sake you two!" she screamed. "What's going on here?"

"I came over to talk sense into yore boy, but he would rather hack me into pieces, like he done to that woman." Uncle Ted explained to his sister, not taking his eyes off of the axe wielder.

"William! Put that down right now, or I'll ..."

"You'll what? Phone the cops! You won't make it to the phone you stupid bitch!" he yelled at his mom. "I want HIM out of here, now!"

Mary looked her brother in the eye and said, "please go Ted, please." She gave him a half-hearted smile and told him she would call him later.

"Aw-right, I'll go ... but I'm warning you Willy boy, if you so much as harm a hair, on yore momma's head, I will kill ya, you understand? Kill ya!" Uncle Ted swore loudly, as he took his index finger and swiftly ran it, from one side of his thick neck to the other side, in the cutting motion.

William took two steps towards his burly, drunkard of an uncle, with the double bladed axe raised above his puny, kid shoulders, and screamed from his twisted, gnarled mouth, "GET OUT NOW YOU FUCKIN' PRICK!"

Uncle Ted stumbled backwards towards the back door, with his left hand in the air, as if to shield himself from the thrust of the deadly axe. "Don't hit me Will! I'm goin', I'm goin'!" he said as he grabbed the already open door and swung it open wider, so that he could jump out onto the porch.

"My God William! Are you out of your mind?" his distraught mother asked.

"You people make me crazy, why can't you just leave me alone?" William blurted out.

Mary shook her head slowly in disbelief and started to cry. Her brother Ted, was already out the door and around the side of the house, heading straight for his pickup truck.

Through tears of upset and anger, Mary quietly asked her son to, "please put the axe down, Will."

It was pitch black inside the storage room. Sunny felt around on the inside right of the heavy steel door, as he slowly closed it shut. He found the light switch, clicked it

DOG WITH A BONE

upwards and "presto" the hum of electrical energy from the fluorescent ballasts filled the concrete room. The flickering light gradually changed to a bright luminescence.

Sunny scanned the layout of the room. It wasn't just a room, it was a small warehouse, hidden from view of the parking area. The place was partitioned into individual storage units, built with two-by-four wood framing and heavy gauge chain-link wire fencing. Each storage unit was approximately eight feet wide by twelve feet deep, with a regular size chain-link door. The units were laid out down a long corridor on either side, coming to a "T" at the end, with more storage units down each end of the "T". The tenant's unit number, was displayed across the top of the door. Every door had some sort of a padlock on it.

No security cameras inside here either! Sunny lifted his Panama Jacks off his eyes and sat them on top of his head. He gazed through the chain-link at all of the junk, in the residents separate storage units, as he hurriedly moved along the narrow corridor, eyeing the numbers above the unit doorways. Finally he reached number ten. Sunny stopped at the tenth unit and peered in through the diagonal shaped galvanized wire.

Inside were some cardboard boxes piled up to the ceiling's height of ten feet. An old pine coffee table and four brown wooden chairs were stacked on each other, upside down. More cardboard boxes and two sets of skis, standing up against the cardboard boxes, with ski boots hanging from the chain-link wire. One mountain bike, with an old green plastic helmet strapped to it's frame. An old car battery sitting on some plastic, on the concrete floor and ... *wait... what's that behind the two sets of skis? YES! One pair of roof-racks! Those racks look like they have been deliberately hidden behind those long skis. YES again! Shiny black, electrician's tape wrapped around the racks. It's got to be the killer's car! But where is the damn killer? Upstairs in his apartment? Who was that woman? His wife? His daughter? Too old to be his daughter! His friend or sister? I have to find out!*

Sunny looked long and hard at those racks and determined that they must be from the killers car. But he knew now, that the only way to know one hundred percent, was to see the man who drives the Pontiac, to be sure. Only Sunny and Ellen have seen the suspect face to face. The police don't even know what he looks like. Their best witness, Frederick Redmond, never even saw the killer's face on the night he observed the car with the roof-racks and with it's trunk open, near the murder scene.

Beyond the storage room door, out in the concrete parkade, Sunny heard the booming sound of a car door slamming. Then seconds later, the echoing of a starter, engaging the flywheel of the engine and resonating into the loud acceleration of the pistons firing!

He dropped his shades back down and quickly headed for the door. Sunny peeled his Mechanix gloves off and shoved them into his front pocket. He then reached up underneath his t-shirt and grabbed hold of the door knob, with his t-shirt covering the handle. *Can't leave any fingerprints, or have someone see me, with gloves on leaving this room.*

As Sunny emerged from the storage room, he saw the Pontiac Tempest reversing from parking space number ten. He casually strutted across the cold, gray concrete floor and glanced over at the blue car as the driver put it in forward gear and turned towards the exit. Almost in slow motion, the driver looked toward Sunny as he spotted him walking across the parkade. No more than ten feet away, the driver of the car and Sunny stared directly at one another. Sunny tipped his head, nodded and smiled at the guy driving. He smiled back at Sunny and then drove out and up the ramp slowly.

Sunny had just exchanged smiles with the devil himself! *It's him! The child killer! Scruffy, dark, curly hair, unshaven, about forty-five years old and those icy-blue piercing eyes! Those eyes are a dead giveaway! That was him, no mistaking, I could never forget that sinister face!*

It's no surprise the killer wouldn't have recognized Sunny. He had his sunglasses covering his eyes and besides, the murdering psycho saw so many people a day in his hunting grounds, that Sunny Kruzik would be just another pretty face in the crowd.

Sunny watched as the Pontiac drove out of the building and then turned left. He ran to his Accord and started it up. He backed up and then drove out of the underground parkade and hung a left.

The icy-blue eyed killer drove down Sussex to Kingsway and then made a left on Kingsway. Sunny followed but stayed a few cars behind. Through the lights and intersections the blue Pontiac drove, with the black Accord in covert mode.

A few miles later, the child killer made a left turn off of Kingsway onto 33rd Avenue, unaware that he was being followed by Sunny. About six blocks along 33rd, a police siren filled the air. Sunny looked in his rear-view mirror and cringed when he saw the flashing red and blue lights coming up fast behind him. He pulled over to the curb and the unmarked police cruiser rushed right past his car, passed three more cars and then slowed as it came up behind the blue Pontiac.

Mr. Icy-Blue Eyes wheeled his crime car over to the curbside. Sunny sat for a minute in his car, still pulled over. *Those bastards beat me to it! I'll wait and see if they know who they're dealing with.*

Sunny sat and waited and watched, but didn't want to sit there too long, cause there really wasn't a pull-off lane.

The cops were obviously running his plate numbers as they sat in their cruiser behind the Pontiac with their lights doing the "disco duck" dance.

Sunny had to drive on, he looked too inconspicuous just sitting in his car behind the cops. So he drove past reluctantly and decided to drive around the block to get another glimpse of the bust.

The traffic was backed up and Sunny couldn't go anywhere. He was at a crawl, until the next side-street came up. *Freakin' metro Vancouver traffic! Always when I'm in a hurry!* After about ten minutes of inching along, he turned right and headed down the side-street. Then he hung another right back onto Kingsway heading full circle onto 33rd Avenue again.

By the time Sunny arrived back, the cop cruiser was still sitting there, but the Pontiac had vanished! *What the! Did they tow him away? No! He would be in the back of the cop car. A tow truck couldn't have impounded his car that fast! They must have let him go. But why? They don't know what I know. I know three numbers of his license plate and I know what he looks like. I know he had roof-racks on that car. Stupid cops! Too bad for them. Good for me!*

Sunny had a big "shit-eating" grin on his rugged face, as he drove past the black unmarked police cruiser, with the two detectives sitting in it, doing their paper work and munching on donuts.

NINETEEN

Sunny could hear Babe waiting behind the door as usual as he slid the key into the lock and she heard the click of the dead-bolt open. She was always anxious to greet her master; he gave her a pat on her golden head.

"Hey Babe, lets go outside," he told her as she followed him out for a pee.

Back inside the loft, Sunny checked his phone messages. There were several voices to call back. Geena, mom, and Ellen all seemed eager to talk to Sunny. The message from his mother was letting him know, she wanted to take him for lunch. Geena wanted to hookup for dinner, and Ellen didn't say what she wanted.

There was no time to phone anyone right now. Sunny still had an unfinished job to do. He had a raging compulsion to meet up with Mr. Icy-Blue Eyes again.

Sunny fed his faithful companion her dinner and then he looked at the clock on the kitchen stove. It was 4:45 pm already. *Shit time flies, when you're having fun!*

He grabbed an apple from the fridge and guided his pearly white incisors into the crispy antioxidant, as he rounded the bamboo dividers and ventured into his bedroom. Sunny took another bite of the forbidden fruit and then set it on the dresser. He knelt down and pulled the small rectangular, brown cardboard package out from under the bed. Sunny plopped himself on the bed. From his belt-loop he removed "buddy", the Spyderco blade that went with him everywhere. He slid the serrated stainless steel blade into the edge of the package and cut through the packing tape. Two opposite ends and along the top, with the sharp knife edge and into the box he stared.

It wasn't very large, in fact it was quite small or maybe compact would be a better description. *Compact, yeah that's it!* Sunny lifted the charcoal black, device out of the box. *What a beauty!* It was the size of a small cellphone and looked very similar to the older model flip-up phones, except it delivered 975,000 volts instead of text messages. The little beauty, wasn't the first one Sunny had owned, but it was smaller and carried more "snap, crackle and pop". Like all electronics on the market today, they get better and better as time advances. His last "stun gun" was clunky and not very concealable; it was definitely "old school" and it eventually ended up at the bottom of the murky Fraser River.

The stun gun, as it was known in the security and surveillance industry was not manufactured in Canada, nor was it legal to own one, but easy enough to have shipped into Canada. And it was top of the line! Nothing but the best!

Millions of packages are shipped internationally across borders every day, and although every single package goes through security scanners, not all contraband or prohibited products are detected. The reason is simple enough; human error! Security measures at the borders are only as effective as the agents working the machines and checking the packages. Many items are just processed without any type of internal inspection of the packaging.

DOG WITH A BONE

It's not the first time Sunny has received foreign mail with something inside, that's forbidden in Canada. Sunny's idea, was to use the old, "I didn't know it wasn't legal in Canada" card; if the package had been confiscated as illegal merchandise. Generally, any confiscated goods are supposedly destroyed, by Canada Customs and the receiver of the illegal wares would be issued a warning letter, stating the consequences that may be dealt by the authorities, if it was to happen a second time.

Sunny was a gambler! His motto: "Do it Now!" Why not take a chance and *do it now!* What's the worst that could happen? They (the border patrol: Canada Customs) destroy the stun gun, or probably one of the corrupt border guards would keep it and take it home for him or herself. And Sunny would be out some money. *Big fucking deal!* No jail time for receiving something other than drugs in the mail. Hell, rapists don't even get jail time in some cases!

Sunny carried the handy little treasure into his kitchenette and pulled open the junk drawer, beside the cutlery drawer. He opened up a package containing two, nine volt batteries. The instructions that came with the stun gun, indicated, installing one, nine volt battery into the back of the electronic device.

After he installed the battery, he held it firmly in his right hand and pressed the black button on the side of the unit. Zzaaapppp! The voltage created, inside the copper wire wrapped coils, shot out of the tiny electrode on the end of the gun and danced across to the other tiny electrode beautifully, like a miniature bolt of sky-blue lightning! It was a magnificent sight to behold!

The digital clock on the kitchen stove now read 5:00 pm. Sunny whipped over to the couch, plunked himself into the soft leather and grabbed the TV remote. The early news was on Global and he wanted an update on the tragic events that normally took place around the world, but mainly he was interested in the crime scene around the lower mainland.

Two vehicle hit and runs, one bus driver assault, drug busts, gang violence and shootings and the wretched dog killer from Burnaby. No updates on the Fraser murders.

As the story of the beaten rottweiler aired, Sunny could feel his blood run cold. He clenched both fists as tight as he could. He looked over at his own dog; she was drinking from her water bowl. Sunny wondered in his mind, how could anyone, on this godless planet do something so horrible to their own faithful best friend. He just found it incomprehensible.

The only word that came to his mind, for persons of that nature, was "bully". Those sub-humans that tortured or killed innocent and helpless animals, children or women were nothing more than bullies! Sunny abhorred bullies!

He sat intently on the edge of the Italian black leather sofa, glaring at the fifty inch flat screen TV, listening to the reporters and the SPCA members gathered around the outside of the Cottonwood Manor. The cameras showed the news media inside the hallway of the old building. A quick flash of the cameraman's handiwork revealed the door and unit number of the animal mangler's apartment.

Number thirty-one! Thank-you Mr. Cameraman, thank-you very much! Wow! They hardly ever show the public where these assholes of the earth live!

Sunny made a mental note of the unit number and the address of the perpetrator. He was really good with numbers. He had a natural ability to remember numbers and calendar dates. All of his credit card numbers and drivers licence numbers were stored in the archive department of his brain.

Sunny went into his closet and grabbed his black leather fanny pack. He bought it in Mexico, about twelve years ago, when he was on vacation in Mazatlan. Only paid five bucks for it. Something like that made in Canada, would have cost at least forty. He threw the stun gun, his black Mechanix gloves and several other items into the leather pouch. The beauty of this particular fanny pack was that it was very streamlined and fit to his waistline snugly, so that when his t-shirt hung down over it, it was completely concealed. Like a magician, he called it his "fun bag".

Sunny's cellphone rang again. He checked the incoming display. It was Geena again. *Pick up or not? Might as well pick up.* "Hi cupcake! I did get your message, but I was going to call you later."

"Just wanted to know if you were up, for going to dinner?" Geena asked.

"Would love to, but I can't right now, maybe a late dinner? I will call you later, okay?" Sunny said.

"Well I guess if you're busy now, later will have to do!" Geena said.

"I'm just heading out the door, I will phone you later on tonight, cupcake!" Sunny reassured her. "Bye."

He set his phone on the kitchenette counter, patted Babe's head, grabbed another apple for the road, then clipped his fun bag around his waist, underneath his black t-shirt. Out through the door he sprang.

Detectives Johnson Fong and Bernard Drake rolled into 312 Main Street's parking lot and exchanged waves and nods with the other members coming and going from the

Station. As they entered through the back way, Detectives Kuban and Rhodes were just on their way out to interview a suspect.

"How's the hunting trip going Bernie?" Rhodes asked, as she smiled at both men.

"Victory!" Drake retorted.

Kuban threw up his hands and made an inquisitive gesture. "Really? No shittin' us guys, this is serious business here!"

"Fuck Mikey, do you really think we would make a joke out of this case? Some of us have kids too, you know!" Drake scoffed.

"Yeah I know, relax man, it was just an automatic dumb reaction," Kuban said.

"Well, tell us!" Rhodes asked impatiently, as she flicked her hair over her right shoulder.

"It was a freak thing. Johnny and I were just heading south on Victoria Drive, about to cross 33rd Avenue, when this car runs the amber light, coming from the east. We were going to let it go until Johnny noticed that the car kind of matched the description of the vehicle we're all searching for. So we pull him over," said Drake.

"The dude was real nervous, but he produced his drivers license and registration. But get this ... while I'm waiting for him to hand me his license and registration papers, I notice faint scratch marks on the roof of the car. The car isn't registered to him, it's registered to a woman, he says it's his sister, but they have different last names. A married name. So we ran a check on the registered vehicle list, and she checked out as the owner all-right. We also ran a check to see if it was stolen, but nothing reported. The address on his license, is the same address as the registered owner. An apartment on Sussex Avenue in fucking Burnaby!" Fong explained.

"You know what that means!" whined Drake. "Fucking RCMP! We will have to jump through hoops and red tape in order to get a search warrant for that apartment. We could have impounded the car, but we need a little more than just the guys license. But when we ran a check on him, nothing came up. No warrants, no outstanding tickets, no previous convictions, not a darn thing. I'd sure like to know if those roof-racks are stashed at that apartment."

"Those racks and the tire treads are our first real piece of evidence!" Rhodes chimed. "If we can get a search warrant for the apartment and find the roof-racks, we can impound the vehicle and then let forensics go over the car with a fine tooth comb. But let's be real, that car is only one of many, still on the road, it may not even be the one we're looking for."

"Yeah, but it's a great start and the way things have been going, I have a good hunch that we may be on the right track," Drake noted. "We're on our way up to see Winters, to see if he can get this search warrant in action," Fong said, as he scratched the back of his head.

"What was the suspects name?" asked Kuban.

"Clayton Webber, age forty-seven," replied Fong. "We'll do some more background checks on him, after we talk to Winters, just to make sure we don't miss anything."

"May the Good Lord be with you two, we'll cross our fingers for that search warrant. We're on our way to interview a suspect over on West Broadway. Turns out that a registered driver of a '96 blue Chevy Corsica is a twenty-eight year old habitual felon. Two counts of robbery and attempted rape of an eighty year old woman. He did his time and is now out on parole. He has been out of jail during the time the murders had occurred," Kuban said.

"Not a nice boy!" Rhodes added.

"Good luck on that one too, keep your pepper spray handy! A little prick like that needs to be sprayed, just for being a prick!" Drake chuckled.

"Yeah ... he's not really a little prick ... apparently, from his rap sheet, he stands six foot four, and has a violent streak," Rhodes said.

"Like I said, keep your pepper spray handy!" repeated Drake.

"I prefer my Smithy!" Rhodes replied as she patted her service pistol on her hip.

The four detectives all had a good laugh and then parted ways.

The place was dimly lit, with low-level mood lighting and medium length aromatic candles, sitting on each white satin cloth covered table; accompanied with glistening silverware and crystal wine glasses, begging to be filled with the finest Burgundy from the south of France.

"Ahh, Dr. Wilson ... how are you this evening?" asked the maitre d'.

"Very fine, Pierre, very fine indeed!" replied Dr. Randall Wilson.

"So nice to see you again Doctor. Your table is ready for you and your beautiful lady friend ... right this way please!" instructed the energetic headwaiter, as he led them through a maze of tables to their own private little booth.

"Tommy will be your waiter tonight sir, and if you would like anything special, please do not hesitate to ask."

"Thank-you Pierre," Wilson said as they sat down in their cozy little booth, across from each other.

As the maitre d' scurried away, Dr. Wilson's dinner date looked at him and quietly giggled, "Tommy? That doesn't sound French to me?"

"Well you know, they no doubt, try to get the real 'McCoy', but I'm sure the B.C. Labor Relations Act would come down on them as being discriminate or racist if they only hired employees with French names. Besides the French are becoming a minority in British Columbia now," the doctor answered.

"Maybe he could just pretend to be Jean or Gustave and try to fake an accent just for fun," humored the lady named Winona, sitting across from the doctor.

The plastic surgeon laughed and reached across the small table and held Winona's delicate hand in his. He caressed it tenderly. "We could ask him," he said.

"I haven't seen you laugh in a long time Randy, it really looks good on you," she said with a sparkle in her lovely blues eyes.

"Good evening Dr. Wilson, and Miss ..."

"Winona, my name is Winona."

"Miss Winona ... I will be your server tonight, my name is Tommy. Would you care for a drink while you are perusing the dinner menu?"

"Tommy, we would like a bottle of Dom Perignon if you don't mind please?" asked the good doctor.

"Yes sir, Dr. Wilson, I will be right back," Tommy answered.

The French restaurant was filling up quickly as it usually did on Friday nights. Expensive dinner jackets and silk and satin evening gowns decorated the well-heeled patrons who were dining. It was the doctor's favorite place to dine, although he hadn't dined here in months.

"I'm so happy Randy, that you asked me out for dinner tonight. I was really worried about you ... you seemed to be greatly withdrawn in the last four months," Winona said.

"I don't know what's come over me, I feel better than I have for months, that's true!" Wilson replied. "Do you believe in Angels, Winny?" he said with a crooked smile.

"Angels?" she curiously asked.

"Yes, Angels," as he kept smiling, "Angels?"

"You know, I think I do ... I mean I haven't really had any personal experiences with Angels. Although, I believe there may be different types of Angels among us. Randy, can I ask you a personal question? And please don't be offended, but have you been taking any medication, since ... well ... you know ..."

"Since Stephanie was murdered?" Wilson interjected.

"Yes, I'm sorry, I know it's a difficult subject, but I was wondering if ..."

"If I'm whacked out on prescription drugs?" he chuckled as he shook his head slowly from side to side. Well right after Stephanie's murder, I was taking anti-depressants, but I'm off of those now. I haven't taken any meds for about six months. No Winny, I'm not poppin' pills, I just ..."

"Ahh, here we have the special Dom for you my good Doctor and the Doctor's lovely lady, Miss Winona!" Tommy cheerfully said, as he uncorked the champagne, and then gracefully tipped and rolled the slender neck of the smooth bubbly, into the crystal wine glass, perched in front of Winona. Just enough for a taste!

She gently lifted the shimmering crystal to her cherry red voluptuous lips, almost in slow motion, as she seductively swirled the contents in the glass. Her lip gloss reflected glistening highlights of white, as if her mouth was wanting something more, than just the sweet choice of champagne connoisseurs. With the grace of a butterfly, she delicately sampled the nectar and then gave her nod of approval.

"Most excellent Miss Winona!" Tommy said as he then poured half a glass each into the couple's fine crystal. He then proceeded to ramble off the dinner specials of the night, and then told them he would be back in five to ten minutes for their order.

"He probably thinks you're my girlfriend, Winny," the plastic surgeon laughed.

"Oh my God, you're right! You know, I never thought about that. Why would he think, I'm your sister, I mean it's not like we look alike, do we?" Winona giggled. "Maybe I should have a name-tag pinned on me, that reads 'sister'."

"It's no big deal, we're out having fun, who cares what people think? Let them think what they want," said Wilson, with another big smile. "We should spend more time together Winny ... remember when we were kids growing up. We always hung out with each other and all of our friends too, down at the park and the skating rink, and stuff like that. Strange! Then people become adults and crawl into their own little shells and become hermit crabs!"

"It's so true Randy, we all spend most of our life, trying to make a name for ourselves and in the meantime, life is passing us by. And then something tragic happens ... like ... Stephanie, and then we stop and realize, that life isn't about material things, it's about family and friends and memories, not 'stuff'. That's what's really important, Randy!" his sister explained, as a tear rolled down her rosy, prominent cheek.

He reached out again, across the table and with his masculine hand gently enveloped hers. "I love you sister," he whispered to her, with tears welling in his eyes.

"I love you too brother," she said back.

And then they both burst out laughing, with tears running down their faces.

Winona opened her purse, looking for a tissue, while Dr. Wilson rubbed his face with his hands, drying off the emotional wetness.

As his sister dabbed away the dampness from her blue eyes, he told her, "I believe in Angels, Winny. Did you realize, that there are ten different types of Angels?"

Sniffling, she said, "no not really, I hadn't really gave it a lot of thought ... although I'm sure there are different kinds, I suppose ... just like people?"

"Exactly, sister, exactly. At least ten types of Angels, but in my books, maybe more!"

"Really? Ten different types of Angels ... how do you know that Randy?" Winona asked with another curious look.

"Well it's not a secret you know, anyone familiar with the Bible, would know that. I mean I'm not going religious on you Winny, but since Stephanie was taken from me ... sometimes it makes it easier to cope with life knowing that the Angels took her to a beautiful place, you see."

"I understand Randy, you know I do," she said.

"We have Angels around us all the time, Winny. There are Archangels, Cherubs, Virtues, some called Thrones and I can't remember all the rest, but did you know that each and everyone one of us, has a Guardian Angel with us daily? It's true! But what I don't understand ... is where was Stephanie's Guardian Angel? How come she wasn't guarded against danger? Maybe that's why I am not a religious man, Winny," the doctor said solemnly.

"I don't know Randy, I don't."

"You know what I do believe in, though? Karma! I believe in the 'Angels of Vengeance'!" Wilson blurted out. I believe that son-of-a-bitch will be dealt the 'Ace-of-Spades' for what he did to my poor, lovely Stephanie. Mark my words, sister!"

"Randy, keep your voice down, people are starting to look this way," Winona said quietly.

"Ahhh, Dr. Wilson and Miss Winona, is everything okay?" Tommy asked with concern, as he wandered over from his station.

"Everything is just fine Tommy!" Wilson said.

"Are you ready to order?" Tommy asked the couple, while smiling.

"Why yes we are, Tommy," he happily answered. "We've never been so ready!" as he winked at his sister.

TWENTY

As Sunny cruised along Kingsway, in his shiny black Accord, his mind started to wander. He started thinking back to an earlier time, when his dad's mom, "Grandma", used to take him for walks through Stanley Park, when he was just a little boy.

After her church meeting on Sundays, Grandma would phone up Annie and Wade and ask to take little Sunny for a walk through the big park and afterwards for ice-cream to Dairy Queen or Ice-Cream World on Granville Street. She loved her grandson and often felt that spending the afternoon with him was just like the sweet icing on the cake!

Grandma was a very religious woman, a devout Christian and studied the Bible since she was a little girl. Her upbringing, by her parents had molded her into a believer of the Lord and the the Holy Ghost. Grandma's mother and father were adamant about the whole family attending the church every Sunday. It was like clockwork. They never missed a Sunday! All her friends of course were Christians as well. All except her own flesh and blood.

Her two sons, Wade and Timothy were made to go to church when they were youngsters, but they hated going, so Grandma let them off the hook. She couldn't get her husband to go to church either, so she always went with her church friends or by herself. Grandma was a very independent and stubborn woman, and decided that even if her own family were not interested in God or Jesus Christ, it wouldn't stop her from believing.

Eventually, when Sunny was old enough, Grandma asked permission from Annie and Wade, if she would be allowed to take young Sunny to Sunday School once or twice to see if he would like it. Of course they let her, after all, he was too young to really understand what all that "stuff" was really about anyway.

Sunny seemed to have lots of fun at Sunday School. The first time Grandma took him, he received a free chocolate bar, a Cadbury Caramilk. He sat in the basement of the Presbyterian House of the Lord, on 45th Avenue in Vancouver and sang gospel songs with all the other little children. Sunny didn't know that the songs he was singing to, was all about Jesus Christ and his Apostles. But he sang his little heart out anyway.

Grandma was very proud of her little religious grandson. So proud that she brought him back to church a second time. This time the Pastor handed little Sunny a red shiny Bible. He held it with both hands since his hands were so small. The Bible was an impressive sight to behold. Such a well made, thick and sturdy bound book it was.

And those words inside the Bible, with all those inarticulate phrases and meanings and passages of pre-modern day literature couldn't give any realistic meanings, other than rhetorical mumbo-jumbo to a small boy of six years old. But Grandma was proud, nevertheless to see her young grandson standing there at that moment, holding that red shiny Bible, in his wee hands, with a big smile on his face.

I can remember that day, just like it was yesterday!

After church was done for the day, Grandma would bundle little Sunny into the car and then they would head off to Stanley Park for the rest of the afternoon.

Grandma would drive her shiny Buick down Georgia Street, and then find a shady spot to park the car, near the entrance of the sprawling park. That way, the two churchgoers could easily stroll over to nearby Lost Lagoon and feed the ducks and geese. Sunny loved feeding the birds. The nineteen sixties style concession stand, near the lagoon, sold the birdseed for the waterfowl. Grandma would buy a bag of seed for a mere dime, for her and Sunny to scatter for the hungry birds.

Sunny and Grandma walked hand in hand until they would come upon a park bench and then they would set up base camp. Grandma always thought ahead for the two outdoor adventurers. This included packing a lunch for both of them. Peanut butter and jam or Swiss cheese and ham sandwiches, accompanied by a fruit juice drink. Sunny would take a few bites of his sandwich, and then grab a small handful of birdseed and run over to the group of ducks and geese and throw the seed with his best underhand, into the quacking melee.

The colorful birds would gobble up the seed and Sunny would give cheers of joy, clap his hands and stamp his feet. Then he would run back to the bench and take another bite of his sandwich as if to give him continued strength, in order to repeat the process over and over.

His favorites in the flock were the Trumpeter swans. Partly, because they were virgin white and as tall as he was, but mostly because they represented a "thing of beauty", even to a young boy, they were amazingly magnificent, something out of a fairy tale.

Of course, after feeding the birds and having finished their lunch, the next thing Grandma would like to do was to ask Sunny what he thought of Sunday School. She would listen intently to the young boy and answer any of his questions, and then she would offer some of her own random thoughts on the great "Savior" of the universe.

Quite often, Grandma would reach into her handbag and extract her own well worn copy of the Old Testament, the first of the two chief divisions of the Christian Scripture, and then pick out selected verses that she had earlier highlighted. Grandma would sit on that park bench on those sunny Sunday afternoons in her Sunday "best" and recite her own sermon to her inquisitive grandson.

Some of the Bible verses that she read to little Sunny, really made no sense to him, so with the utmost patience Grandma would interpret the ramblings in her own simple words, so that they made some kind of sense to the six year old boy.

He liked Revelations 6:8, the one about *"and I looked and behold, a pale horse, and he who sat on it, his name was Death, and Hell followed with him"*, probably because of the horse and that the swear word Hell was in the sentence. To hear his Grandma say the word Hell, was pretty amusing to a kid. Sometimes she wondered if he was getting any of this Bible stuff at all.

Sunny's favorite verse of the entire book that she had preached to him on those cherished Sunday afternoons, was the famous *"eye for an eye, tooth for a tooth"* principle.

"What does that mean Grandma? An eye for an eye?" Sunny asked the wise woman.

"Grandson, an eye for an eye means that if someone hurts another person, then the person that did the hurting, will be punished in the same way, that they hurt that person. Do you understand what I am saying to you Sunny?" Grandma asked her innocent grandson.

"I think so Grandma. Kind of like, if that white swan hurt that goose, then that goose can hurt the swan back?" he wondered as they looked over at the waterfowl.

"Yes Grandson, yes that is exactly what it means. The same goes for people Sunny, if anyone was to cause harm to your mother, then that person should be harmed the same way! God watches over everyone Sunny and He would want no harm to come to anyone, but if it did, for whatever reason, then He wants 'an eye for an eye', do you understand this?" Grandma asked curiously.

"Yes Grandma, I do!" he replied.

Sunny snapped out of his mental reminiscing and remembered why he hadn't stayed on the religious road like his loving grandmother. He learned as he was growing up, that there was no God above, after he had kept praying night after night for Denny Barker to quit kicking the shit out of him daily! *If there really was a God, he or she wouldn't let all the bad things happen on this planet! Or maybe this planet really is "Hell on Earth" after-all!*

Sunny cherished those early days with his Grandma, and although she may have had her own views on life and religion, the one principle that she had drilled into his head and that he lives by, to this day, is "an eye for an eye".

Sunny turned the car stereo on low and looked in his rear-view mirror. *Too much damn traffic on this street!* He was nearing Burnaby, getting closer to Sussex Avenue.

Chief Constable Joe Winters was in his office, talking on his phone, when Detectives, Johnson Fong and Bernard Drake knocked on his door. Through the door window, he motioned with his big hand to come on in as he kept yakking on the phone. The two policemen entered and both took up seats on the opposite side of Winters' cluttered oak desk.

"Gimme a sec!" Winters said as he covered the phone mouthpiece with his right hand.

Fong fidgeted and Drake looked down at his scuffed up shoes, with his hands folded together, in between his knees. "Okay, I'll get back to you," Winters said to the caller. He then hung up the receiver and sat back in his big black leather chair, "what's up guys?"

"We need a search warrant Boss," Fong blurted out.

"Yeah, I heard something about that ... word travels like lightning through this department," Winters said. "Tell me why you think you need a search warrant, and we ARE talking about the Fraser case, right?"

"Yes sir, we are," added Drake. "We pulled a car over on 33rd Avenue, earlier today and well ... the guy just seemed 'out of sorts' you know. I mean he seemed real nervous, and there were scratch marks on the roof of the car. It was a blue Pontiac Tempest sir. The car does match the description we've been pursuing."

"Look Bernard, scratch marks on the roof is definitely a good indication that it could be the suspect vehicle, but we need more proof than that, in order to obtain a search warrant of the premises. You know that more than one car in this city, is capable of having roof-racks installed on the roof. We can't ask for a warrant on that alone, or that the guy seemed nervous when you pulled him over. All kinds of folks get real nervous when a cop walks up to their window. You guys should do some more investigating on this guy. Did you check out his tire treads when you had him pulled over?" Winters asked.

"Not a thorough search. I mean it was on the side of the road and the traffic was non-stop. I know that a visual probably wasn't good enough. I guess we should have taken some pictures of the tire treads and then we could have matched them up with the evidence," Drake explained.

"You're damn right a visual isn't good enough. We can't obtain a search warrant on a suspicion, we need something more, we need to know that those tire treads actually match the ones that were left at the murder scenes. If you had taken pictures of those treads and they had even looked remotely similar, well then we could request an Impound Warrant and seize the car for inspection. Then we could compile our Information to Obtain (ITO) documents and warrant form and then present it to the judge to obtain the Feeney Warrant in order to search the guy's residence," Winters said.

"More homework needed!" Fong said as he shook his head up and down.

"Yes, boys, more homework is needed! We know where this asshole lives now, so go back to his place and get some closeup pictures of his tires and then we can go on from there. Kuban and Rhodes are going to check out some ex-con over on West Broadway. The guy could also be a possible suspect; his DNA was never registered, my guess is that the presiding judge on his attempted rape of the eighty year old woman forgot to order the DNA submission. For some strange reason, my gut tells me that it's not him. He doesn't fit the profile of a child killer. But we need to check everyone out, just in case," Winters said.

"It's already six fifteen! We'll go and have some dinner first and then we'll head over to Sussex Avenue and do some surveillance and see if we can get some digital images of those tires," Fong said to Winters as he looked over at Drake and nodded.

"As soon as you get those photos, send them over to forensics," Winters commanded.

"You bet, Boss!" Fong answered with a smile.

The two detectives walked out of Winters' office and down through the corridor to their waiting cruiser.

"Where do you want to eat Bernie?" Fong asked his partner.

"Let's head over to Whitespot and bug Carol," Drake said. "It's on the way."

"Thanks for meeting me here Ellen," Geena said as the two gals sat down at a table in the corner.

"No problem, Geena, I needed to get out and have a drink anyway," Ellen said loudly, as the crowd was getting rather noisy.

"How have you been lately?" Geena asked her.

"Great, really," Ellen fibbed. *Actually not great at all,* she thought to herself. *I can't tell her what happened to Sunny and me ... unless she already knows? If she knows, I'll let her bring it up.* "And how was your trip to Seattle?"

"We had so much fun ... my sister and I. Did lots of shopping, for shoes, clothes, and took lots of pictures, I like taking pictures. I'm like a photo-nerd!" Geena laughed.

"Good evening ladies, can I get you some drinks? Oh, hey you two, how's it going? I didn't recognize either of you at first!" Lola chimed.

"Hey, we're great, Lola, you know ... two hotties out on the town, for a drink!" Geena quipped.

"It's good to see you ladies out having fun, but where's the man tonight?" Lola asked.

"That's what we're wondering, he seems to be real bloody busy lately. He hasn't been here tonight has he?" Geena wondered.

"No, he hasn't, but I could have used his help earlier ... it's been real busy, payday for most of the patrons I guess," Lola said to the ladies.

"You know Sunny ... always on the move, that's what keeps him fit," Ellen surmised.

"That's so true. Throwing assholes out of this bar also keeps him fit ... so whatcha having girls? Paralyzers are on sale tonight!" Lola sang.

"Sounds good to me, Lola," Ellen said as she looked over at Geena.

"Me too! Make mine a double!" Geena said with a big happy grin.

"Okay ladies, I'll be right back with your drinks."

"So Ellen, have you noticed anything bugging Sunny lately, I mean when you saw him last?" Geena asked.

Ellen knew, that if Sunny wanted to tell his girlfriend about what happened in the woods a week ago, he would have told her. He had told her not to mention it to Geena, so she wouldn't worry about it. *It's not my place to say anything and Sunny said he wasn't going to tell her,* Ellen thought to herself. "No not really Geena, I know Sunny always seems to be preoccupied with everything around him, but it's ... it's just who he is, I guess," Ellen reasoned.

"You don't think that he might be seeing someone else, do you Ellen?" Geena asked nervously.

"God no! Sunny isn't like that, you know that Geena!"

"Yeah, I know, I don't know why I even thought that, it's funny how the mind can imagine stuff like that," Geena said as she shook her head, as if disgusted with herself for even thinking that.

"Guys are guys, they act different than us, it's sometimes best not to try and figure them out," Ellen said.

"Funny, that's exactly what Sunny says to me, in reverse ... he says he doesn't understand what makes us tick. Women run on emotions and guys run on reality, is what he tells me," Geena laughed. "I hate to admit it, but sometimes I think it's a true statement."

"Hey look! There's Big Bob over by the pool-table," Ellen said as she pointed.

"That man is as big as a mountain, he's the guy Sunny talks about, the guy who he helped kick some ass in here one night, apparently," Geena added.

"Here's your drinks ladies!" Lola chanted as she laid the beverages on the oak table. I tried to get Sunny to pull a shift earlier today, but I guess he had other shit going on?"

"He's busy, he may join us later though," Geena said.

"You gals have fun and I'll be back in a bit to check on you," Lola said as she turned and went to the next table.

Ellen and Geena raised their glasses and clinked them together. "Cheers!" both ladies said at the same time as they sampled the potent delicious concoctions.

As Sunny neared Sussex Avenue, he slowed his car down and clicked his right turn signal on. He wheeled his Accord around the corner and could feel his adrenaline molecules starting to recharge. Driving south on Sussex, he turned left at the first side-street, and then parked his car at the curbside, about fifty yards from the corner. He reached into the glove compartment and removed an item. He then pulled up his right jean pant leg and slid that item down his sock. Sunny grabbed the newspaper that was lying on the passenger seat and rolled it up. He checked out all his surroundings, casually, up the street, in his rear-view mirror and both sides of the street, while sitting in his vehicle.

All looks quiet around here! Do it now! Sunny exited his car and put the rolled up newspaper under his arm. He clicked his remote to lock his car and then strolled down the sidewalk towards the older apartment building. Within minutes he was nearing the concrete ramp leading to the underground parking.

Sunny pulled the newspaper from under his left arm and unrolled it. Pretending to read the front page of The Province newspaper, he nonchalantly walked down the concrete ramp into the darkness of the parkade.

Sunny surveyed the parked cars in the dimly lit surroundings of the concrete underground. The Tempest wasn't there. *Perfect!* Nobody else in sight either. Just the shadows of his own body stretched out across the cement floor.

He opened his fanny pack and removed his Mechanix gloves and slipped them on. The stun gun he slid into his right rear jean pocket, all the while keeping a watch on the ramp entrance.

Sunny pinched his lock-pick and torsion-bar between his careful fingers and moved towards the storage room door. Within seconds he had violated the tumblers inside the lock, and as if in slow motion the dead-bolt slid sideways with a clunk and the steel door opened. It was dark inside the room, just like the last time. Sunny reached for the light switch and turned it on. *Nobody here in the dark, except maybe a spider or two. Must check to make sure though!*

Sunny walked the length of the corridor and then quickly looked both ways at the end of the "T", just to be positive that no one else was in the storage room. He then quickly went back to the door, as he heard the rumble of a vehicle entering the parkade. Sunny flicked off the lights and cracked the door open, just a sliver, so he could peer out, without being noticed.

It was a red Mazda 3, driven by a woman from what Sunny could see, peeking from his hiding spot. She parked in number twenty-eight, on the far side of the lot. He watched her exit from her car, set her alarm with her remote, and then she headed for the elevator.

He waited for the elevator doors to close behind her and then he stepped out from the shadows of the dark storage room. About twenty feet from the storage room was one of many concrete pillars throughout the parkade. Sunny ambled over to the wide pillar and hid behind it, out of site from the parkade entrance and out of site from the elevator door.

Now the waiting game. *Just like a black widow spider lingering for an unsuspecting fly,* he thought to himself. The pumping action of his heart was so distinct, it was as though, he could actually hear it. He kept his newspaper with him, folded up and laying at his feet, just in case he needed to pretend he was reading the news. *The sound of another car entering!*

The Whitespot Restaurant was crowded with Friday night hungry patrons, mostly families. As always at the Whitespot, there was the dreaded lineup at the door. Never a good place to stand or sit. People blocking the entrance, seemed to be a great deterrent to make a hungry person go somewhere else for grits.

But not Detectives Drake and Fong, no sir, they always got seated, when Carol was on shift, even if there was a family ahead of them waiting to be seated. They would somehow, always get her attention and then she would find them a small table, somewhere out of site. She had no problem telling the waiting customers, that the cops partners, were already seated at a table and that the detectives were just late and would be joining them. Carol loved cops and she loved lying to people!

Fong and Drake were good detectives, but they never missed an opportunity to butt in front of the lineup of the hungry diners. They justified their arrogance, by reasoning that they were out to find a "bad guy", rapist or killer or whatever their mission was at the time, and that they were doing their public service for the people, so the people should let them eat first, so that they could get on with their job.

"How's your food?" Drake asked Fong.

"Great, as always. Sure is busy in here. I wonder if the child killer eats here? You think?" Fong asked Drake.

"That's a weird thought Johnny, but you know something, that piece of shit *could* be in here right now," Drake whispered.

The two detectives glanced around the restaurant, as they ate their meals.

"Another round ladies?" Lola chirped as she sauntered over to Geena and Ellen.

"Hell yeah! We want another round, and make them doubles, my good friend," Geena shouted over the noise.

The bar was packed, as it always was on a Friday night. East Side had no shortage of drinkers, lots of Irish and Italians in the 'hood. It was getting noisier as the night went on.

"Hey, do you ladies know those guys sitting up at the bar?" Lola asked, as she turned around and pointed at two

DOG WITH A BONE

men on the far right side of the bar. One guy was wearing a jean jacket and the other had on a green and yellow plaid shirt.

"No, never seen them before," Ellen said.

"Me neither," Geena added, "why do you ask?"

"They keep rambling on about you two, like they know you or something," Lola explained. "I'll be back with your drinks," as Lola turned and walked away.

"I wonder who they are?" Ellen asked Geena.

"Probably nobody. Two horny fuckers, who left their wives at home," Geena laughed out loudly.

"That one dude keeps looking over here, Geena," Ellen said nervously. "He's getting off his seat ... I think he's coming over this way ... yeah, I think he's coming to our table."

"Well quit looking over at them," Geena said.

"Hi ladies, how's it goin'?" the dude with the jean jacket asked

"We're fine, just real fine!" replied Geena.

"My buddy and I were just wondering if you ladies, would be interested in us, joining your table?" he asked.

"Uh, not tonight, we're busy talking and besides we're waiting for my boyfriend," Geena answered.

"Well, we could hang out with you, till your boyfriend gets here if you like?" Mr. Jean Jacket insisted.

"Like I said, we're BUSY, so why don't you take a hike back to your boyfriend!" Geena said rudely.

"Easy bitch! Maybe you need some medication or something!" he snapped back at her.

"Is there a problem Geena?" Lola asked, as she set their drinks on the table.

"Not really, this creep was just leaving," Geena said.

Lola turned to the guy and said, "if you cause trouble, or harass these ladies, or anyone else in my bar, you'll have to leave!"

"Whatever!" the guy said as he turned and went back to his seat at the bar.

"Such an asshole! What the hell is wrong with people anyway?" Ellen said to the girls.

"Brainless, Ellen ... most people walking around today are brainless!" Lola said, raising her eyebrows. "Let me know if they bother you again, okay."

"Sure Lola, no pronlem, we won't let two idiots ruin our night, will we Ellen?" Geena said.

"Not a chance!" Ellen answered, as she raised her drink in the air for a toast.

It wasn't the suspects car, coming down the ramp. It was a newer, lime green, Volkswagen Beetle. Sunny hated those new Beetles. He had owned an older seventies model VW Beetle, and that car actually resembled a beetle bug. The newer ones just didn't have it, as far as he was concerned.

Sunny carefully watched the Beetle back into unit number nineteen, in the next row of cars, down from the killers parking spot.

A man of about forty years old, got out of the car, with a cigarette in his mouth and lifted a bag of groceries from the passenger seat. He then proceeded to the elevator door. Waiting for the elevator, he dropped the cigarette on the ground and stepped on it. Then he glanced around the concrete parkade slowly, as if he sensed someone lurking in the semi-darkness.

Slowly, Sunny eased his body back, behind the gray cold pillar, keeping watch of the man's shadowy silhouette on the wall. Finally the elevator door opened with a clunk and a thud. The smoker looked over his shoulder one last time as he entered the elevator.

Sunny could feel his anxiety building up and then releasing, over and over, like the ocean waves crashing into the beach and then retreating back out to sea. Minutes seemed like hours. *What if the fucker stays out all night? Maybe he's hunting his next victim! If only those damn cops hadn't pulled him over, I would still be tailing him right now. Instead I'm sitting here like a hungry spider, in the dark! Don't complain, he has to come back at some point. Hopefully tonight!*

Another twenty-five minutes had passed, before the next car entered the underground parking lot. It was a white mini-van. A late thirties couple and their young child got out of the van with a wooden box, full of stuff. It looked like kids toys. They headed for the storage room. *Damn it! They'll see that it's unlocked.*

The man carried the box over to the storage room door, while the woman stuck the key into the dead-bolt lock and turned it. She opened the door and then turned on the light. It was as if she didn't even realize that the lock was already open.

Sunny chuckled to himself. It was like the old saying goes ... *"If you're going to break into a place, save your energy and try the door first, it might just be unlocked"*.

The couple emerged from the storage room, about ten minutes later without the box. The man then proceeded to lock the door and off they went straight to the elevator. Sunny watched them disappear into the outdated contraption. *That's just bloody great! He locked the darn door.*

Sunny waited a few minutes, to make sure the "coast was clear". As he left his covert location, he rummaged through his fun bag, for his lock-pick and quickly walked back over to the storage room door, looking over his shoulder. Within moments he heard the dead-bolt slide open with a clunk!

The sound of a car was approaching the entryway. Sunny ran back to his secluded post and hid behind the wide pillar out of site.

The vehicle rambled down the ramp into the half-full parkade. Sunny kept tight to the concrete pillar, like a pancake stuck to a cast iron frying pan without grease. The rubber tires squealed on the smooth cement floor as it wheeled off the ramp and around the corner. It was the blue Pontiac Tempest!

Sunny could feel his heart pounding again, just like the Scottish drummer in an Irish parade! But he knew how to keep calm and cool in a situation like this. His Master in karate school had taught him to always "stay calm and think; in dangerous situations; only a fool rushes in".

Besides, Sunny knew first hand, that this man was violent and more than likely armed, since he had pointed a handgun right at Ellen and himself, that scary day in the woods.

The Tempest slowly eased into the number ten parking space. Sunny watched intently from his secret spot. The man turned off his engine. From where Sunny was watching, it looked like he was leaning over his car-seat and reaching into his glove compartment for something. But the crappy light in the underground parkade was very dim, so it was near impossible for Sunny to see what the guy was reaching for. After a few moments, he sat up and wiped off his dashboard with a rag. Then he then lit up a cigarette and sat in the car for a few minutes blowing smoke out of his window. The minutes seemed like hours to Sunny, but he had to time everything just right, with no mistakes! After all, he had Babe to look after, and Geena would surely miss him, and his parents too.

Sunny spread his forefingers and index fingers on each hand and then brought his hands together to push the fingers of the gloves tight. He did this with each set of fingers and thumbs, so that his gloves fit like a second skin on his stocky hands. He patted his right rear pocket, kind of like he was patting Babe on her golden head, in a motion of confidence, to know that the stun gun was still there.

"That hit the spot Bernie! I was famished, now we can get on with our mission," Fong said to his partner. "Flag down Carol so we can get the hell out of this place."

"Maybe she'll give us a super discount like last time," Drake said as he winked at Fong.

"Well maybe you should wink at her instead of me, she seems to have a 'cop crush' on you Bernie."

"Anything for a free meal, eh?" Drake replied, as he then waved Carol over to the table.

"How was dinner gentlemen?" Carol asked them.

"Superb as always sweetie? Drake answered back. He flirted with her for a few minutes and then she said she'd be right back with their bill.

Fong looked across the table at Drake and asked him, "what if the suspect isn't at his residence, how long do we wait? I mean we're already two hours into overtime."

"Shit Johnny, we'll wait all night if we have to, the force doesn't care how much time we put in, besides it's the taxpayers footin' the bill anyway. As long as we can stay awake, we'll be there all fuckin' night if we have to! Old man Winters will blow his stack, if we don't get some pictures of those tire treads or some other evidence,"

Drake scoffed. "Let's get a couple of coffees to go, the extra caffeine will keep us awake!"

Fong drummed the table top while Carol made her way back to the detectives with their bill.

"Hey Sugar, can we get a couple of large coffees to go, pretty please?" Drake mushed.

"Of course Bernard, I'll get them right away for you and it's my treat," Carol insisted as she placed the check on the table top.

"Your turn to pay Johnny, I got it last time, besides it looks like she gave us fifty percent off, again!"

Fong reached for his wallet as he perused the check laying in front of him.

The cops waited patiently for their coffees, scanning the restaurant, similar to vultures waiting for their prey to finally succumb in the scorching desert heat. Both cops were wondering what the night would bring.

Carol brought the coffees "to go" back to the police detectives and accepted the money from Fong. The men got up from their cozy table, bade farewell to their little hussy server girl and then wound their way through the busy restaurant.

Drake glanced at his watch, "it's already seven thirty Johnny! Shit times flies. We better get our asses over to that guys place before we turn into pumpkins for Christ sake."

Finally Mr. Icy-Blue Eyes emerged from the car, with his cigarette stub, stuck to his fat lips and the blue smoke curling upwards into his piercing eyes, as he squinted from the acrid, cancer causing smoke burning his orbs. The creep looked around the parkade as if he was expecting someone to be there.

Sunny could see him perfectly from where he was stationed. He was a large individual, standing about six foot two, maybe weighing about two hundred and twenty-five pounds, with a beer gut protruding out from his rumpled, brown corduroy jacket. His brown cowboy boots were scuffed and worn. With that five o'clock shadow stuck to his face, and the way he held that short cigarette butt in his mouth, painted the picture of a man that was a fat, lazy slob of a bully!

Mr. Icy-Blue Eyes spat the cow-assed butt onto the concrete floor and then deep within his sinuses, he commanded his nasal fluids with a loud inward growl to form a massive snot wad in his throat. With a loud disgusting spew, he "horked a loogie" right onto the windshield of the car parked next to his. He snickered at his handiwork as he slammed his car door shut and then lumbered to the back of his car. Looking around the underground parking lot again, the man slowly made his way to the elevator.

Everything about the man seemed suspicious and sinister to Sunny. The way he looked, the way he sneered, the way he walked. *And those eyes! Those pale icy-blue piercing eyes! They could give a person nightmares,* Sunny thought to himself.

Sunny could feel his adrenaline racing. It was now or never. *Do it now! Do it now!*

Sunny Kruzik morphed his body into his stoic predatory mode. Out from the cold, gray concrete pillar he slunk unobtrusively towards the back of the intended target. In his black sneakers, he silently and quickly, crept up behind the larger man, removing his stun gun from his back pocket, as he moved closer in.

The man was almost at the elevator door, by the time Sunny was about seven feet from his back. Without hesitation, the guy turned around to see Sunny right behind him. His icy-blue eyes widened with surprised fright. He reached into his corduroy jacket with his left hand to grab something. Sunny could see the butt end of a pistol sticking out from his coat.

With the "speed of sound" Sunny jammed the electrodes of his stun gun into the monster's Adam's apple. Sunny could feel the compact unit in his hand heat up instantly as it buzzed like a mosquito on steroids!

The big man made a loud gagging noise as he started twitching almost immediately, with his eyes rolling upwards into the eye sockets, so that only the whites could be seen. He lurched forward, shaking uncontrollably and then his large overweight repulsive body toppled to the concrete floor, with a dull, sickly thud! His face smashed into the ground with a crunch. The big guy laid on the cold floor, his nerves still twitching involuntarily.

Sunny didn't have much time. He knew that the high voltage from his little friend, zapped the guy into unconsciousness for only five to ten minutes.

Sunny rolled the heavy-weight over onto his back. He could see that the fall, had broken the creep's nose. Pretty much flattened it right out, with blood leaking from both nostrils. Spittle oozed from both corners of his mouth from the deadly shock of the stun gun.

With both gloved hands, Sunny grabbed the dark curly hair on the incapacitated man's head and dragged him over towards the storage room. *Thank God, this floor is smooth!* The weight of the big man, made Sunny thankful for his great physical condition. Working out and staying in shape, gave him the advantage of dragging the heavy load. *Only twenty more feet to go!*

Sunny opened the unlocked steel door and held it with his foot as he inched the man inside. Once inside, Sunny locked the door and then proceeded to drag the big guy by his greasy hair, down the corridor to unit number ten.

TWENTY-ONE

The accident happened just moments before Detectives Drake and Fong left the Whitespot Restaurant. Two cars and a pickup truck were involved in the gruesome crash.

One police cruiser with it's flashing red and blue lights was already at the scene. Another siren, wailing in the night air, was close by. A small crowd of onlookers were starting to gather on the sidewalk. A few of the curious people ran over to the crumpled vehicles to see if they could help in any way.

"Shit! We'll never get to Sussex!" Drake fumed.

"Relax Bernie, one thing at a time! There may be injuries, and we're second on the scene," Fong said, as they pulled their car up to the crash and turned on their flashing lights.

As the two homicide detectives left the confines of their comfy car, they could hear several sirens coming from all different directions.

That's the way it is with emergencies. Someone phones 911 and then the dispatcher makes the distress call to all available emergency personnel within the area; firetrucks, ambulances and police. Everyone shows up at the accident scene, usually more emergency personnel than needed. Better more, than not enough! And always at the taxpayers expense. Heaven knows that most accidents are not really accidents at all, usually it's stupidity, someone not paying attention to the road. Texting or talking on one's cellphone, seems to be overtaking the drinking and driving so-called accidents.

"This looks like a bad one!" Fong said to his partner as they got closer to the smashed up vehicles.

As the two detectives surveyed the situation, they both realized that the passenger in the Toyota Echo was already dead. It looked like a female, but the face had hit the windshield or dash board, and the blood had made the gender unrecognizable. The driver of the car was already out of the vehicle and sitting over on the curb, holding his head, with several witnesses attending to him.

The driver of the other car, an earlier model Subaru was still sitting inside; an elderly man of about sixty-five years old. He was just sitting there, calm as a cucumber. So calm, that Drake thought he too, was deceased. That is, until he turned his head slowly to look at the homicide detective.

Steam was hissing out from under the crumpled hood of the old man's car. The front and rear driver's side tires were flat. The back-end of the Subaru was pushed upwards towards the roof. Drake and Fong figured that if this guy didn't have some sort of a neck injury, it would be two winks short of a miracle!

Two more police cars careened into the bloody smash-up. Within minutes, the ambulance and firetrucks had arrived, with the emergency personnel attending to the victims in their vehicles.

Detectives Drake and Fong were interviewing possible witnesses that were milling about the sidewalk. Some of the bystanders were trying to get a closer look at the banged up steel, taking pictures with their cellphones.

Two policemen were directing the backed up traffic around the tragic accident.

The paramedics from the ambulance attended to the Toyota Echo, but quickly realized that the person sitting in the passenger seat, was in fact deceased. They then checked out the driver of the Echo, who was sitting on the curb. He was in shock and kept babbling about being late for work or something to that effect.

The first cop that had arrived on the scene, was at the truck with Drake and Fong. Three firemen were also assisting. Inside the pickup truck, were two young men, both unconscious, and slumped over forward. The potent stench of "skunk weed" lingered in the cab and a broken bottle of Canadian Club Whisky lay on the floor of the truck.

"These guys ... shit! Okay we need to check their vitals and get them out of there. It looks like a DUI (Driving Under the Influence) to me," Fong said to the firemen and other cops.

"I have to agree Johnny. A couple of the witnesses said they saw the truck driving erratically before the accident. And then they were tailgating the Subaru. One of the witnesses said the truck slammed into the back of the old man and the old man rear-ended the Echo," Drake said.

"Yeah ... and an innocent passenger dies!" said the first cop on the scene. "Fuckin' drunken dope addicts! Makes me sick!"

"We hear you, boy do we hear you!" Fong replied.

Drake walked back to the cruiser and grabbed their coffees. "Here Johnny, drink it before it gets cold," he said as he handed the cup-of-Joe to his partner, "drink up, and then we better get over to Sussex. There's enough heads here now, to figure things out. They don't really need us," as Drake looked at his watch. "It's eight thirty now."

The Barking Dog was a full house! The East Side bar was hopping! The tables were packed, and there wasn't a seat to be had. Everyone was having a great time. It was so noisy, the patrons had to talk extra loud to be heard above the music. The bar had a jukebox, but sometimes on weekends, the management would bring in live music. Rock n' roll cover bands were definitely the crowd pleasers. Other times it was a solo act or a duet, but the real entertainment was the rock bands.

Geena and Ellen were knocking down the drinks. Paralyzers, martinis and appetizers! The girls knew better than to just drink and not eat something.

"So do think Sunny will show up Geena?" Ellen asked.

"He damn well better! He told me he would call me later and that we would hook-up. Who knows what later will be? Ten o'clock, midnight? As long as he shows ... hell it's Friday night. Let's have another martini!"

"Where is Sunny, anyway?" Ellen asked.

"You know what Ellen?"

"What?"

"I don't ask him, I trust him, I don't ask ... cause ... well he's Sunny, he sometimes just goes off and does his own thing, he's kind of a loner. I mean, he knows all kinds of people and he's very outgoing and he's kind of like a wanderer, I guess? I don't know ... now I'm babbling on. I think I'm getting drunk! Let's get Lola over here and get some alcohol, gurrrl!" Geena slurred.

"Maybe he's out fighting crime, like a superhero!" Ellen joked.

"Yeah, now that's a hilarious thought!" Geena laughed.

Reaching unit number ten, Sunny had only moments before the big man "came to". He was already starting to stir. Sunny propped him up against the chain-link door of unit number ten.

Sunny unzipped his fanny pack and pulled out two zip-straps. He quickly lifted and stretched out the man's left arm, horizontal to his body. He ran the zip-strap through the chain-link wire and around the man's meaty wrist, and then pulled it as tight as he could. His wrists were so fat, the strap just made it around, with an inch to spare. Sunny did the same to the right arm, stretching it out as far as he could, and then zip-strapping the wrist to the chain-link.

He pulled two more zip-straps out of his black leather pouch and then connected them together, to make a longer strap. Mr. Icy-Blue Eyes' head was hanging down forward and he was already starting to mumble.

Sunny fed the extended plastic strap through the chain-link wire and around the fat, ugly neck of the big creep. Then he cinched the zip-strap real snug, just below the guy's Adam's apple, pulling the man's large head upwards and against the wire mesh. The zip-strap was indenting the flesh of the man's thick neck, almost to the point of asphyxiation. His breathing was restricted, but enough to keep oxygen flowing into his massive lungs, in order to keep him alive.

His eyes snapped open wide and he tried to turn his head but was unable to, from being strapped so tightly to the chain-link wire door. The look of fear in his face, made Sunny realize that now the tables were turned. It was the same look of fear, that Sunny and Ellen must have had that day in the bush, when this bad man pointed his gun directly at them.

Pulling frantically at his tight plastic bonds, the suspect child killer realized that he wasn't going anywhere too soon! He tried to talk, but his words came out in a low raspy dribble, caused from the neck strap putting extensive pressure on his vocal cords. Swallowing was an effort and his breathing was shallow.

"Whaaat ... do ... yooou ...(gasping) want ... wiiiith ... meeee?" came the words slow and labored from the big man's wretched mouth.

Sunny reached into the man's jacket and yanked out the gun that he was concealing. It was a .38 Smith and Wesson revolver with a six inch barrel. Sunny checked the weapon for bullets. He found four slugs in the chambers of the cylinder.

Sunny removed all four bullets and then placed them and the empty revolver on the floor between the man's legs, so that he could stare at them. "Why did you do it?" Sunny asked the terrified man.

"Dooo .... (gasping for air) whaaaat?" the man replied.

"You know!" Sunny remarked, as he held the stun gun up in plain view of the immobile prisoner. He moved the compact, deadly device closer to the man's face.

Sweat beads were forming on the suspect's brow. His eyes widened again as he looked at the electronic device, that was just mere inches from his fat pulsating neck.

"Tell me why you murdered those innocent kids?" Sunny asked with anger in his voice.

"(Gasp) what ... (gasp) kids," Mr. Icy-Blue Eyes asked shaking uncontrollably from fear.

"You know!" Sunny reiterated.

He had to be positive this was the right guy. He slowly pushed the stun gun into the guys Adam's apple, as the big prisoner frenetically tried to resist the assault. The prisoner tried to scream, but the pressure on his throat, subdued all attempts of any loud yelling.

Sunny had turned the stun gun switch to "OFF". He held the high voltage unit's electrodes firmly against the man's neck.

"This is the last time, then I flick the switch! Why did you do it?" Sunny barked.

Crossing Boundary Road and driving into Burnaby, Drake and Fong were fast approaching Sussex Avenue. With only minutes until the turnoff, they wondered if the suspect was even at his residence.

"When it rains it pours, hey Bernie?" Fong said to his partner in a question.

"No shit! That was a real bad accident back there. Those two assholes driving that truck are in deep shit!" Drake responded.

"It never fails, the driver that causes death and destruction on the streets, almost always lives and gets to walk away 'Scott fuckin' free'," Fong said with some anger in his voice.

Drake slowed the cruiser speed down and flicked on his right turn signal, as they neared Sussex Avenue. The unmarked cop car hung the corner as darkness started to descend upon them. They drove at a slow pace down Sussex, driving right past the side street, where Sunny had parked his black Accord, only fifty feet away from the corner.

Fong fumbled around in the cruiser glove compartment for the digital Pentax camera.

"If those RCMP bananas knew what we were up to, they'd most likely have a 'shit attack', Johnny!" Drake laughed out loud.

"Oh yeah, they think they're above us for some reason? We should all be on the same fuckin' team. All of us against the criminals, for Pete's sake! Fong reasoned.

The big man's cold blue eyes seemed to be bulging and turning a darker shade of blue, from the lack of oxygen.

"I ... (gasping for air) I ... don't ... (gasp) ... know ... I ... haaated ... (gasp) my ... brutherrr ... when ... (gasp) weee ... were ... kids ... (gasp). I haaate ... kids! They ...all deserved ... it," the self-confessed killer wheezed out slowly.

Sunny lowered the stun gun, stood up and shoved the electronic wonder back into his rear pocket. He then turned around and grabbed hold of the man's right cowboy boot. The guy tried to kick out at Sunny's legs, but the lack of oxygen made it a fruitless endeavor. His lower limbs just flailed about hopelessly. Tugging and twisting with a firm grip, Sunny pulled that size eleven boot, right off of the monster's foot.

Sunny glared at the murdering son-of-a-bitch with a nauseating emotional look. "An eye for an eye!" he said to the sickening waste of skin in front of him. "You will never hurt another child ever again!" as he bent down and pulled up his right pant leg, removing something from his black sock.

As Sunny straightened his posture, he held the object up for the killer to see. He then proceeded to slowly run his gloved fingers along the short length of the shiny thing, as if to taunt him.

The big man's eyes bugged right out, like two huge glass marbles pushing out from the end of a drinking straw. He tried to scream again, but intermittent gasps of air and reverberating sounds were the only noises escaping his fat pulsating throat.

It was obvious that the shiny eight inch chopstick, that Sunny held in his hand, didn't seem to appeal to Mr. Icy-Blue Eyes at the moment.

With the dowel in his left hand and the size eleven boot in his right hand, Sunny bent over and whispered into the killer's left ear, "this is for those eight kids!" and then he shoved the end of the chopstick into the guy's ear canal.

The prisoner struggled immensely, trying to escape the violating dowel, emitting garbled, wheezing sounds of partial words, which were not making any sense.

Sunny held the chopstick, solid like a rock, and wound up with the size eleven boot. He pounded the end of the resin rod, as hard as he could with the scuffed up western heel of the cowboy boot. There was a heavy dull thud, from the heel as it connected and a soft crunching noise was heard from the side of the man's head.

A deep throaty, horrifying, continuous grunt erupted from the child killers mouth. Furiously he tried to escape his restraints.

Sunny repeated the hard blows to the end of the chopstick with the heavy boot heel, over and over, driving the smooth instrument deeper and deeper into the murderer's brain.

The dreadful grunting and thrashing continued for about twenty seconds and then abruptly ceased. Only three of the eight inches of the chopstick was visible. The big man's body convulsed involuntarily for another ten to fifteen seconds and then went limp, his head dropped forward, blood oozed from his ear, nose and the corner of his mouth. Death had arrived!

It was an eerie sight. The demon's pale blue eyes were still open, and he had an evil sneer on his face. The same sneer, when he had pulled the gun on Sunny and Ellen that day in the woods. Sunny felt a chill run up his spine and got goosebumps all over his arms.

Sunny unzipped his leather pack once again and removed a black mini, Sharpie felt pen. He grabbed the curly hair on the dead man's head with his left hand and raised it up. Looking into those dead blue eyes, was enough to give a person insomnia. Sunny had prayed for this moment. With the felt pen, he scribbled "CHILD KILLER" across the lifeless forehead of the big fat man.

Sunny is a killer's killer! Not just a killer, but a justifiable assassin that modern society needs and yearns for. He is the solution to the reprehensible criminal element that the justice system repeatedly ignores. The public is constantly being let down by the courts. As far as Sunny is concerned, the justice system, doesn't keep society safe from violent crimes! It's a system for the criminals. And because of this greatly flawed system, Sunny has created his own set of laws, the kind his religious Grandma implanted into his brain when he was a youngster; "an eye for an eye". He knew that what he did was against the law, but what is the law? The laws constituted by governments are simply mere formulations of nouns and adjectives; just words, nothing else. Heinous crimes against humanity or animals deserves the same as! Real life retributive action is needed, not bullshit words that let the violent offenders back on the street.

Sunny did the deed and now he has to make himself scarce. *Shit! A car coming in!* The echoing sound of a vehicle entering the underground parkade. *Got to move it!*

Sunny slipped his pen into his fanny pack, zipped it up and quickly headed for the exit door. He turned out the lights, cracked the door open just a hair and peeked out.

The unmarked police car had entered the underground parking lot at Sussex Avenue. The cops wheeled around until they spotted an empty parking space and then backed up their cruiser into it. The two detectives sat in the car for a few minutes, talking.

Sunny could see the car and the two people inside, but didn't know who they were. *Just a couple back at home no doubt,* he thought to himself. *Time to exit, in case they come to the storage room!* He glanced over at the concrete pillar and saw his newspaper laying on the ground.

Sunny pulled off his black Mechanix gloves and turned them inside out, then he shoved them into his front jeans pockets and reached up under his t-shirt with his right hand, and pulled the door handle inwards with his shirt covering the handle, so as not to leave any fingerprints.

He emerged from the storage room and strolled over to the pillar, bent down and picked up his newspaper. As he stood up, pretending to read the paper, he peered over the top of the paper towards the vehicle that had just parked. Slow, but steady paces he took towards the ramp, Sunny didn't want to look suspicious, all the while pretending to be interested in the newspaper.

The two got out of the car, and looked over towards Sunny. He glanced over at them, with only the top of his head showing, the rest of his face buried in the paper. Both men were casually dressed, nice clothes and one had a camera in his hand.

Maybe they're gay? Or going to some woman's apartment for a double date. Probably gay, not that there's anything wrong with that.

DOG WITH A BONE

The men passed by Sunny as one said, "good evening" and the other just simply nodded.

"Evenin'," Sunny replied with a fake accent, while looking intently at his newspaper, heading up the ramp.

Almost to the top of the ramp, Sunny quickly looked back and was startled with what he observed. The two men were inspecting the killer's Pontiac and taking pictures of it. *Fucking detectives! Those are the guys that had him pulled over on 33rd Avenue! I thought they looked familiar!*

Sunny picked up the pace, heading up Sussex, to the side-street where his Accord was parked. Still reading his newspaper, even though darkness had arrived and avoiding all possible eye contact with any would-be passerby's that would be able to identify him.

Within minutes Sunny was in his car, heading home on Kingsway. About two miles from Sussex Avenue, he turned down a side-street and then up an alley. The first storm sewer he came to, he stopped his car, looked around and saw nobody. Sunny stepped out from his ride and pushed his gloves through the thick steel grate. He then drove back out to Kingsway, looking for a phone booth. He promised Geena he would call her tonight and hookup. Three blocks later, Sunny spotted a phone booth. "Hey cupcake, are you at The Dog?"

"You betcha, and we're having a good time!" Geena replied.

"See you in twenty minutes!" Sunny barked.

Back in his car, he turned on the stereo and then inserted his Foreigner CD and listened to "Dirty White Boy" on the way to the bar. *"I'm just a dirty white boy ... dirty white boyyyy!"*

The drinking crowd was now thicker than ninety-weight gear oil. Sunny pushed his way through the lingering partiers who stood around up by the bar and near the entrance. The smokers would stand around and drink and then go out for a smoke and then back in and drink and then back out again. Ever since the government made public places illegal to smoke, there seemed to be more in-and-out traffic. A revolving door would be "the cat's ass" in a place like The Dog. But a cat's ass at The Dog would be in trouble!

"Hey cupcake ... hi Ellen. You two look like you've had a few already!" Sunny laughed.

"Only a couple Sunny, where the hell have you been?" Geena asked.

"I just let Babe out for a pee."

"It took you all night to let her out for a pee?" Geena snipped.

"Of course not ... I was ..."

"We thought you were maybe hunting criminals, like a super-hero!" Ellen drunkenly joked, as she turned to Geena and laughed out loud, under the blanket of the thunderous bar racket.

The two ladies laughed and clinked glasses again, for the umpteenth time!

"Well it's about time you showed up!" Lola chanted, "these hotties had to fight off a crowd of hungry wolves!"

"I don't doubt it Lola, how about a drink, girl? The usual, please," Sunny asked.

Lola brought Sunny, a Sailor Jerry's Rum and diet-Pepsi and the ladies each, another martini.

"Cheers!" Sunny said aloud as he raised his glass to the girls glasses. "Let's celebrate! To a most excellent fulfilling and splendorous night."

TWENTY-TWO

Saturday

"Could you please take the garbage out for me Will?" Mary Marcus asked her son politely.

"In a minute!" William snapped back at his mom.

William had shuffled out of his bedroom, looking like "death warmed over". His hair was sticking out all over the place and he had big puffy bags under his eyes, confirming that he hadn't slept all night. Surfing the internet for porn, no doubt!

Rubbing his eyes, with the palms of both hands, he asked his mother, "what's for breakfast?"

"Sausage and eggs," came the reply from Mary.

Something caught young William's eye, through the window, from outside. He turned to look, in his half dazed sleepy state. "It's that damn cat!" William yelled, as he headed for the back door.

"Will! Leave that cat alone, it's Mr. Bobrick's cat, and he's a decent neighbor," his mother said.

"I hate cats and I hate you! Don't tell me what to do! Everyone is always telling me what to do and I'm sick of it!" William yelled to his fearful mother.

"Please settle down Will, you need to quit being so angry about everything. I'm here to help you. I'm not against you, I'm your mother and I love you, but you need to trust me, Will," Mary pleaded.

"I don't need any help! I need to be left alone!" William said as he stared intently at his mother, with an evil grin.

Icy chills ran down Mary's spine. She felt nauseated and dizzy. She pulled out a kitchen chair, sat down and placed her head into her tiny hands and wept quietly.

William was already out the back door with a broom, swinging at the friendly tabby, that was perched on their porch banister. He hit the curious mouser broadside with the whisk-end of the corn broom. The cat let out a screech, spiraled off the dilapidated porch and landed on all fours on the overgrown grass below.

William ran down the stairs, screaming and waving the broom around as the terrified tabby cat ran through the yard and jumped up onto the dividing fence, then disappeared into the next yard.

"Old man" Bobrick was in his yard and witnessed the commotion. His cat ran right past him and up onto his back porch for safety.

Mr. Bobrick came over to the "good-neighbor" fence and pointed his crooked finger at William. "I know what you did, son! I know your kind. Leave my cat alone or I'll phone the police!"

"FUCK YOU old man!" came the reply. "Phone the police and see what happens, I'll burn your house to the ground!" William taunted as he turned and walked back to the porch stairs.

Mary was peering out through the kitchen window. She saw and heard everything her son said and did. She was horrified! *He seems to be getting worse, not better. I think he may need medication, I have to do something, before he hurts someone again!*

DOG WITH A BONE

Mr. Bobrick shook his head in utter disbelief and hobbled back to the safety of his house, muttering to himself and looking for his cat.

Mary stayed inside her house, determining it would be healthier for all, if she didn't add fuel to the fire. Her son was already riled up and the only way to calm him down, was for her to say and do nothing. She was deathly afraid of her son and he knew it, and he was taking full advantage of her.

Sunny and Babe had been up for a couple of hours. He drank three cups of coffee already. The girls were still sleeping, Geena in Sunny's bed and Ellen on the leather couch. It was now 10:00 am and there was no sign of either of the ladies, waking anytime soon.

The three had walked to Sunny's place, from The Barking Dog late last night. None of them wanted to drive, so they all crashed at the loft.

Sunny filled his coffee cup one more time, sat down at his desk and fired up his laptop. He kept the volume down, so the ladies could sleep off last nights spirits. Waking up two women with a plethora of martini's running through their veins could turn out to be a disaster. Better to let them "saw logs" for awhile. Also, he didn't want them seeing the news right away.

Sunny surfed the news channels. The Province newspaper website had plastered "FRASER MURDER SUSPECT FOUND DEAD" on the front page. A short paragraph followed the headline. Not too much information, being that the news was only a few hours old.

Next he Googled the Global TV site. On the front page of the website, it read:

"BREAKING NEWS"

SUSPECT FRASER KILLER FOUND DEAD

"Authorities have confirmed to the media, that about 6:00 am this morning, a man believed to be the serial killer of the so-called "Fraser Murders" involving young male and female victims, in the Greater Vancouver area has been found dead. The RCMP won't elaborate on the investigation, but have told local media outlets that it appears, the suspect himself, was in fact murdered. The identity of the person has not yet been revealed. These reports have not yet been confirmed. More on this story as information is obtained from the police."

Sunny smiled to himself. He sipped his coffee as he turned off his computer. Babe was sitting next to him, looking up, almost like she understood what had happened. He patted Babe on the head and said, "let's go for a walk and let these girls sleep, wadya say Babe?"

She let out a short, low growl and wagged her tail, with her hips swaying, as if to say, *yeah, let's go!*

Chief Constable Joe Winters was bloody ecstatic! Everyone down at the station had a big smile on their faces. The call had come in from the RCMP's Chief Superintendent of IHIT, at about 6:50 am this morning.

At 7:30 am, Chief Winters was addressing a group of homicide detectives in the board room. "I want everyone's attention please. I have some great news and some, not so great news!"

All of the present members of the homicide department were quiet, except for the sound of a few slurping coffee.

"First off, people ... the great news! If you haven't heard the buzz yet, the body of Mr. Clayton Webber, the number one suspect in the Fraser case murders, was discovered by a tenant at the suspect's apartment building, around six o'clock this morning. He was found trussed up, in the storage room, located in the underground parking facilities at the apartments. Apparently, there was no doubt, that he was stalked and murdered. Murdered in the same MO (modus operandi) as how he killed all those poor kids. Forensics will be getting DNA samples from the body in order to confirm a definite match to the sperm samples left at the various crime scenes," Winters explained.

"How do we know this guy was the number one suspect, prior to the DNA match?" Detective Ambleside asked.

"Last night, Detectives Bernard Drake and Johnson Fong went on a fact-finding mission. Earlier in the day they had pulled over this same guy, for a routine check. His vehicle was of similar description to the models we have been pursuing. While they had him pulled over, they noticed marks on the roof of the car. Obviously, this led us to believe ... possible roof-racks! Not quite enough evidence to bust someone, so they went on a witch-hunt for more. And guess what?" Winters cleared his throat as he looked around the boardroom at all of the homicide police, "the pictures they took of the suspects tires, are an exact match to the tread patterns left at some of the crime scenes!" the Chief exclaimed proudly. "Of course we still need the DNA to make positively certain."

"You said he was trussed up?" asked one of the detectives from the back of the room.

"Trussed up like a fuckin' turkey being served for Thanksgiving dinner!" Winters laughed. "With a chopstick stuck in the side of his head! Someone out there had a hard-on for this cretin. Whoever did this, knew exactly what Webber was up to ... which brings me to the 'not so good news', and that is ... we have another killer out there to deal with. Someone more intelligent than Clayton Webber. He beat him at his own sick game!"

"So if Webber was killed the same way as he murdered his victims, do you believe it could be an accomplice of his, that was in on his sick shit?" asked a rookie homicide detective.

"Wish I had a 'crystal fucking ball' Detective!" Winters answered to the young cop. "We don't have all of the facts yet, we're waiting for more from the RC's ... should have more in a couple of hours. The damn media is hounding us for everything we have and we gave them the scoop early this morning, to put the public's mind at ease. Hopefully this is our guy! Now ... back to this other killer," Winters took a deep breath and then continued, "Detectives Fong and Drake noticed a guy coming out of the storage room, seconds before they approached the suspects car. The guy was reading a newspaper as they passed each other. They even exchanged pleasantries. And then the guy walked out of the underground!"

The room full of gumshoes fell silent. They stared at the Chief, waiting for more. He just stared back at the group.

"WELL?" Winters chirped. He waited silently for about twenty seconds and then asked, "are you detectives or what? He waited another fifteen seconds, and then, "come on people wake up! What's wrong with what I just told you?"

The members looked around the room at each other, some shrugging their shoulders, others with "what the hell is he talking about" looks on their faces.

"He WALKED out of the fucking parkade! Why wouldn't he drive out or take the elevator, late at night? And who reads a bloody newspaper in the dark, while walking? So either Clayton Webber had a partner in crime who he pissed off, or we have a vigilante walking the streets!" Winters said. "Sure, he saved the taxpayers a ton of money, and I'm happy that bastard is dead, but now we have to explain to the press, that we didn't do our job properly ... someone else did it for us! It doesn't look good for the Vancouver City Police force, people!" Winters lectured the cops.

"This isn't the first time, is it Chief?" the same rookie as before, asked.

"No sir, it's not the first time! There have been several cases over the last few years of vigilante justice in this great city of ours. We're not certain if it's the same individual responsible for all of the murders of the violent offenders, or if it's copycat killers. Whatever the case may be, it seems, that the person or persons, deliver the same punishment to the criminal, as the criminal has delivered to their victim," Winters explained to the members. "In the previous cases of the 'Retribution Murders', as we have dubbed them; the culprit has never left a single clue at any of the murder scenes. And the MO's have never been the same, because the murderer kills them the same way they had killed, so every killing is different. That's the reason it's so hard to pin it on the same person. It's crazy! If it is one person responsible, he or she is one intelligent human being.

William Marcus stomped into the house and glared at his mother. Mary went about her business of getting brunch together for her troubled son.

As she was frying up the sausage at the kitchen stove with her back to him, she asked, "what was the problem out there Will?"

"None of your stinking business!" William replied angrily. He stormed into his bedroom and slammed the door.

She followed him, opened his bedroom door, looked in and said, "Will, I can't take this anymore, you have a nasty streak and you need to stop! You need to get some help Will! You can't keep behaving this way. You and I have to see your probation officer next Tuesday and if you don't smarten up, I will tell him how you're REALLY behaving!" Mary said with her voice breaking up.

William lunged at his mother and grabbed her slender neck with both of his hands. He slammed her frail body up against the bedroom wall and squeezed her throat. His mother started choking and flailing her arms around, trying to pull his arms away from her neck. Gasping for air, he finally let her go and she fell to the floor, clutching her throat and crying hysterically.

"Don't you ever threaten me again, do you hear me, do you bitch?" William screamed, "you have NO idea what I'm capable of!"

Mary crawled on her hands and knees into the kitchen slowly, then pulled herself up to the kitchen stove and turned off the element. Crying softly, she made her way into her bedroom, shut the door behind her and laid down face first on her comfy bed. Mary wept gently into her feathered pillow.

Sunny and Babe returned from their walk to the park. The girls were up and had already showered. Peppermint tea fumes wafted through the loft and the smell of fruity shampoo invaded the nostrils. It was a good, clean smell, unlike the odorous reek of last nights bar stench.

"Mornin' ladies!" Sunny crooned, as he entered the lofty digs.

"And a good morning to you my hunky man!" Geena said with love in her eye.

"Did you two have an interesting walk?" Ellen asked as she stroked Babe's head and neck.

"Always, we always have an interesting walk. I like to think of it as an adventure. Life is an adventure Ellen, isn't it?" Sunny said as he winked at her, thinking about their adventure in the woods a week ago.

He didn't want to say anything about the morning news of the police, finding the body of the child killer. The mood of the girls was much too positive to bring up something like that. Besides, he figured they would hear about it soon enough, and then he could act surprised.

"Ellen and I thought we would do some shopping downtown today, would you like to come with us Sundance?"

"No, I have some things to do today, maybe see my folks and get Babe some more dog chow. You ladies don't need me as an escort." Sunny reached into his pants pocket and pulled out a fifty dollar bill. He placed it on the kitchenette bar and said, with a smile, "lunch is my treat today, ladies".

"Sunny you don't have to do that," Ellen quipped.

"I insist, don't argue or I'll cry!" he laughed.

"Oh thanks, Sunny, that's so nice of you." Ellen said.

"Thanks honey, sure you don't want to come with us?" Geena asked again.

"Positive! You two have fun today," he insisted, as he gave Geena a kiss and Ellen a hug. "Now it's my turn for a shower. Lock the door on your way out, please," as he headed straight for the bathroom.

Babe watched her master close the bathroom door, and then she went and laid on her comfy bed. She stared at the girls and let out a long, contented sigh, then closed her big, brown, beautiful eyes and drifted off to sleep.

Geena and Ellen smiled at one another, as they both watched Babe sleep soundly. They finished their tea and then quietly tip-toed to the door, hoping they wouldn't wake the princess. As they exited, Babe slowly opened her eyes half way, watched them shut the door and then dropped her eyelids tight.

TWENTY-THREE

Saturday Afternoon

The distant sound of the lawnmower could be heard as soon as Sunny turned the ignition off. It was a clear, beautiful, hot August afternoon and the Kruziks were cutting their lawn, as they usually did, about once a week.

Babe jumped out of the passenger side of the Accord, as Sunny held the door open for her. She knew exactly where they were; at Grandma and Grampa's. She sauntered over to the freshly cut green grass of the front lawn and sniffed a few different areas. When she finally found the right spot, she squatted on her haunches and "did a pee". A girl just doesn't pee anywhere, it has to be the perfect spot!

The monotonous roar of the lawnmower was coming from the back yard. Sunny and Babe went through the side gate, around to the back. Annie Kruzik was lounging in the crystal clear, in-ground pool, while father Wade was toiling away, with the mower in hand, doing laps on the "greener than green" grass, instead of laps in the swimming pool.

Annie waved at her son, from the inflatable chair that she was floating around in, while sipping a daiquiri. Wade hadn't noticed the intruders, as he was deeply immersed in his precision grass manicure endeavour.

Sunny moseyed over to the patio furniture and sat down on the lounge chair, underneath the big beige umbrella, safe from the scorching sun. Babe followed him over and plunked herself down, underneath the table in the shade beside him. Sunny sat and waited for his dad to make his rounds. The sound of the mower was deafening. He wondered how his mother could sit in the pool with that God-awful noise. *Maybe she's going deaf. She will be deaf, if she stays out here too long!*

Annie gradually paddled over to the edge of the pool and grabbed onto the chrome ladder, to steady herself. She set the drink on the ledge of the poolside and then stepped onto the lowest ladder rung and pulled herself out of the plastic floating lounge. Up the ladder she came, with the sunlight sparkling off of her wet skin.

"Wade ... Wade!" Annie yelled over the deafening sound of the lawnmower, waving her arms, trying to get his attention.

He looked at her, as she pointed over to the umbrella. Wade saw his son and Babe. He reached for the STOP button and turned off the dastardly noisemaker.

"Getting your exercise I see, both of you!" Sunny teased.

"Hi dear, I'm not getting as much as your father, but we do usually take turns. When he gets too hot, he jumps in the pool. Sometimes we cut it in the evening when it's much cooler," Annie explained to her son, as she towelled the dripping water from her firm body.

Sunny's dad sat down beside him, and opened up the cooler, which sat beneath the patio table. He pulled out two ice-cold Pilsener beers. He handed one to Sunny. The men opened their beers and then clinked them together.

"Cheers!" Sunny said to his pops. They both chugged the suds like there was no tomorrow.

DOG WITH A BONE

"Can I get you something to eat Sunny? Your dad and I were going to have a late lunch, will you join us?" Annie asked with delight.

"Sure mom, I'll have a bite. Also can you bring me a dish for Babe. She looks mighty thirsty!" Sunny said.

Annie went into the house to get the lunch ready. Wade looked at his son and said, "darn grass grows faster every week. It seems the more I cut, the quicker it grows."

"Don't water it, dad. If you don't water, it won't grow," Sunny said jokingly.

"I should cement the whole bloody yard, for Christ sakes!" Wade surmised.

"It's good to see you dad," Sunny said.

"It's good to see you too, son," Wade replied as they clinked beer bottles again, and then polished off the tasty suds. "Another one?" Wade asked.

"One more, why not, it's Saturday!" Sunny reasoned.

"How's my granddaughter doing? Come here Babe," Wade called, as he bent over to pet the little princess. "Spoiled rotten isn't she? But why not, she's a damn good companion. Man's best friend!"

"You got that right, dad! Faithful, right to the bitter end, like no other!" Sunny said with a big smile.

Annie was on her way back with snacks and a bowl of water for Babe.

"Need a hand mom?" Sunny asked.

"No, It's all on this tray. Sandwiches ... I already had made them up earlier for your dad and I."

As they ate their lunch, Sunny's dad asked him, "did you see the news today, Sunny?"

"Ah, yes I did, why do you ask?" Sunny queried.

"They figure they got the serial killer who murdered all those young adults and children. Well *they* didn't actually get him. He was found dead ... murdered, they think. Probably by a vigilante. Thank God that bloody maniac is dead! That should happen to all those perverts and psychopaths! We would save millions of dollars, by not wasting taxpayers money on ridiculous court costs," Wade vented angrily.

"That person who disposed of that kid killer deserves a medal and should be running our country," Annie added.

Dispose! I like that term, just like throwing out the garbage! Well, a medal okay, but I don't want to run the country. At least I know your on my side. Thank-you, mom and dad! "Yeah, that monster got what he deserved all right! Hopefully, other would-be psychos would 'take note' and learn from that," Sunny said.

"If the government doesn't want to bring back the death penalty for these sickos, then they should put them all on an island, and let them fend for themselves," Annie said.

"You're right mom, they should ... great lunch by the way, very tasty," Sunny said, changing the subject. "I was wondering if I could leave Babe with you guys for the evening, if that's okay? I have to pick up a few things, her dog chow and some other items."

"Of course it's okay, she loves hanging out with us, anytime, Sunny, anytime!" his mother said.

"Great, thanks. Now you be a good girl Babe, I'll see you later," Sunny said, as he patted her soft blond head. Then he got up and kissed his mother on the cheek, hugged his dad, like he always did and then headed for the back gate. "I'll be back in a few hours."

Mary Marcus came out of the bathroom, from having put on her makeup. She went to the kitchen sink, picked up a glass and poured herself a drink of water. Then she grabbed her purse from the back of the kitchen chair and dug her keys out of the purse.

"Will ... Will are you there?" she called to his closed bedroom door. "WILL!"

The bedroom door flung open. "WHAT do you want?" he asked angrily.

"I'm going out for awhile, I will be back later tonight," Mary said.

"WHERE are you going?" William demanded.

"Just out to visit a friend, for coffee and cards. Please be good Will, that's all I ask," his mother pleaded.

He went back into his bedroom and slammed the door shut. Then he turned his stereo up real loud.

Mary could hear the music out in the carport, as she climbed into her vehicle. She looked back at the house and just shook her head from side to side, in utter disgust. Mary started her car, backed out of the driveway, and then drove away from her house. She felt an overwhelming, emotional state of relief as she looked in her rear-view mirror and saw her house shrinking smaller and smaller.

While most people felt safer inside their homes, she actually felt safer, away from her home. She was living with a human time-bomb and feared for her life. Mary needed to get away for awhile and visit a friend for comfort.

The murder scene at the underground parkade, in the Sussex apartment building was still cordoned off with the yellow "Crime Scene – Do Not Cross" tape. One of the rookie RCMP officers was assigned to watch the storage area, from his cruiser that was parked in the underground parkade, while the homicide detectives came and went. The officer on watch duty, was stationed there, to inform tenants that may need access to the storage area, that they would have to wait forty-eight hours in order to gain access. Forty-eight hours was the window of opportunity that was most crucial after a crime, to allow the forensic investigators to find any clues left behind by the perpetrator.

Most of the evidence had already been collected earlier in the day; and the child killer's body was already being examined by the forensic pathologist at the Burnaby Central Morgue.

A few more homicide investigators from the Vancouver City Police's FIU, met with the RCMP's IHIT at the crime scene to recheck for any missed evidence.

Besides Clayton Webber's gun, bullets and the chopstick stuck in his ear, the police really had no clues of any sort. At this point, they had no idea, if the assassin who killed Webber, had left the gun or if it was actually Webber's own weapon. He wasn't on record for owning any legal handguns or rifles.

After all, none of the eight murdered children who Webber had killed, were shot. They were all choked to death or incapacitated with the chopsticks to the brain.

There were no security cameras in the building and no eye witnesses that the police have come across yet, only the two Detectives Fong and Drake, that believe they may have spoke to the assailant briefly. There were numerous fingerprints in the storage area, but they could belong to any number of the tenants living in the building. All fingerprints would have to be checked. A very time consuming effort indeed, but must be done nevertheless.

The RCMP were a wee bit upset with the Vancouver Police's members, Fong and Drake, having done surveillance in their municipality without permission. But knowing that they hopefully have the right serial killer off the streets killing kids, quelled the authoritative hierarchy of territorial policing rights.

Chief Constable Joe Winters knew he should have informed the RCMP, that his men were crossing the line, but figured once they got the information they needed, it really wouldn't matter. Especially if the information turned out to be false, he didn't want to get anyone over excited.

TWENTY-FOUR

Saturday Night

The sun was dropping behind the west-coast mountains and casting long shadows on the earth's blanket. The warmth of the ground brought the evening crickets to symphonic ring-tones, echoing throughout the air. Except that one had to be almost a block away from the Marcus's bungalow, to actually hear the delightful chirping of the insect's back legs rubbing together. Heavy metal music, resonating from the worn and weather beaten house, drowned out the beautiful, melodious, high-pitched crickets.

William Marcus was drinking beer and listening to Judas Priest's "You've Got Another Thing Comin'" at the eardrum-shattering level, of decibels. Partially wasted from six beers and too many cigarettes, he kept the music loud.

Poor Mr. Bobrick was too nervous to let his cat outside anymore. He kept all his windows and doors locked tight, to keep the noise and the crazy neighbor kid out, just in case he decided to come-a-knockin'. Bobrick wasn't taking any chances!

Down the dusky street, roared a carload of teenagers who passed the walker on the right side of the road.

"FUCK YOU ASSHOLE!" yelled one of the teens hanging out of the passenger window, as he flicked his cigarette at the man. The cigarette spewed a burst of bright orange sparks as it hit the pavement about fifteen feet from the intended target.

The pedestrian walking along the sidewalk paid no attention to the troublemakers. He just minded his own business and ignored them. The vehicle drove on past. After a minute or so, the red taillights of the car disappeared in the distance of the night.

The music became clearer as the person walking, neared the middle of the block. Slowing down his pace, the music was very decipherable now. Standing opposite of the house, from where the head-banging tunes were coming from, the man looked and listened.

The street was dark, empty and quiet, except for the racket from the Marcus's home. It was a rough neighborhood at times! Punks driving around screaming obscenities at people, rundown houses, older cars parked at the curbside, and loud music, loud heavy-fucking-metal-headache music reverberating from William Marcus's bedroom.

Ready to take a step from the curb, the walker noticed headlights in the far distance at the end of the street coming towards him. Stepping backwards and waiting, he realized it was the same car with the belligerent punks driving back towards him. The pedestrian moved back from the road and hid behind one of the big, old oak trees along the dark, grassy boulevard.

He watched the car approaching at a rapid speed, until it neared his location. Then the car full of teenagers slowed down. Hiding behind the massive tree trunk, he peered around to get a look at the vehicle. The fellow knew that the street punks were looking for him. He heard one of them say, "he must have gone into one of the houses, probably lives around here. He disappeared fast ... chickenshit! Let's circle around the block, maybe the guy cut through someone's yard!"

The vehicle sped off down the street and hung the corner with the screeching sound of rubber.

Out from the shadows of the big oak tree, the man appeared. He looked both ways down the dusky street of the neighborhood. Without hesitation he crossed the road and vanished through the front cedar hedge fence of Bobrick's property. From the intermittent, bluish low-lighting glow and flashes coming from Bobrick's front window, it was evident that he was watching television, with all his inside lights turned off.

Hidden from view of the front street, the prowler slunk down the fence line that separated old man Bobrick's house and the Marcus's. Nobody was around in either yard. Not even the cat! The only lights on at the Marcus's house were the front-room, kitchen and his bedroom.

The half-moon was high in the sky with heavy clouds, filtering out the moonbeams, making the night as black as coal.

Watching from Bobrick's yard, over the "good neighbor" fence, the motionless trespasser could see shadowy movements through the stained, sheer cotton curtains on William's bedroom window. But a closer peek was needed. Carefully, but swiftly, Burt scaled the rickety cedar fence and landed in the Marcus's messy back yard.

The music was still blaring from the tattered walls of the house. Burt stood and examined the back of the house and the yard. The back porch was in total darkness. He made his way to the porch and stealthily crept up the worn out stairs. The third stair up, rocked a little and creaked. Nails were loose! It didn't matter much, the music was too loud for William to hear the board squeaking.

Burt tried the door knob, it was unlocked! Slowly he turned the handle, until it clicked. He waited about five seconds and then gently opened the door.

Off to the side of the entryway, strewn about, was an untidy pile of shoes, dirty boots and coats. The light over the sink illuminated only part of the kitchen. The hallway leading from the kitchen to the front-room was dark, with only a sliver of light emitting from the bottom of the door of William's room.

The music was quieter now, but still loud. William must have turned it down a notch.

Burt quickly moved down the darkened hallway past the ex-con's bedroom door. He did a visual inspection of the front-room and the adjoining bedroom. No one else was home! Burt suspected William was home alone, when he had observed that the car was absent from the carport, but nevertheless, he wanted to be one hundred percent sure.

Burt gently slid open, the wooden bi-fold closet door in the hallway, diagonally across from William's bedroom, stepped inside and then closed it shut. He peered through the slanted slats into the dark hallway. Burt could see the sliver of light under the door from across the hall.

Listening to the thumping of the heavy bass sound, through the thin wall of the closet, proved to be nerve-wracking. The noisy song on the stereo was nearing the end, so the sound was fading out somewhat. Burt took this as his signal. He banged hard on the wall of the closet twice with his open palm. Then he waited five seconds. Then again, twice more he banged hard on the closet wall.

William leaned over from his big-ass chair and turned down the volume of his stereo, and listened. Another BANG! "Wha' the fuck?" William said to himself quietly. He turned the music right down and listened intently. He'd already drank six beers and was downing his seventh. William wasn't quite sure if he was hearing things or if there was actually something or someone out there. He tried to focus beyond his drunken stupor.

"Meeeeooowwww!" came from outside William's bedroom door.

"That ffff...ugging cat! How the shit ... did it get ... in?" William slurred loudly, in his intoxicated state. "I'll get ... that fugger!" he threatened as he got up from his big comfy chair. The well oiled-up William, grabbed a fish bonker from his fishing gear, that was stashed in his bedroom closet and then stumbled to the bedroom door. He opened the door and holding the fish bonker up at chest level, he entered the darkened hallway.

Down the hall he staggered, towards the kitchen. "Here kitty ... kitty!" William called. He wandered through the kitchen, looking under the table and behind some boxes sitting by the entry way. Into the entry way he swayed, looking around the boots and coats.

"Meeeooowww!" came from down the hallway.

"Mutha ... fugger! The front-room ... are ya at? I'll kill ya ... fuggin cat!" William furiously remarked, as he turned and headed through the kitchen towards the front-room.

The madman swung his head around from side to side as he entered the front-room, desperately searching behind the sofa, lazy-boy chair and other furniture jammed into the little area. He bent over and looked under the coffee table. Nothing! "Whuut thu fuuck? Where are ya ... stoopid cat?"

"Meeeooowww!"

William Asshole Marcus standing in the center of the tiny front-room, snapped his head around, looking towards the closet in the hallway. "Hhhhmmmm," as he slowly swayed towards the bi-fold closet doors.

As he put his left hand on the door-knob, he held his fish bonker out towards his right side. He gripped the knob and as he pulled the bi-fold door open towards himself, he said, " gotcha ... dead kitty!"

Horrified, as if he had witnessed Satan himself, William's eyes damn near bugged right out of their sockets, as he stood face to face with the intruder in the closet, instead of the feline he thought he was hunting.

Like a bolt of lightening, the twenty-four ounce carpenter's hammer came down smack in the middle of William's unsuspecting, sweaty forehead. With a dull sickening thud filling the airwaves, the young, unlucky William crumpled to the floor. He was moaning incoherently and twitching all over! The hammer came down again and again, until his crushed skull opened up and gave birth to his pinkish white, gooey, twisted brain matter. No more twitching. His body was as limp as freshly boiled spaghetti noodles.

The assassin dropped the hammer on the floor and went into the bathroom. Burt turned on the bathroom light and looked into the mirror. No blood on the face. He turned out the light and left silently through the back door.

On the hallway floor, peacefully staring up at the ceiling, with eyes wide open, young William lay.

TWENTY-FIVE

Sunday Morning

The morning sun, cast it's warm beams of light through the crystal clear windows of the spacious sun-room, where Dr. Wilson and his young daughter Melissa, were enjoying their freshly baked waffles, with whipped cream and strawberries, when the phone rang. The sweet smell of cinnamon and fresh fruit drifted through the morning air.

"I'll get it daddy!" Melissa excitedly offered, as she sprang out of her white, cushioned wicker chair and ran to the phone in the kitchen. "Hello?" she answered, "um, yes he is ... okay, I'll go and get him. Daddy! It's for you," Melissa called out as she carried the phone out to the sun-room, full of tropical plants. "Here daddy," as she passed the phone to the doctor.

"Yes this is Randall Wilson, how may I help you?" asked the plastic surgeon as he set his cup of coffee down.

Wilson listened intently as he fidgeted with the table cloth hanging off the edge of the white wicker table. His daughter stared at him as he made several different faces, forgetting that she was sitting right across from him.

"Dead? He's dead? I see ... yes I understand. Next week? Okay, that's fine. Yes, of course. Thank-you for informing me. Goodbye," Wilson said as he hung up the phone, and set it down on the table.

Melissa was making a reverberating sound through her straw as she sucked up the last of the chocolate milk in her glass. "Who was that daddy?" she asked.

Dr. Wilson was a straight shooter with his daughter, never one to side-step the truth or lie to her. He looked at her with some hesitation, as he formulated in his mind, how he would explain to her, the information he had just received over the phone.

"Melissa, my darling, that was the police," he said.

"The police dad!?" she quipped, "well, why? What do they want? Is it about mommy?"

"Actually honey, it is. It seems that the bad man who hurt mommy ... well ... they found him ... dead!"

"He's dead? How?" Melissa asked her dad.

"I'm not exactly sure honey, but they want to talk with me next week about what happened. Sometimes when something bad has happened to someone, all of the people involved or concerned are notified by the police," the doctor explained, as he took a sip of his coffee. He realized his hand was trembling as he brought the cup up to his mouth.

"Are you okay daddy?" Melissa asked. "You're hand is shaking."

"Yes, honey, I'm okay ... in fact I feel great," he exclaimed as he tried not to get too excited in front of her. He knew that his trembling was brought on by the overwhelming joy of knowing, that his wife's murderer was dead.

The phone rang again. This time the doctor picked it up. "Hello, Wilson residence!" he said.

"Randy! Have you heard the morning news or read The Province this morning?" Winona asked with exhilaration in her voice.

"No I haven't heard the news yet Winny, but I just got off the phone with the police, and they gave me the news, but only very little information. They want me to come in, early next week for a meeting. Just a sec ... Melissa, please go and play in your room, while I talk to your auntie, okay?

"Oh my God, Randy, it's just like what we talked about at dinner on Friday night ... Angels ... fucking Angels of Vengeance! You don't think that they want you to come in, cause they believe you're a suspect do you?" his sister questioned.

"No! No that wouldn't be why ... would it? No ... they always inform the victims families when something happens to the perpetrator," the plastic surgeon reasoned.

"But you said it yourself, you just got off the phone with them. They DID inform you, over the phone! Did you ask them why, they want you to come into the station?"

"No I didn't, but I'm positive that they probably want to give me explicit details of what happened in person, rather than over the phone. Besides the media never gives all the right information, they always leave out the details. But that prick got exactly what he deserved!" Wilson said as he checked out his hands. The trembling had stopped.

"It's like a miracle! It all seems so surreal, Randy! There's definitely Angels out there brother. We are going to have to celebrate, and go for dinner again. Does Melissa know?"

"I told her briefly what happened, I will tell her more when I find out everything. I want her to know the complete truth," he told his sister.

DOG WITH A BONE

"I saw it on Global TV at nine o'clock this morning, just before I called you. They said that he was 'brutally' murdered, and that it was most likely a targeted 'hit', done by a professional. I'm quite sure that they're probably letting the public know that, so they don't think that there's a maniac randomly killing people," Winona explained with excitement in her voice.

Wilson said goodbye to his sister and put the phone down. Melissa slowly walked around the corner and towards her dad. "Angels, daddy? Are there really Angels?" she asked, tilting her head.

"I thought you went to your bedroom to play?" as he shrugged his shoulders, shook his head back and forth and smiled at her. "Yes, my darling, there are Angels! They took mommy to heaven so she could rest," the doctor said as he hugged his daughter tightly. "I love you Melissa."

Stanley Park was starting to fill up with the Sunday crowd. Sunny pulled his clean, shiny black Accord into the parking lot at Lumberman's Arch. The few remaining water droplets from the car-wash, clinging to the acrylic clear-coat, for "dear life", glistened like brilliant diamonds in the sunshine. Sunny always made sure, that he washed his "ride" once a week.

"Come on Babe!" Sunny said as he opened the passenger door. She jumped out and sniffed the fresh, salt water air.

Sunny let her "do a pee" and then he hooked her leash to her pink collar. Dogs are not allowed to run free in Vancouver City parks, only in designated dog parks.

He clicked his remote to lock the car and then the two of them headed for the seawall. The seawall was teeming with walkers, joggers, cyclists, and roller-bladers already. Vancouverites loved their big playground of a park. The seagulls were also fond of the park. They were abundant along the seawall, waiting for the odd snack left behind by a tourist.

Sunny and Babe would normally walk for about an hour, when they came to the park, which was fairly often. Down the seawall and back. Today was a very good day!

Mary Marcus had been taken to the Surrey Memorial Hospital emergency ward, late last night, after discovering her son's battered body. She had come home just before midnight and almost stumbled right over William in the dark hallway. She managed to call the police moments before she collapsed on the kitchen floor.

The RCMP IHIT were dispatched to the Marcus's rundown house within minutes of Mary putting the 911 phone call through. When they arrived at the house, they found Mary still unconscious on the floor.

Her brother Ted was at the hospital by her bedside. The RCMP homicide detectives had informed him, that they wanted to interview him later in the day. The neighbor, Mr. Bobrick had told the police that he had heard an argument between William and his uncle the day before, while tending his vegetable garden in the backyard.

Some of the neighborhood folks were passing by the bungalow, taking pictures with their cellphones. The whole yard had been wrapped with the yellow crime scene tape, as the homicide investigators were still scouring the Marcus's house for clues.

Mr. Bobrick was out in his front yard, holding his cat in his arms, petting the purring feline and talking to a nice couple of neighbors who lived across the street from him.

DOG WITH A BONE

"I feel terrible for Mrs. Marcus," old man Bobrick said to the middle-aged husband and wife. "She is such a good, generous woman. She did everything for that boy and he treated her very badly, you know. I used to hear them argue all the time. He would swear and say horrible, disgusting things to her."

"I know. We could hear him from across the street. It's a shame for their whole family, but maybe now there will be peace for her, I hate to say," the husband of the couple said.

Global TV and other reporters had already been at the crime scene earlier in the morning. The news about the murder was all over the media.

The phone at Dr. Wilson's residence was starting to ring non-stop. Some of his family members were calling to talk to him. A reporter from The Province newspaper as well as one from Global TV were hounding him for the scoop on his thoughts about William Marcus's death, being a possible revenge killing.

Wilson started screening his phone calls. He wasn't a "texter", so he didn't have to worry about texting anyone back.

As he was grinning a huge smile from ear-to-ear, standing at his kitchen counter, he poured himself another cup of hot vanilla flavoured coffee. He listened to his answering machine, record the morning enquiries of the anxious reporters, wanting to interview him.

Then a message came in a low, gravelly voice, *"Hi Dr. Wilson ... it's Burt, please pick up the phone."*

The doctor almost dropped his coffee, and then spat out what he had in mouth, into the kitchen sink. Quickly, he wiped his shirt sleeve across his lips and then grabbed his phone. "He..llo, hello Burt!" he stammered. "It's Randall ... how are you?" he asked nervously.

"*Fine, Doctor ... very fine indeed,*" Burt responded. "*I take it, that you no doubt, have heard this beautiful morning's news?*"

"Yes, as a matter of fact, I have ... and I'm very ..."

"*Don't say anything more on the phone Doctor! We need to wrap this up. Meet me at the same place, in one hour, okay?*" Burt instructed.

"I'll be there sir!" Wilson promptly said. Then the good doctor hung the phone up.

He stood in the kitchen for a moment, thinking about what he just talked about, until he heard, "daddy ... who's Burt?"

"Oh, honey ... he's just a friend from the office. I have to see him about something, to do with work," her dad lied.

Shit, I thought she was in her room! I hate lying to her, the doctor thought to himself. *Well, I guess it's not really lying, after-all, it was a job done. And a job is "work".* "Melissa, I'm going to drop you off with Auntie Winny for a couple of hours and then we'll go out for some ice-cream, okay honey?"

"Ice-cream! Sure daddy ... yippee!" Melissa cheered, as she clapped her tiny hands together.

The doctor phoned his sister and made arrangements to drop Melissa off for a while. Then he gathered up his things and got his daughter ready and out the door they went.

The duck pond was extremely active with all the feathery fowl quacking and honking as they were being fed by the park enthusiasts. The children playing on the swings nearby and the sun bursting through the willow trees, made Dr. Randall Wilson glad he was alive. It was too bad he couldn't have brought Melissa to the park today, she would have enjoyed herself. But today he had some important business to finish up.

The nervous doctor pulled out a cigarette from his shirt pocket and lit it up, as he sat on the same bench that Burt and him had shared together before, not very long ago. Taking a long drag of his cigarette and opening up his Province newspaper, he spotted "it" on the third page. "It" wasn't a very long article about the murder of William Marcus. Not much information or detail either, since it was only reported last night and was scooped to the press, no doubt at the last minute for the Sunday edition.

Again Dr. Randall Wilson smiled. He laid the paper in his lap as he took another long drag of his smoke. He was very relaxed and felt good today. And why not? After all, the sun was shining, the ducks and geese were happy, and his wife's sadistic killer was dead! Murdered "brutally", according to the press, hopefully in the same fashion his wife was killed. *How fitting, how wonderful, how justice was finally served properly,* the doctor thought.

"Good morning Dr. Wilson!" came a voice, from behind the plastic surgeon.

Wilson turned around to see Burt standing there. With his moustache trimmed neatly, bright blue eyes sparkling in the sunlight and his hands on his hips, he looked just like an Angel to the doctor. An Angel of Vengeance!

"Such a lovely day, isn't it Dr. Wilson?" Burt said as he checked out the activity in the park.

"A lovely day indeed Burt," Wilson replied. "Have a seat, my good man," as the doctor patted the bench next to him.

"Actually, Doc, I prefer to stand, if you don't mind," Burt said as he walked around the bench to face Wilson.

"I heard the news this morning from the police and just read it in this paper a few minutes ago. I want you to know, that I'm a very happy man today, Burt. I can't thank you enough! Here's my donation, to the "Good Will" of man. I hope it's satisfactory," as the doctor pulled a small, puffy white envelope from his shirt pocket.

"Slide the envelope into the newspaper and then hand me the paper," Burt instructed the doctor.

He did as he was told. "Burt, the police want to interview me next week," Wilson stressed.

"You'll do just fine, Dr. Wilson. Look how cool you are right now. Don't worry about it. I have to go Doctor," Burt stated.

"Thanks again for everything Burt," Wilson said as he put his hand forward to shake hands.

Burt backed away, without shaking or saying anything more. He smiled at the doctor and tipped his head up and down quickly, as if to say "your welcome". Burt then rolled the newspaper up, slid it under his arm and walked away in the same direction he came from.

Wilson lit up another cigarette and sat on the bench, watching the kids in the park playing.

At the far end of the busy park, Burt inconspicuously surveyed the surrounding area, removed the envelope from the Province newspaper and then tossed the tabloid into the trash can. He walked across the street and got into his car. He bent over and pulled up his passenger floor mat and stashed the envelope underneath it. Burt started his car and then drove off from the park.

As he headed down the freeway towards Vancouver, he looked in his rear-view mirror and smiled to himself.

He opened his sunroof and then slid a CD into the disc player. "Dirty White Boy" wailed from the dash speakers!

One at a time, Burt peeled off the blue colored contact lenses, from his eyeballs, and then held them up through the open sunroof, first the right, and then the left, until they blew off from his finger and into the wind. Then, very carefully, he pulled the fake mustache off his upper lip and let it fly from the open sunroof too.

Burt looked into his rear-view mirror again, with a wide devilish grin and saw the crystal clear reflection of the professional hit-man, Sunny "the Bully Basher" Kruzik, staring back at him! *"Cause I'm a dirty white boy ... yeah, a dirty white boy ... dirty white boyyyyy!"*

Made in the USA
Charleston, SC
27 June 2013